# SEA OF LOST SOULS

## THE OCEANUS SERIES - BOOK ONE

## EMERALD DODGE

# ALSO BY EMERALD DODGE

**The Battlecry Series**

Battlecry

Sentinel

Mercury

Ignite (Prequel Novelette)

**Enclave Boxed Sets**

Of Beasts and Beauties (Excalibur)

**The Oceanus Series**

Sea of Lost Souls

House of the Setting Sun (coming soon)

Valley of the Shadow (coming soon)

Crown of Sorrows (Prequel Novelette)

**Other Works**

Novenas for Mothers

Novenas for Students

Novenas for Singles

*For Sarah Spivak*
*My favorite part of writing this book was that I had a brand-new excuse to talk to you all the time.*

# GLOSSARY OF NAVAL TERMS

- **Deck** - Floor
- **Bulkhead** - Wall
- **Ladder** - More properly, a stairwell. They are extremely steep.
- **Head** - Bathroom
- **Klaxon** - Alarm
- **Stern** - The physical rear of the ship
- **Bow** - The physical front of the ship
- **Aft** - Toward the back of the ship, when speaking of directions
- **Forward** - Toward the front of the ship, when speaking of directions
- **Starboard** - Right, when speaking of directions
- **Port** - Left, when speaking of directions
- **Fantail** - A portion of the back end of the ship above the water.
- **Rates** - Jobs/professions within the Navy

- **Taps** - The tune played over the intercom to signal the end of the working day.
- **Berthing** - Living spaces where sailors sleep and recreate.
- **Racks** - Beds, often stacked three high.
- **Officer** - A member of the managerial, and highest, ranks of the armed forces. Officers are accorded special honors such as saluting, and they are given higher pay. Officers have a presidential commission, and as such are sometimes referred to as "commissioned officers." This is in contrast to "non-commissioned officers," a type of enlisted serviceman.
- **Enlisted** - A member of the lower ranks of the armed forces. They join for a specific period of time, at the end of which they can choose to reenlist or not. Enlisted personnel tend to make up the system experts and technicians.

*How varied are your works, LORD! In wisdom you have made them all; the earth is full of your creatures. There is the sea, great and wide! It teems with countless beings, living things both large and small. There ships ply their course and Leviathan, whom you formed to play with.* - Psalms 104:24-26 NABRE

# 1

"**M**an overboard! Man overboard! Starboard side!"

The alert came over the ship's intercom system, echoing down the USS *Taft*'s passageways and making my ears ring as the sound bounced around the steel.

I tore my eyes away from the white-red fire of the F-18 that had just landed on the flight deck, and began to sprint into the hanger bay, leaving behind the exciting maelstrom to muster for the third man-overboard alert in six hours. The roar of the jet, the howling of the storm, the crashing waves, and angry shouts from other sailors all mixed with a new sound: the alert klaxon.

I thudded down the stairs and dashed into the reactor office, where I was supposed to be manning the phone during my time on watch. I'd only taken a few seconds during an errand to admire the jets, but there was every chance I'd be written up for not being at my station at the beginning of the man-overboard.

I grabbed the juicy superhero novel I'd been reading and tried to look engrossed. It had already been ten seconds, and I couldn't hear my favorite person cracking skulls.

"Up! Move! Move! Make a hole! Hurry up!"

There he was.

The tired yells came from beyond the open door, mixing with the klaxon. The yeller, Chief Swanson, sounded like he'd just woken up. Considering that it was half past midnight, he probably had.

His concern was all for show. After the first two false alarms, I was positive that nobody cared about the man-overboard. Now, if they found the chucklehead who kept throwing emergency chem lights in the water... yeah, there was going to be an actual man-overboard situation, and every sailor on the carrier was going to cheer.

Chief Swanson stumbled into the reactor office, bleary and half-dressed. I tossed him the clipboard. "Petty Officer Second Class Goldstein comma Rachel present, in body if not in spirit. My spirit is back in my rack getting some sleep."

"Shut up, Goldstein," he said without looking up from the clipboard. "Where's Bickley?"

A booming voice over the intercom interrupted us. "Time plus one!"

It had been a minute since the man-overboard. If all five thousand hands on the ship hadn't mustered by time plus twelve, they'd launch the helicopters and search teams. Considering that I'd seen thirty-foot waves just a few minutes ago, I did not envy anybody who had to search for a single person in that ocean.

I flipped my book open to where I'd stopped. "I took over for him. He's probably on his way here from his rack."

The ship rolled slightly, and a pen fell off the desk with a clatter. Huh. Maybe someone *had* fallen off the ship. The storm was getting worse.

There was the sound of a train passing over head, followed by a vibration that resounded in my chest. It wasn't a train, of course—it was an F-18 landing on the flight deck. I'd overheard an airman say that four planes had been called back to the ship as the freak storm had overtaken us. I'd watched the first one return. Two down, two to go.

Groans and mumbles carried down the passageway as the rest of my muster group wandered into the office. In my opinion, we were the best possible muster group, comprising three good-looking nuclear electricians. Not that our appearances were remotely important, of course. It was just that our good looks made it funnier when people found out that we were nukes, since most sailors thought that nukes were pasty, squishy sewer monsters. *I* thought I was rather pretty, with my fair, lightly-freckled skin, and soft brown curls that stuck out every which way.

Bickley, the oldest of us, led the pack. Pillow marks lined the brown skin of his face, and his white tank top allowed us to see his impressive nautical-themed tattoos that he'd gotten during each of his four deployments. "'Sup," he said through a yawn. When he'd finished, he gestured toward the clipboard. "Petty Officer First Class Jack Bickley, ready for duty or whatever."

"Thank you, Petty Officer," Chief said. "Your eagerness to serve is much appreciated."

I hid my smile. Bickley's military bearing always went up in smoke after midnight.

My best friend, Torres, moved like a zombie down the hallway. She still had a crusty spit trail on her cheek and was blinking rapidly as though she were confused by what was going on. Her pixie cut stuck out oddly on one side, and her feet were clad in actual bunny slippers. Her intricate collarbone tattoo—I'd egged her on into getting it in Marseilles—was on clear display underneath her tank top.

Chief ticked off her name. "Petty Officer Second Class Marisol Torres, check, and nice slippers, by the way. Where's Rollins?"

"He's definitely on watch," I said. He'd complained about it for an hour before I'd kicked him out of the reactor office and told him to go whine to the generators instead. It was a forgivable offense, though; he wasn't normally so prone to complain, but it was the middle of the night in the sixth month of a deployment. We were all getting a little fatigued.

The carrier leaned to the side suddenly, tossing my colleagues to the floor. My rolling office chair merely scooted across the small office like a lame theme park ride. A familiar wave of nausea hit me, and I began to mentally calculate the physics of the motion to take my mind off of it. It was unfortunate that I got motion sickness so easily. I loved the *idea* of going fast and wild. My stomach did not.

"Time plus two!"

Bickley put the wastepaper basket back in its spot. His movie-star good looks, all symmetry and deep brown eyes, were muddled by his lack of sleep.

"Is this a hurricane?" I asked, casting a glance toward the ceiling. "I would've thought we sailed around those. I like some excitement, but this..."

Torres shook her head and patted my shoulder. "Nope, they'll sail right through. Don't worry, though. We sailed through Hurricane Ben during my first deployment, and we were just fine. Not much can sink a carrier."

As if to underline her point, the ship pitched again, and this time they all braced themselves for support. I just rolled back to my desk, little calculations and figures flitting across my mind. *Please don't barf. Please don't barf.*

Another jet landed, the same train-like cacophony rumbling above us. Three were now home safe.

Bickley sat down on the desk, and we bumped fists. I turned to the Chief. "Since you're here, I'll say that there's nothing to report. But I did pass the reactor classroom on the way here, and there was definitely signs of"—I coughed to hide my laugh—"the reactor ghost. Someone had pulled out all the chairs."

Bickley waggled his fingers. "Oooh, the reactor ghost is back."

"Goldstein and I were talking earlier about who it might be," Torres said. "We think it's the ghost of Admiral Rickover."

I couldn't help but crack up to hear my own theory again. The Father of the Nuclear Navy *would* haunt a reactor classroom. Maybe he'd come back to wreak his terrible vengeance on the guy who kept throwing chem lights overboard and tricking the lookout teams.

"Time plus three!" The ship leaned hard to the starboard side, and we all fell to the deck.

Or maybe he'd come to shuttle us all into the afterlife when the ship capsized.

Chief got to his feet with a huff and pointed down the passageway. "Goldstein, go find Rollins. Drag him up here by his ear if you have to."

It was on.

I sprinted down the passageway to the heavy gray door that led to the main part of the reactor department, along the way calculating the most efficient route. I heaved it open, wincing against the blast of air that was hotter than the sun, then all but leapt onto the stairs and slid down the rails. There wasn't even time to blow on my hands—I simply went down another flight and hoped I didn't have blisters later.

Small groups of sailors were huddled here and there for their musters, all waiting for the announcement that they'd either rescued the poor guy who'd fallen overboard or keelhauled the idiot who'd called a false alarm. They couldn't go back to sleep or work until I'd found Rollins.

Where *was* that big lug? *If he's somewhere with his girlfriend, I'm going to kill him.*

"Time plus four!"

I hurried into the reactor control room, a relatively cold room compared to the rest of the reactor spaces. I glanced at the watch bill —yep, Rollins was supposed to be on watch now. I hadn't seen him on the flight deck, so he wasn't the man overboard.

Lieutenant Murphy looked up from her work at her desk. "Goldstein, aren't you supposed to be at muster?" The watch officer didn't leave her desk for anything, as far as I knew.

"Rollins is missing. Do you know where he is?"

"He stepped out to get a log reading in the engine room."

"Thanks, ma'am!" I called over my shoulder as I ran out, heading toward the engine room.

Another heavy metal door, and—

I covered my ears against the deafening blend of engines, generators, various high-tech machinery, and a few things that ran on diesel. Generators the size of school buses roared on many sides, causing my chest to vibrate. There was no point yelling for Rollins, and if he'd been in here when the man-overboard had been announced, it was plausible that he hadn't heard it.

The ship pitched again, and I almost lost my footing right next to an exposed metal pipe.

I hurried through the narrow walkways around and between machines, squinting for my colleague, a relative newbie to the ship along with myself. Rollins and I had gone to nuke school together, though I didn't know him well.

Somewhere, far above the never-ending blast of noise, the

intercom called time plus six, setting my teeth on edge. I had six minutes to find Rollins and get him upstairs.

The ship swung again, slamming me into a railing that knocked the breath out of me. When I'd caught my breath, I noticed that a pen had slid out from behind a generator, where I hadn't looked yet.

And it had left a bloody trail as it went.

I dashed around the generator and gasped. Rollins was sitting up against the bulkhead, unconscious and bleeding profusely from a large laceration on his forehead. Blood had poured down his front and onto the engine log, seeping into his green camouflage uniform and all over the metal floor. I'd never seen so much blood from a wound that wasn't in a war movie. Blood dripped off of a jagged piece of metal that stuck off the generator—he must've fallen and banged his head. All things considered, Chief *probably* wouldn't get angry at him for being late to muster.

I steadied myself and slipped my arms under his, wrapping them around his barrel-like chest, and began to pull him toward the door. There was no time to worry about a broken neck; I had to get him to Lieutenant Murphy, who could call the medical team.

I back-stepped, slowly but surely, toward the door, making sure to not catch my uniform on anything and praying that the ship didn't dance in the waves again. Rollins' blood dripped down my arm and onto my hand, making my grasp slippery.

I ignored the tiny voice in the back of my mind that noted how utterly still Rollins was.

"Time plus eight!"

The announcement sounded just as I'd stepped through the door to the passageway. I repositioned my arms, then took a breath. "Lieutenant Murphy! I need you! Now!"

The petite redhead poked her head out, then shrieked. "Get him in here! I'll call the medical team!"

I slowly walked the final few yards into the reactor control room, then laid Rollins down on the steel floor. Lieutenant Murphy, who was on the phone, tossed me her uniform's blouse and gestured for me to put it under his head as she wrenched the intercom speaker from its cradle. "Medical emergency! Medical emergency in the reactor control room!"

Her voice echoed throughout the entire ship, immediately followed by, "Time plus nine!"

I didn't wait for her to dismiss me. I ran at top speed back down the shadowy steel passageway, underneath the endless line of pipes and wires, past the same groups of sailors. They pointed this time. "Hey, yo, where'd the blood come from?" one asked.

I took the stairs three at a time. "Chief! I found Rollins!"

"Time plus ten!"

The hasty thuds of Chief's boots disappearing many decks above me, and the descending boots of the medical team, let me know that all was going to be well—sort of. Rollins was obviously in a grave state, but we wouldn't catch hell from the officers for not reporting during a man-overboard. The helicopters and search teams wouldn't have to be deployed in a near-hurricane...for Rollins, at least. Maybe someone on the flight deck really had been blown off, and if that was the case, I hoped they were found soon.

I finished my journey to the sound of claps that immediately ceased as soon as they saw me: disheveled and covered in blood.

Torres put a hand over her mouth. "Sweet mother Mary. What happened?"

I fell back into my office chair. "From what I could tell, he hit his head. I don't know if he'll be okay, since that was a nasty cut."

"Time plus eleven!"

Chief needed to hurry up and submit that muster report.

Bickley sat on the desk. "I wouldn't worry too much. Head

wounds bleed a lot, but they're usually not that bad." He clapped me on the shoulder. "You did good. At breakfast, everyone is going to know about the heroic nuke who saved the day during the man-over-board. Maybe you'll even get a medal. Your parents will have to admit that a medal for valor is pretty cool."

I picked up the book I'd been reading. "And yet, I'm still on phone watch."

Such was life in the Navy. And besides, my parents wouldn't care if I'd gotten a medal for rescuing the Admiral from a great white shark. The last conversation I'd had with them had hammered home their disapproval in my career choice.

My colleagues snickered, and they settled in chairs around me while we waited for Chief to return and let us go back to bed, or watch.

Torres picked up a squeeze toy shaped like a football and tossed it to Bickley. "So, who do you guys really think is the reactor ghost?"

"My money's on Diaz," Bickley said. "That dipstick is a big-time practical joker. I can see him moving our stuff around."

The captain's nasally voice came on the intercom. "Time plus twelve. All hands accounted for. The aft lookout team spotted a chem light in the water." He sounded equally exhausted and annoyed.

We all sagged with relief. Now we just had to wait for Chief to come down and dismiss us.

"It's not just moving stuff around, though," Torres said. "Remember that drawing?"

There was a pregnant pause as we recalled the unexplainable incident the week before. We'd all exited the reactor classroom at the end of a training session, chatting amongst ourselves and heading up to lunch. Torres had doubled back to get her notebook, then shouted for us to "come see."

I nodded thoughtfully. "Okay, yeah, that was weird. But a giant drawing on the whiteboard isn't... isn't... it's not paranormal by itself."

"A drawing of an F-18 suddenly appearing on the board ten seconds after we left the room is just plain fre... what was that?" She slid to her feet, her hand held up.

We hushed, looking at her for an explanation. She strode out the door, turning her head back and forth. "Hello?"

"What is it?" I asked.

"I swear to God, I just heard Rollins. But like... he was far away, but also just on the other side of the wall. Didn't you hear him?" She studied the bulkhead, as if the chart-covered space would suddenly produce Rollins.

"What did you hear?" Bickley asked. "I didn't hear anything."

Torres rubbed her forehead. "I don't even know. Just... just an impression of his voice, I guess." She gave her head a little shake. "I'm probably hearing things because I'm so tired."

"I hear the reactor phone ring sometimes, if I'm using the head on watch," I said. "You're just worried about him." I tossed the squeeze ball to her. "You might as well stay up with me. Your watch slot begins in twenty minutes."

"Ugh. Thanks for reminding me." She raised her hand to throw the ball back to me, but then lowered it, her eyes narrowing as she looked toward the door. "I just heard him again. I'm positive I did."

I sighed. "He's probably getting stitches right now. I didn't hear anything. It's just the late hour, Tor."

"What did he say?" Bickley asked.

Torres closed her eyes. "He said... he's *saying*... 'I'm standing right here, guys.'"

Bickley suppressed a smile. "You've been reading paranormal stuff again, haven't you? I'm telling you, quit hitting the library in your downtime and start playing dominoes, like a normal sailor."

"I *like* ghost stories," Torres said, affronted. "I'm psychic, you know."

I pinched the bridge of my nose. Not this crap again. It was one thing to say you were connected to the "beyond," but it was just tacky to joke about Rollins. "Being able to guess that the galley is going to run out of food on any given day does not make you psychic. It means you have a good grasp of statistics."

Bickley grinned. "Yeah, the hungrier you are, combined with the variable of whether or not you're luckless enough to be a nuke, determines—"

"Shut up, you guys!" Torres said. "I thought you were on my side. You're just as much into the ghost stuff as I am." She smacked my shoulder.

I smacked her back. "Not to the point that I'm joking about saying you hear Rollins's ghost or something."

"I wasn't joking! I really did!"

"Hands to yourselves, you two," Bickley said. "It's way too late at night for me to break up a catfight. "He held out an arm between us. "I know something that'll make you both happy: there's never any line at the pay phones this time of night. Since you're awake, why don't you both call your parents? Tell them you're calling live from a hurricane. It always impresses the civilians. Goldstein, it's only bedtime in Virginia, right? And Torres, you're from around Chicago, right? I bet your dad's up."

Torres lightened up. "Oh, good idea!"

Our resident Navy brat was the daughter of a retired Master Chief, and she was the most complete daddy's girl I'd ever met. Even more than me. Before this deployment, she'd cut her hair like his when he was in the service, accidentally making her look like a little boy from afar. Still, she was proud that he was proud, so we didn't give her grief about it. Much.

Torres began to idly flip through one of the nuclear manuals from the bookshelf, but I turned away and swallowed the new lump in my throat. Before I could resume pretending to read my book, Bickley asked, "You going to call anyone tonight?" His tone carried his real meaning.

I glanced up at him, then away. "I don't think that's a good idea."

His warm hand on my shoulder made me look up again, and he had the expression on his face that underlined why he'd been promoted so quickly through the nuke ranks: stern, yet understanding. "Call home, Rachel."

I gulped and nodded. I needed to, but damn, I didn't want to. What was there to say to the people who'd called me selfish for joining the Navy? Hashem knew, I loved my parents more than life itself, but the wound was too deep, too raw for a mere phone call.

And I knew how the call would go. Once again, they'd recite the list of things they'd given their only child: the best schools, a private *shul* tutor, the most elaborate bat mitzvah Virginia Beach, Virginia had ever seen, shopping trips to New York, all of it.

"But I want *adventure*," I'd hissed at them, that turbulent day on the pier, minutes before walking onto the USS *Taft*. "I want to see the world, serve my country, and grow *up*. I'm not a little girl anymore. Can't you just be happy for me?"

And that's when my father had spat the worst thing he'd ever said to me. The words had wrapped around me like a curse, sinking into my insides. Even there, in the reactor room, I could still feel the sting of them.

"I'm not selfish," I whispered, the words of my novel blurring together. "I'm not."

Bickley checked his watch. "And I know you're not. As for me, I'll be calling my kids, if Chief ever gets back down here. I wonder if the officers gave him trouble about being so late?"

I let out a long breath, then blinked and smiled up at Bickley. "I doubt it. More likely, he's biting his nails up with the guys on the bridge. There's still a jet out there. I've been counting them. The flight deck guys said four jets were out when the storm came up. I've only heard three land."

Torres snapped the manual shut. "You couldn't pay me enough to try to land a jet on the carrier in a storm like this. They'd be safer flying straight back to Oceana Naval Air Station. We're in the middle of the Atlantic, right? It's not that far."

The sound of boots descending the stairs made us all turn toward the door. Torres poked her head out, then turned back with a relieved smile. "It's Chief."

Finally. "Well, good night, everyone," I said, turning back to my desk to pick up my book. "Enjoy your phone calls. After everything, maybe we all should go vis—"

My vision was snuffed out like a candle.

## 2

*This is a nice pillow.*

My first inane thought upon waking was immediately chased away by another, more serious one: *where am I?*

I hadn't even opened my eyes yet and I knew I wasn't anywhere I'd been before. The rack felt wrong, much too hard for anything I'd ever encountered in the Navy. I scraped my fingertips across the surface and felt a thin, rough material, almost like taut burlap. The smell was also wrong, vaguely sterile and cold, like a hospital. My berthing smelled like an old factory—of oil, paint, dirt, and sweat.

I opened my eyes. A metal beam above my head bore the spray painted words NO SMOKING IN YOUR RACK.

Well, that answered that question. I wasn't on the USS *Taft* anymore. For one thing, smoking was only allowed in a few designated areas on the *Taft*, so the message was redundant. For another, I was lying on a framed canvas hammock attached to the bulkhead with two chains. Beds like this hadn't been on ships since World War II, at least.

My hammock was one of many in the large room in which I'd woken, but only a few of them were occupied. Bickley slept to my left, a hand on his chest and a babyish peace on his face. On the far end of the room stood two proper racks, complete with mattresses and sheets. Torres was bundled sweetly in the top rack, breathing slowly and soundly. The bottom rack was in disarray, as if the occupant had vacated it in a hurry.

The storm had passed; there was nothing to feel but a smooth, relaxing lull as the ship moved through still waters. But what ship were we on? What had happened? I closed my eyes and massaged my eyelids, straining to recollect anything at all.

A sound.

A feeling.

And then...nothing. But it was a *deep* nothingness, a meaningful nothingness. I'd experienced similar mental void in nuke school, when I'd partied too hard on the weekends. *Nuke life is a grind*, they'd said. *Drink away your frustrations*, they'd said. I'd woken up on Sunday mornings, weekend after weekend, having no clue what had happened in the last twelve hours. But the weight of those hours was still in my mind, just as it was now.

Something had happened to us.

I threw back the thin wool blanket and swung my feet over the edge, then hopped down. "Hello? Is anyone there?"

A USS *Taft* aviator walked out of a nearby room, his head turning all around until he found me. He carried himself with a tense alertness that hinted that he, too, didn't know where he was. He was fairly young, perhaps around thirty, and on the squirrely side, with thin, pointed features, and quick movements. His flight suit identified him as Lieutenant Commander Hollander.

Self-consciousness rose up in me; he outranked me quite a bit. I automatically began to recall everything I knew about dealing with high-up officers. *Remember to call him Commander, not Lieutenant Commander. Address him as "sir." Stand at attention until he tells you otherwise. You don't have to salute him right now because you're inside.*

He spotted me and hurried over. "Sailor, are you from the *Taft*? Do you know who the others are? I woke up just a few minutes ago."

I snapped to attention. "I'm Petty Officer Goldstein, sir. I'm a nuclear electrician stationed on the *Taft*." Now was not the time to get dinged for improper military bearing.

Commander Hollander, on the other hand, didn't seem to care. He pulled me close and whispered, "At ease. We're not on the *Taft* anymore. In fact, I'm not even sure we're on a US Navy vessel. I've seen a few people around, and they won't talk to me. They're dressed wrong, too. I think maybe we've been captured, or possibly transferred here under suspicious circumstances."

They did *not* cover this in nuke school.

I swallowed. "What are you saying, sir?"

His dark gaze darted toward the door and back to me. "I'm saying that as soon as the others are awake, we're going to organize an escape. I'm the only officer, so if we're apprehended, I will speak for all of you. Is that clear?"

I nodded. "Crystal. Sir, if I may ask…?"

"What is it?"

"What do you remember before coming here? Because I don't remember anything. I was just talking with the other nukes after the man-overboard, and then… nothing. Just nothing."

He shook his head. "I don't remember anything, either. I was on a training mission during that storm. The captain radioed in for the rest of the guys out there with me to come back to the ship, and I was the last one. I remember being totally focused on coming in for landing, and then nothing. Just like you."

"Goldstein?" Torres's sleepy voice made us turn our heads. She sat up and scrubbed the sleep from her face, then got out of her rack. She put her hands on her hips and looked around, finally raising an eyebrow and giving me an expectant expression. She was no longer in her pajamas, but her navy blue jumpsuit-like coveralls she wore during work hours.

I realized then that none of the nukes were in pajamas or camo, as we'd been during the man-overboard. All of us were in our coveralls. When had we changed? Who'd changed us?

"Before you ask, we don't know, either," I said to Torres. "Sir, this Petty Officer Torres. We're all in the reactor department. In fact," I said placing a hand on Bickley's shoulder and giving him a little shake. "I think it's time to wake everyone up. Bick, get up."

Bickley sat up and blinked around in sleepy confusion. "Did I wake up inside *Saving Private Ryan*? Where the hell are we?"

Nobody offered an answer. In fact, we all had the same what-the-heck looks on our faces—especially when two women in forties-era starched white nurse uniforms fluttered into the sick bay like two bedsheets with makeup. *Old fashioned* makeup.

The shorter of the two, sporting coiffed brown hair and bright red lipstick, grinned from ear to ear. "Oh, you're awake! I'm so sorry y'all had to wake up alone. That's never easy. Peggy and I had to talk to the skipper at a moment's notice." She had a rich, thick southern drawl that reminded me of my cousins from Savannah.

"Peggy" was blonde with rosy pink lipstick, and her hair was done up in a grandiose style that I knew had a specific name, but couldn't quite recall.

"Why are you two dressed like you're in a Danny Kay movie?" Torres asked. Leave it to her to be point-blank.

"Petty Officer, I'll speak for us," Commander Hollander said sharply. He directed his no-nonsense look at the nurses. "I'm Lieutenant Commander Hollander, United States Navy. Where are we? What's happened to us?"

I angled my body between my colleagues and the unknown nurses as subtly as I could. Maybe I was petite, but I was fierce. My high school lacrosse coach had always told me so, especially after I'd sent one girl to the hospital during a game.

Peggy and the brunette faltered, and I couldn't help but feel a little sorry for them, since they *seemed* nice. Indeed, Peggy's happiness fell away as she said, "I... the captain said that since you're such a big crowd, he wanted to tell you himself. This is unusual, you see. Usually it's just one person. We've never had four new crew members at once. That's why some of you had to be in the extra racks. We didn't even have mattresses for them because we've never had to use them before."

She spoke with a classic north-midwestern accent, the words themselves stretched into a verbal smile as she spoke them. I placed her from Wisconsin, or maybe Minnesota.

The brunette held her hand out toward the door. "But I will say that I'm Nurse Dorothy Majors, and this is Nurse Margaret Houston, and you're on the USS *Saint Catherine*. You can call us Dot and Peggy, though. Everyone does. You're on a friendly ship, ya'll. Come with us and everything will be right as rain." She spoke with such warmth that I believed her.

We all exchanged a look, then headed toward the door with Commander Hollander taking the lead. While we walked, Torres leaned over and whispered to the rest of us, "There is no such ship as the USS *Saint Catherine*."

I whispered back, "You're sure?"

"My dad made me memorize all the possible carriers I could be assigned to. I'm sure."

Bickley pointed to the back of Peggy's head. "Did your dad ever make you memorize something that would explain why she's wearing victory rolls?"

I mentally slapped my forehead. That's what they were called, "victory rolls." As in, victory against the Axis powers.

The mystery deepened. We squared our shoulders and continued walking toward whatever awaited us on the enigmatic USS *Saint Catherine*.

---

THE SHIP WAS OLD.

That was the biggest takeaway from our scenic route through the USS *Saint Catherine*. Peeling paint, leaky pipes, and generally dated everything were impossible to miss. We passed a few sailors at their work, and it truly was like we were on a movie set from the 1940s: the men—there were no other women to be seen anywhere—were clad in navy blue bell bottoms, chambray shirts, and white Dixie cup hats. I half-expected them to strike a jaunty pose and tell me to buy war bonds.

As we walked past, many of the crewmen would jump up and bid Torres and me appreciative hellos. Some even offered their hands, but Dot and Peggy would hiss at them to get back to work every time. I understood the appeal of the opposite sex as much as anyone, but why were they acting like this? Some of them were so dumbstruck, they didn't move out of the way for Commander Hollander, nor make any sign they knew an officer was in their presence.

We were probably aboard an *Essex*-class aircraft carrier, which made no sense whatsoever; *Essex*-class ships had been deployed in World War II. None were still in operation, their design having been rendered obsolete by the nuclear powered *Nimitz*-class carriers, the pride and joy of Admiral Rickover.

Another oddity was how few sailors there actually were. As we walked through the hangar bay, sun poured in through the hangar bay doors, so where were the thousands upon thousands of people it took to run an aircraft carrier during the day? We'd passed a dozen men in one room, and a handful of diners in a small galley, which itself was staffed by just two cooks instead of the normal eight.

The proportions of rank were wrong, too. There were a great deal of lower enlisted sailors, but almost no chiefs. It was ten minutes before we passed another officer, a young ensign in a uniform I'd only seen in movies, with tan shoes instead of black. He caught sight of Commander Hollander and saluted. "Welcome aboard, sir. I'll see you later in the officer's mess."

Commander Hollander saluted in return, his face betraying the exact same confusion I felt. He looked over his shoulder at us. "That man was dressed like my grandfather was in his service portrait."

Peggy didn't seem to hear us. Instead, we went up three flights of stairs, and then she pushed open a large steel door. We stepped onto the flight deck—and gasped in unison.

We were definitely on an *Essex*-class carrier, complete with airplanes that looked like a squadron straight out of a World War II epic. Hellcats, Helldivers, Avengers, and Corsairs glinted in the sun on the deck, their crews happily chatting while they cleaned, waxed, tightened screws, and tossed tools back and forth to each other.

Three planes flew over in formation, and I stumbled backward as I craned my neck to follow them with my eyes. Two more flew in a different direction, so low that I could see their large payloads.

There was no mistake—they were armed for war.

And now that I knew what to look for, I could see that the *Saint Catherine* had indeed seen war. Scorch marks marred the hull, and men were cleaning the guns and crew-served machine guns, chatting away as they worked. Wooden crates sat here and there, some marked ORDNANCE.

"What is going on?" I whispered.

I turned around where I stood, searching for the lie. All of these planes were the stuff of childhood models and vintage collections. I knew for a fact that some of them were on display at the National Air and Space Museum Annex in northern Virginia. None of them were in service. They were all propeller planes, for heaven's sake.

Moreover, we were on the tell-tale flat, straight runway of an old aircraft carrier. Only new ones had the angled runways. More sailors were visible now, and all of them attended to their work while wearing the dated uniforms. One seaman took a drag from a cigarette while a lieutenant walked past, and the lieutenant didn't even blink.

If this was a dream, it was a trippy one. If it was a hoax, it was on a scale heretofore unfathomable to me. But it was all so real, so lucid and tangible. It couldn't have been a dream. The cool salt spray of the ocean would've woken me as it blew over my face and teased wisps of my hair. The leather bomber jackets and scratched goggles worn by the aviators were too lived-in to be costumes. Those were real people attending to those planes.

Torres grabbed my hand and yanked me toward the rest of the group. "Your mouth is open," she said. "Let's try to act natural."

Dot opened yet another steel door, and we all stepped into the cool darkness of a large passageway. With no further ado, she rapped on a door to our right, which bore a brass placard that read:

*Captain Edward Gorman, USN*
*Commanding Officer*

A man's deep voice replied: "I'm busy!"

Peggy managed to make even her eye roll delicate. "Sir, it's—"

Someone ran to the door and opened it. An older gentlemen with a commander's braiding on his sleeves began to usher us in. "You should've said it was you right away," he muttered, more to himself than anyone else. "So much to do, so little time, come in, come in, please take a seat. Thank you, nurses. That'll be all." His nameplate identified him as Commander Muree. He was tall, graying, and clean-cut, like an old lawyer in the courtroom dramas I loved to watch.

We were not in a stateroom, but rather a conference room. The mahogany table was covered in nautical charts and instruments. The warm wooden paneling along the walls lent the whole compartment a noble quality. The velvet upholstery on the chairs was finer than anything I'd ever seen in the enlisted spaces. A decorative ship's wheel, also mahogany, was mounted on the wall. Large portholes let in streams of bright sunlight. I'd been in a conference room just once before, and this one matched the one on the *Taft*.

However, the map on the far wall did not. I failed to recognize the ocean displayed thereon, nor the vast array of islands and small land-masses. It was marked merely *Oceanus*, a name that, while familiar to me from mythology, didn't make actual sense. *What on Earth?*

Dot and Peggy gave us sad parting smiles, then shut the door behind them.

None of us had taken seats around the large oval table, on the far side of which sat the most exhausted-looking man I'd ever seen, with gray hair and eyes, an Edwardian beard, and wrinkles on every inch of exposed skin. He looked up at us after a second, and I was taken aback by the weight of the years I could see in his eyes.

"Captain Gorman, I presume," said Commander Hollander. "My name is Lieutenant Commander Arthur Hollander, United States Navy. I'm an aviation officer aboard the USS *Taft*. You are the commanding officer of this vessel, are you not?" While he spoke, he gestured for the rest of us to stand along the bulkhead behind him.

"I am, Commander. Please, sit. All of you, make yourselves comfortable. You've come a long way."

Commander Hollander straightened. "Captain, I—"

Captain Gorman stood, every action appearing deliberate in its slowness. Yet, he exuded the effortless authority that only age and experience could offer. He raised his chin, his face almost serene, and leveled a polite expression at Commander Hollander. "Commander Hollander, take your seat."

The words were electric, coursing through me like an iron rod jammed down my spine. Indeed, all of us stiffened as he spoke. His voice hadn't changed, but it *had*. His simple statement carried in it a thread of instinctual command: *I am in charge.* It wasn't scary. It wasn't threatening. It was compelling in the fullest sense of the word. I did not want to find out what happened to people who disobeyed that voice.

Commander Hollander sat.

Commander Muree smiled wryly and gestured at the other chairs, which the rest of us hastily filled. He took the remaining empty seat and folded his hands on the table.

Captain Gorman returned to his seat. "I rarely have to use my captain voice, Commander, and under the circumstances I will forgive the situation. I know you have questions. I know you *all* have questions. Since it's protocol for you to speak for subordinate sailors in a situation such as this, I will address you alone unless I have reason to do otherwise." He took a deep breath. "Commander, what is your last clear memory before you woke up?"

Commander Hollander paused and nervously tapped his fingertips on the table, apparently weighing his options. After a few seconds, he said, "A training mission. I had just lowered the wheels for landing. I was speaking to air traffic control about the landing conditions on the deck due to the inclement weather. They were guiding me in."

Captain Gorman nodded. "Yes, last night was a particularly bad storm. Is that where your memory ends?"

Commander Hollander frowned. "I... there's something else. I suppose 'sensation' would be the word. Something happened, but I don't know what."

Tender pity swam in Captain Gorman's eyes for the briefest second, then he nodded. "I need to speak to your sailors now." He looked at Bickley, who tensed. "Petty Officer, what is your last memory?"

"We were all at muster for a man-overboard alert, sir. We were waiting for Chief Swanson to return so we could go back to bed, or watch."

Torres and I murmured assent.

Captain Gorman didn't look surprised. In fact, we must've confirmed something for him, because he nodded with immense soberness. "It doesn't surprise me that you don't remember anything. It was all so fast. I visited the scene myself once I'd heard what had happened."

"What was fast?" Commander Hollander asked.

A gunshot exploded through the quiet room, sending us all to the floor with shouts alarm. We all floundered to get to our feet and away from the maniac: Commander Muree.

Commander Hollander clutched his chest and braced himself on the table, completely silent but for the sound of the air leaving his lungs.

Commander Muree holstered his smoking pistol, smirking. "Settle down, sailors. He's fine."

Commander Hollander moved his shaking hand and uncovered the hole in his flight suit. It was directly over his heart. After a second of staring down, he unzipped his flight suit a few inches and pulled his collar down.

There was no bullet wound.

"How?" he whispered. He shrank away from Gorman and Muree.

I'd grabbed Torres and thrown her into a corner, where I shielded her from Commander Muree with my arms spread wide, and hopefully a look of stony defiance on my face. Bickley and I glanced at each other. Could we take them? Bickley was ripped, but Torres and I were tiny. Gorman and Muree were two old men, but one of them had a gun. This could go either way.

But the captain just surveyed us all with his usual tiredness. "There's no need to rip me limb from limb. Commander Hollander is already dead. In fact, all of you died last night."

# 3

"You flew your aircraft into the stern of the USS *Taft*, Commander. The sensation you all felt was merely that of your bodies being destroyed in a fraction of a second. Truly, it's remarkable that you felt anything at all."

There was total silence in the conference room. Waves lapped gently against the hull of the ship, and the gentle creaking of the vessel provided a pleasant nautical melody that clashed sharply with the conversation within.

Commander Hollander slowly lowered his hand from his collar. "This is all a sick joke. This has to be a sick joke."

"You were coming in for landing, were you not? Considering the movement of the ship in the storm, and the late hour, is it so hard to believe that you made an error and crashed?"

"You're accusing me of killing myself and three other people," Commander Hollander ground out. "This is beyond the pale."

"Twenty-five other people, actually," Captain Gorman said mildly. "The others have all gone to their final rest. It appears that the *Saint*

*Catherine*, on the other hand, desires a nuclear team and an aviator. Your arrival couldn't have been more timely. We have several operations going on at the moment, and the ship is well past due for an upgrade."

I could feel my heart beating against my rib cage. How could my heart beat if I were dead?

Commander Hollander narrowed his eyes. "You are aware that this all sounds like the ravings of a lunatic, don't you? And isn't it convenient that our bodies were destroyed? How do we know that this... this isn't some kind of..." Words seemed to fail him, as they'd failed the rest of us.

"The bullet was a blank," Torres blurted. "Yeah, it was a blank, and there was already a hole in his uniform. That's easy enough."

I cleared my throat as I dug the bullet out of the wooden paneling along the wall. It had missed my head by less than six inches.

Commander Muree sighed. "Like I said before, we visited the scene immediately afterward. Petty Officer Goldstein was thrown from the compartment, so her family may have remains to bury."

Like a car crashing headfirst into a wall, my thoughts stopped. No, absolutely not, abort mission, *no way in hell* was any of this happening. Hannah and Mordechai Goldstein were not the parents of a dead child. They were not going to sit shiva for their twenty-one-year-old daughter. I was not dead. I was not dead. I. Was. Not. Dead.

I closed my eyes, the analytical, annoying part of my brain not playing along with the emotional part. That cursed part of my mind jumped into action and began to parse through the absurd words, traveling backward to the previous night. Torres had heard Rollins speaking to us from somewhere near, yet far away. A ghost would've qualified, separated by the veil of life and death. And Rollins had been so injured when I'd found him. He'd bled out, and been *so* still...

Like a match igniting in the darkness, my analysis and my

emotions combusted into a tiny, growing internal flame. The first possible truth leapt up, a brainchild born of Occam's razor: we were on some kind of ghost ship. Who was I to say that such things didn't exist? No other possibility seemed remotely sensible. It was the simplest explanation, if the weirdest.

"Rollins died in the engine room, didn't he?" I asked, not caring in the least if I was breaking protocol by speaking to Gorman. "That's why Torres could hear him. He was already on *this* ship."

"Be quiet," Commander Hollander said, still sharp. "I'll speak."

The man who had killed me *dared* to tell me what to do?

My fists clenched, and I stomped up to him. "No. You killed us, *sir*, and my contract died with me, so shut the hell up. You're not an officer, I'm not a petty officer, and as far as I'm concerned, you've done enough." My voice was mottled by fury that coursed through my veins like magma.

"I didn't mean to!" Commander Hollander's shout contained an equal venom.

"So you've accepted that you're dead," Captain Gorman said. "You can already feel it in your bones."

"Can it, old man," I snapped. I whipped my head back toward Commander Hollander. "I swore to my parents that I'd be safe in the Navy, and *you* just—"

He held his hands up. "It was an accident!"

He didn't *mean* to. It was an *accident*. Excuses, all of them.

The rest of us were closing in around him, a rippling energy coursing through me... and into the others. And *from* the others. I could feel their fury as it grew in each one of them, distinct from mine. Like an invisible iron cable, our anger and resentment yoked us together, feeding itself. My emotions braided with theirs, circling, yearning for more.

Their thoughts and feelings raced through my own mind,

blending with memories of my childhood, where I'd been held aloft on the shoulders and dreams of my doting parents. In the space of a breath, it had all been snatched from me, and that one truth began to pour forth new truths like pus.

I'd never get married in my childhood synagogue to the elusive "good Jewish boy" they'd always hoped I'd meet. My father would never apologize to me. He'd never tell me he was proud of my achievements.

I'd never again get to tell my parents that I loved them. That I was sorry I'd broken their hearts. That I was still their little girl. That despite temptations and flirtations with the world, they'd raised me well enough that I'd kept our faith and our ways.

And I was privy to my friends' losses and rages, too.

Bickley wanted to kill Hollander all over again for taking him away from his family. He was never going to see his little sons grow up, nor reconcile with the ex-wife he still loved. Torres thought of her father, the Master Chief, and remembered how proud he'd been when she'd enlisted. Her twin brother had died in infancy, and now her parents would have to say goodbye to their remaining child.

There was something more to Torres's thoughts, an additional level of understanding. She was furious about something else, too.

She was staring at Captain Gorman, her face as calculating as it was cold. "You knew," she said quietly, her voice almost dangerous with the force of her anger. "That's why you sent the warning on the chalkboard. You knew what was coming." She balled her fists—and a large crack appeared in one of the portholes.

"It wasn't me! *Stop!*" Captain Gorman commanded, again in the voice that would not be disobeyed.

But we disobeyed, and the world turned red as the cycle of sorrow spun out of control.

The table flipped up by itself, tossing the two old men against the bulkhead. Bickley and I shoved aside the table and tackled Gorman and Muree, our fists flying. Torres jumped on Hollander. Rage poured out of us like a hurricane, tearing apart the curtains, upholstery, and even the carpet, all by itself. The portholes began to shatter, causing shards of glass to rain down on us as we tussled. Some of them froze in the air like lethal rain drops, then flew outwards as if they were blown backward by the chaos, embedding themselves in the walls.

The door flew open and several sailors jumped into the fray, pulling us off of the officers. Male shouts and female shrieks mixed to create complete pandemonium. I swung wildly for any face my fist could connect with.

Everything began to swim together in front of my vision, all the confusion and pain from my own heart mixing with the others, beating wildly through my core like drums in the very center of my soul. I'd lost everything, lost everything, lost everything...

*I'm so sorry.*

The words, more breath than speech, whispered in my head. They were as soft as my mother's kiss, yet solid enough to sever the connection between myself and shipmates. The speaker's sincere condolences washed over me, breaking my heart and freezing the raging inferno that had fueled my meltdown.

I stumbled away from the two seamen who'd put up their fists, challenging me to a fight. "What? Who said that?"

"It was the ship," Captain Gorman said. He was sitting up against the bulkhead, his uniform torn and scuffed in places, but otherwise unharmed. Commander Muree was in Bickley's chokehold. Bickley made a face and pushed him away.

Torres backed away. "What do you mean, it was the ship? What's going on? What just happened? *What is this place?!*"

The door banged against the bulkhead as I sprinted from the room.

*I'm dead. I'm not dead. I'm dead. I'm not dead.* My heart was beating double-time, my blood pounding in my ears. How could this be? How could I still feel and think and hear if I were dead? How could I have a heart to beat and blood to bleed?

A blond sailor seized my shoulders, making me stop in my tracks. "Hey, slow down there, shipmate. You're new, aren't you? Are you okay?"

I shoved him away and kept running down the narrow passage-way, once more sprinting past huddles of sailors who pointed and whispered. I had no idea where I was running, but if I followed the leaking pipes overhead, maybe I'd find a place of safety.

I burst through a door and tumbled onto the flight deck, where the aviators were still attending to their vintage planes. My chest heaving, I sidled alongside the hull and slunk into the shadow of a lone Corsair. I clutched the landing gear, then kneeled on the rubber tires. Sweat, and a few tears, dripped off of my chin.

A man with orange paddles hurried past me to an open section of the flight deck and raised them, his paddles moving in the intricate move-ments of air traffic control. Indeed, he was staring at the sky beyond the stern of the ship. I squinted against the glare of the late-morning sun, and sure enough, a silvery plane was coming in for a landing.

The plane neared, its mechanical drone drowning out all other sounds. Finally, it touched down on the deck and bounced once, the tail hook catching on the rusting cable. Flight deck workers ran out and greeted the pilot, who gave them a friendly wave through the glass.

I couldn't help but watch the team as they worked to bring the plane in and begin routine maintenance, and as my heart settled back into its normal pace, the analytical side of my brain won out again.

Everyone looked so happy and normal here. Adjusted. The happiness automatically struck down the possibility that I was in a place of eternal torment—so was this the place of eternal peace and rest? I'd spent little time studying the afterlife in *shul*. I'd been told that I would be "gathered to my people" when I died, and perhaps meet Hashem, whose true name was so holy that we didn't dare to speak it.

But everyone was working here, and the officer wielding a gun didn't exactly hint at eternal peace. I wasn't surrounded by scores of Jews, from what I could tell. Nothing I'd seen hinted at the near presence of deity, either.

This was all very disappointing.

The door I'd come through opened again, and my shipmates came out, their heads turning. Torres saw me and opened her mouth, but I put a finger to my lips. She nodded, tapped Bickley on the shoulder, and pointed to me.

They rushed over and hid with me in the shadow of the Corsair. After everything that had happened, I wanted to hug these two. However, I just swallowed and glanced around us, then gestured for them to huddle around me. "What happened back there?" I whispered. "I had to leave. I couldn't take it anymore."

Bickley palmed his face. "I don't know. The other sailors cleared out after you ran, but Hollander got into a shouting match with Gorman and Muree. We ran out as soon as we could and followed you."

Torres squeaked. "How do you think they did it? They really did shoot him."

The Corsair that had just landed taxied past us, and the flight deck crew walked in the other direction. Their loud masculine laughter was relaxing, in a way. Familiar. The military I was from was full of happy people at work, teams of buddies who worked together like a well-oiled machine. The people around me had been part of my own team.

I closed my eyes, straining for even the tiniest recollection of my final moment on the USS *Taft.*

*A sound.*

*A sensation.*

*Nothing.*

Fingers brushed mine. I opened my eyes to see Torres peering at me, tiny wrinkles appearing between her eyebrows. "Are you okay?" she whispered. "I heard your thoughts in the conference room. I heard about your parents."

I leaned against the Corsair. "Yeah, and I heard about your dad and your brother. I heard all of that stuff. We had some kind of mind-meld woo-woo mojo thing going on for a few seconds. If anyone has any—"

"We're spiritually connected," Torres said.

"Excuse me?" Bickley said, a sigh in each word.

Torres stood her ground, pulling back her shoulders. "I'm not going to let you guys make fun of me this time. I really am psychic. I woke up to the sound of someone telling me she was happy to have me on board, and now I know who it was. The ship was talking to me. Back there, when we all went haywire, we were feeding into each other's emotions. We became, like, poltergeists."

She blushed pink. "I think I was the catalyst for that. I was so angry. I had all these thoughts running through my head, and then suddenly I could see a little bit of the history of the people in the room, and the ship was there, its own entity. I made the porthole glass crack, remember?"

Bickley shook his head. "No. It's too ridiculous. We're not dead. I can feel the heat reflecting off the flight deck right now. My hand still hurts from punching Hollander. We're alive. Back there, something happened, and I don't know what, but we're not dead. Maybe we've all been given LSD."

Torres and I exchanged a doubtful look.

He took in a steadying breath, then exhaled heavily, clearly thinking hard. "Okay, that sounded far fetched. The way I see it, we're in some kind of fantastical mess. I'm an open-minded guy, right? I can accept that there are forces at work here that I didn't know existed. But we're not dead."

Torres rocked back on her heels. "They kept saying that they'd visited the scene of the so-called crash. Maybe we can, too. That would be hard to fake. Wanna ask the nurses? They seemed friendly."

Bickley nodded. "Stay here. I'm going to ask that guy how we got on board." He pulled back his shoulders and stalked off toward a lone flight crew guy who was taking off work gloves several feet from us.

Though I'd never say it out loud, I was glad Bickley was taking charge.

We all watched as Bickley spoke in a low voice to the man, who replied inaudibly. After a few exchanges, they both walked over to us. His uniform identified him as Seaman Stanholtzer.

Stanholtzer smiled from ear to ear when he saw Torres and me. "I'd heard there were real women sailors aboard, but I didn't believe it. I think I was born in the wrong decade."

Torres offered her hand. "And what decade was that?"

"Born in 1921, ma'am. Died 1943."

I paused, then offered my hand to the dashing brunet. "You, um, look good for a dead man."

Stanholtzer laughed while he shook my hand. "I could say that you look good for a dead woman. Was it the jet? That's what they were saying down in berthing."

I couldn't help a blush. Nobody liked to hear a qualifier after "you look good," supposedly-dead or not.

"We were kind of hoping you could tell us a bit about what happened last night," Bickley said, a thread of imperative in his tone. "You mentioned that we got here through 'weak spots' when you were talking to me a minute ago. What are those?"

Stanholtzer must've heard it too, because he stepped back and deflated. "They're the holes in the fabric of reality. Like a curtain on a window, sometimes the fabric has a spot that's more worn than the rest of the fabric. Some are large enough for a ship to pass through, while others are very small, no bigger than a few feet wide. In the world of the living, there are people who can sense those spots, or at least sense what comes through. In my day we called them fortune tellers, soothsayers, and things like that."

"Psychics," Torres murmured. "That's another term."

"Yes, I've heard that one, too," Stanholtzer said. "We have a psychic on board, actually. Seaman Wayne. He foresaw the crash and..." Stanholtzer stopped, apparently picking his words. "...he *claims* he wanted to warn you all. The way I heard it, though, he actually was going back and forth between the ships and mucking around on the living ship, causing trouble. He got caught last night when he was sneaking back onto the *Saint Catherine*, and the Master at Arms tossed him in the brig. He's lucky, though. There are many weak spots around these parts that pirates use to chase down ghosts like us. He could've easily ran into one of them."

"Causing trouble," I repeated. "Like, maybe, throwing chem lights overboard?" My stomach tightened. If that man-overboard hadn't been called, Torres and Bickley wouldn't have been in the reactor office with me. They probably would've lived.

Stanholtzer shrugged. "Can't say I know what a chem light is, ma'am, but it sounds like something Wayne would do."

Bickley gulped, and I saw the pain and anger in his eyes. "One last thing. Where is the weak spot that Seaman Wayne went through to get to our ship?"

Stanholtzer paused, and a grim look overtook his features. "Oh, I know where this is going. You can't go back. You have to understand that. You're dead, Petty Officer. All of you are. I've had this talk before. There's nothing to be found but trouble on living ships."

"Where is it?" I repeated.

Stanholtzer's eyes flickered over to a corner of the hangar bay, then back to us. "I have to go," he said in an undertone. "If—no, *when* you get caught, you never talked to me, okay? It's not worth getting dumped in Port des Morts."

"Right," we all said. I didn't care enough to ask where Port des Morts was. I wasn't going there.

Stanholtzer hurried off, throwing a dark look at us once before disappearing through a doorway.

Bickley slammed his fist against the Corsair. "Did I just hear that we were all in that room together, and thus died together, because some asshat on this ship was throwing chem lights overboard as a prank?"

"That seems to be the measure of it," Torres grumbled. "And we're obviously not in Heaven. I wouldn't say this is Hell, either. Ergo, Purgatory. We're being purged of—"

"Shut up, Torres!" Bickley's shout caught the attention of several passerby, and we retreated deeper into the shadows. "Knock it off," he hissed, quieter. "Can we just...quit it with the afterlife stuff? I don't think we're in any kind of afterlife any of us has heard about." He shot me a quizzical look. "What did you learn in *shul*?"

I rolled my eyes. "Well, gee. Right after the part about how to clean the temple, there's this long description of Hashem's instructions on how to build a ghost ship, and He gave it to Noah's cousin Brad, who—"

"Enough," Torres barked. Her hands were on her head, and her stricken expression, with tears on her cheeks, was enough to make me regret my sarcasm.

I pulled her into a hug, and let her sob unrestrainedly on my chest. "I'm sorry," I whispered. "We'll figure this out." Tears spilled over on my own cheeks, and we wept together, just Marisol and Rachel, two friends lost at sea.

Torres hiccuped. "I can feel it."

"Feel what?" I said dully.

"The weak spot that Wayne went through. It's definitely right over there. It's billowing out all this... energy, I guess. Like an open window allowing a draft to come in."

I couldn't feel anything.

"Everyone, act nonchalant," Bickley said in a low voice. "There are people over there."

We walked into the enormous, shady hangar in which planes were stored. We weren't bothered by anyone, since most of them were absorbed in their daily tasks, probably uninterested in whatever the newbies were doing.

In the corner of my eye, I saw a few men begin to unload crates of ordnance from a cargo plane. Why *was* there so much ordnance? What did this crew expect to happen?

I gave my head a little shake. I didn't care, because it didn't matter.

Torres guided us to a spot near the corner. "It's right here." She craned her neck and looked around, then held out her hands. "I can see the opening. It's all intuitive for me, like I was born for this. Grab on."

The door Stanholtzer had gone through opened up, and he came

back out—this time with the Master at Arms and two of his deputies.
He pointed toward us.

"Hey!" the Master at Arms yelled. "Get away from there!"

"Now!" I shouted.

We took her hands, and her eyelids fluttered. My body fell
through an invisible gauze, as thin as gossamer. The entire world
receded into blackness as I descended into a well—no, a chasm—of
nothingness.

Above me, at the entrance of the well and getting farther and
farther away each second, the Master of Arms held out his hands,
horror etched onto his face.

# 4

I could see the result of the wind that whipped through the charred room, but I could not feel it. That was the first shock.

A stiff sea breeze blew continually through the enormous gaping maw in the side of the USS *Taft*, causing ashes and charred bits of detritus to flutter along the ruined deck plates, but not even the hair on my arms stood up. Instead, I drifted through the ashy space, soundless, and stared at everything.

It was so quiet. Unnaturally quiet.

Why wasn't there any noise? Certainly the two men down the passageway should've made some, since their mouths were moving. The waves that crashed against the hull below should've sent up roars of sea spray and hissing. The helicopter that hovered nearby should've drowned out everything with its thud-thud-thuds.

But all I could hear was my own fake breath. Fake—because I was a ghost floating through where I'd died. There was no denying it anymore.

The room where we were was more of a "space" now. Our cause of death was childishly easy to suss out: Commander Hollander's aircraft had exploded upon impact with the hull of the ship, blasting open the side and filling the reactor office with flames fed by jet fuel. The ceiling, deck, and bulkheads had melted in the heat, creating a cavern that stretched five levels.

We hadn't burned. We'd been vaporized. That was the sensation I'd felt in my last moment, and for the first time, I was grateful that my memory stopped there. I was dimly aware of Bickley and Torres floating nearby, but I couldn't see them. In fact, I couldn't see myself. I was merely that, an awareness.

The carcass of the F-18 had fallen through the deck into the room below. I drifted downward and gasped when I saw the twisted, destroyed wreckage: racks. Sailors had been sliding back into bed when the accident had occurred, and many wouldn't have had time to escape. A burning plane, and the deck it landed on, had collapsed on them. Liquid fuel, so hot the flames would've been invisible, had poured down onto the terrified sailors in their last moments.

Captain Gorman had claimed that my shipmates, those poor people in the compartment below the reactor office, had gone to their final rest... but not us. The USS *Saint Catherine* had snatched three nukes, and the aviator that had caused all the trouble, and tucked us securely into the sick bay.

But why? What could we possibly offer to a ghost ship from World War II? I drifted around the space, alone and bodiless. There were no answers for me here, but then again, what did I expect?

A low, animalistic growl made me turn around, but there was nothing there. "Hello?"

Nothing.

But I wasn't alone. Eyes were on me. I drifted away from the wreckage, the echo of cold trickling down my neck.

"Rachel... bravest woman I ever met..." A female voice called me to itself.

I thought about answering it—and then I was there. I had no recollection of traveling from one end of the ship to the other.

I was in the ship's chapel, a place I'd only been in once or twice. Sunlight leaked through the bland stained glass windows, illuminating the face of a young woman I knew from the reactor department. Her voice came in and out as she spoke to a crowd of sailors.

A memorial service.

I drifted forward and looked over my shoulder at the assembled faces, then froze. It wasn't just any memorial service, it was a department memorial service, comprising my former colleagues.

I had no idea who was speaking about me. Regret and shame twisted inside, and I bowed my head. She was brand new to the ship, I knew that, and I'd said hello to her once or twice in the passageway. But goodness, she looked cut up about poor, dead Rachel Goldstein.

Dang it, *what was her name?*

She was still speaking. "...when Lieutenant Murphy told me that she'd dragged Petty Officer Rollins all the way to the reactor control room, I wasn't surprised." She laughed through her tears. "Petty Officer Goldstein always made sure to say hello to me when she saw me. I guess she knew I was new, and..."

Had I always said hello? My mother had always accused me of being too lost in my own head to ever acknowledge when she was talking. Maybe I had grown up a little in the Navy.

Portraits were lined up behind the woman, no doubt hastily printed off in a yeoman's office. My portrait sat between Bickley's and Torres', while Rollins was on the far right. The remaining picture was of Chief Swanson, who was actually smiling in his portrait.

The nuclear navy had taken a heavy loss, indeed.

It made sense that the nukes were holding a private, departmental memorial service; nobody from the rest of the ship would've known who we even were. Nukes were always relegated to the bottom of the ship, behind heavy doors and stern keep-out signs. We were a close-knit community whose lives revolved around the reactors. The ship-wide memorial service would be larger and fancier, but this was the real one. This was the one where people were truly mourning me.

I went through the aisles of seats, taking in every single face.

The Reactor Officer, the highest officer in the department, was crying. He'd always made sure to visit us during long night watches. His wife had liked to send in home-baked treats for us when we were in port.

I kissed his cheek and whispered words of thanks.

Lieutenant Murphy wept into a lace handkerchief, and it occurred to me that she was probably aware that she was the last living person to speak to me. In fact, she'd been unfortunate enough to call the medical emergency for a dead man just minutes before.

I kneeled down in front of her. "Hey, I'm okay," I said as kindly as I could. "Rollins is too, I think. We didn't feel any pain."

"Speak for yourself, chick."

I spun around.

Rollins, still in his bloody uniform, was leaning casually against the bulkhead. He gave me a little wave. "*You* went poof in that crash, but *I* banged my head. Hurt like hell."

Despite the blood, he looked as healthy as ever. And he was visible. "Why can I see you?" I asked. "I can't even see myself."

He pushed himself up and walked through a handful of sailors to get to me. "I can see you. You see what you expect to see. Our perceptions create reality here. At least, I think that's how it works. You're a ghost, so you expect to be invisible, right? I didn't realize I was dead for a while, so I was just walking around and trying to get people's attention. Here, give me your hand."

I stuck out my hand, and he grasped it. The firm pressure of a human hand jump-started my appearance. Color flooded through my hand, coursing up my arm and swirling into my torso like paint in clear water.

Something flickered in the corner of my vision, in the doorway. I looked over, but saw nothing. The same trickle of cold from before raced down my spine. We were not alone.

I pointed to the doorway. "Did you see—?" But it was already gone.

He brushed off my shoulder. "Looking good. Sorry about the accident." His face softened. "I was just putting two and two together when the plane hit. I was there when... well, I was there. It was actually me who got you all onto the *Saint Catherine*."

I was getting a headache from all of this. "What do you mean, it was you?"

He pointed all around. "According to Dot and Peggy, when you have one psychic on a living ship and one on the *Saint Catherine*, you can hook them up like a plug into a socket. Torres was the living one, and some guy named Wayne is the *Saint Catherine*'s. So when you all died and Dot and Peggy popped through one of the openings with their stretchers, I told them to save their energy, and I carried all five of you through the openings myself. You guys were in some kind of stasis, probably from how fast the deaths happened."

This all begged one question. "So why are you still on the *Taft*?"

His expression darkened. "Gorman gave me the whole speech. I'm not getting involved with any of that. I pledged my life to the Navy, not my afterlife. I'll stay right here and watch over this ship."

I rubbed the back of my head. "Um, pretend I attacked Gorman and Muree during the welcoming speech, and therefore didn't get to the shocking information you're insinuating."

He paused, then laughed. "Was it just you, or was it all of you?"

Two invisible awarenesses joined us, their identities automatically obvious to me. Instead of greeting them, I reached out and touched where I knew their hands to be. Color raced up their arms like it had mine, and my confused, ghostly teammates stared at their hands like people seeing the sunrise for the first time.

"Yeah, we're definitely dead," I said quickly. I turned back to Rollins. "You were saying?"

Rollins arranged his legs Indian-style, making him appear to be sitting on an invisible chair. "There's a war on," he said, his tone dark. "And the *Saint Catherine* is a warship. Gorman was going on about some magic crap, and how the ship needs sailors to do its part in the conflict. That was the weirdest part—he kept referring to the ship as a person."

"It *is* a being," Torres said, pulling her legs into the same floating style. "It's spoken to us."

Rollins didn't miss a beat. "I don't care. I'm not getting involved in some magical war of the ancients. I have that choice. If any of you want to stay behind with me, I don't mind. I'll haunt the *Taft* forever if that's what it takes to not get embroiled in someone else's fight."

We all looked at each other. Torres pursed her lips. "I think I'd rather explore the other world than haunt the *Taft* forever."

"I want to go home to my parents," I said. "They're—"

"No, you don't." Bickley shook his head. "Guys, I know every single one of us has someone to go back to, but we can't. For the sake of our sanity, we can't haunt the living and watch them grow old without us. I'm not going to watch Tanya marry some other guy. I'm not going to watch my boys call him 'Daddy.' It's the natural order of things, but I'm not sticking around to see it. I'm going back to the *Saint Catherine* and figuring things out from there." He floated backward and drifted out of the room.

Torres gave me a sad look. "I guess we really are dead, huh?"

"You think?" I grumbled. I still wanted to go see my parents, but I had no idea how to get off the *Taft*, or if I even could.

Torres moved her head side to side, her body trailing along each way as she did so. "I'm going to go pray at the crash site, okay? Take your time. I won't take anyone back until you're ready to go. Call me when you need me."

She floated away through the bulkhead.

I turned to Rollins, but he was already disappearing through another bulkhead, leaving me alone with the living. Their voices came in and out; I could most clearly hear words said about me.

Pouting, I slouched in an empty chair. One of the sailors squinted and blinked in my direction, then gave her head a little shake.

"Boo," I mumbled. "Something, something, dead man's chest."

She tapped her ears until the person sitting next to her elbowed her in the ribs and pointed toward the podium.

Ugh, I couldn't even haunt someone at my own memorial service. This sucked.

Fatigue settled on my shoulders, making me slouch even more as necessary questions presented themselves. What was I supposed to do now? I'd accomplished what I'd set out to do by getting off the *Saint Catherine*, but what was next? What was going to motivate me to get out of this chair when my memorial service was done?

I closed my eyes, forcing back tears. My story was done. The Book of Rachel was closed, and the world had moved on. I was just a remnant of whom I'd been in life.

*Oh, stop wallowing.*

The memory of my mother's exasperated chide, said whenever my lacrosse team had lost, cut through my pity party.

"Yeah, but, I'm dead, Mom," I muttered. "I'm allowed to wallow just this once."

*You wanted adventure, right? Go back to the Saint Catherine and find out more about the war. It sounds like the ship needs you.*

"I'll stay right here, thanks. It's safer."

*My daughter isn't a coward.* My father spoke this time.

"No, your daughter is a selfish ingrate, remember?" I sat up, squeezing my eyes shut as hard as I could. "Well, watch me. I'm not moving. I'll... just... haunt this seat for eternity."

The soft glow of the electric candelabra blurred from tears, and I crossed my arms across my chest. I was definitely allowed to wallow. I was dead. I'd died when I was twenty-one. I had nothing to look forward to, nowhere to go, and nothing to do.

Another low growl made me whip around and stare at the passageway. "Who's there? Rollins, is that..."

My words crumbled into nothing when I focused on what I was seeing in the passageway. It was darker than usual, and rippling, as though heat waves were rising from the deck. A low rustle emanated from the depths of the tunnel—"passageway" didn't cut it anymore—warning me of danger.

My feet touched the deck, providing a blessed feeling of grounding. I didn't take my eyes off the tunnel as I backed through the crowd, passing through them and causing one or two of them to shiver violently.

A figure took form in the darkness, blurry yet distinctly masculine. He rippled along with the waves of dark energy, then stepped onto the deck, holding up his hands in that same confused way my friends had. His features sharpened, melting from an all-over, shadowy charcoal gray to bone white.

His eyes were equally white, with only a tiny black pinprick for pupils. Shaggy blue-green hair, knotted and snarled, hung down to his ears. His clothes, brown rags tied together with leather straps, were bloodstained and torn in many places. The knife on his thigh glinted in the weak sunlight of the chapel.

I backed away even more. "What the *hell* are you?"

He bared his long, pointed teeth and said something in a foreign language. His voice was not human—the vowels and consonants clashed together sharply, forming phenoms that I'd never heard from a human larynx.

"Okay, uh, bye now," I said, my eyes darting around the room. "Bickley! Rollins! Anyone! Help!"

He unsheathed his knife.

Bickley and the others descended through the ceiling at the same time the man hurled his knife at me. I ducked at the last moment, and the knife sailed straight through the bulkhead.

Bickley and Rollins tackled him. The man crumpled under their combined weights, wailing in his strange, inhuman voice.

Torres hurried over to me. "Who is that?" she whispered. "He has that same kind of energy I felt before."

"I don't know," I said, gasping for breath. "He—"

The man grabbed Bickley's face. Bickley shouted into his palm, first in pain, then in terror. Visible little beads of light crawled out of his body, up through his face, and into the palm of the man.

Torres and I jumped into the fray, kicking and stomping the man with as much fury as we could muster. He let go of Bickley, who crumpled. Torres immediately grabbed Bickley's collar and pulled him away, then did the same with Rollins.

She held her arms wide, shielding us, then jabbed her finger toward the tunnel. "Go back where you came from! I know you can understand me!"

The man picked himself up, trembling—but whether from fear or anger, it was not clear. He gave his head a shake. "G...ghosts," he spat, the word accented but clear. "You are... human... waste."

Bickley sputtered, but Torres took my hand in her left one, and

Bickley's in her right. "I'm a psychic," she said, a warning in her tone. "And if you don't leave, we'll make you."

The man growled, a low beast-like rumble that vibrated in my chest. He'd been the sound I'd heard before.

"Last chance," Torres said. "Everyone, remember what we did to Gorman and Muree? Let's do that again."

An electric candelabra by the podium fell over, causing several living sailors to gasp. I stepped up, raising my hand, and focusing on the thread of anger that tugged at my consciousness. I seamlessly joined Torres' mind, and this time there was no hurricane—just power. Bickley jumped in, strengthening the force even more.

Torres lowered her head and narrowed her eyes—and the porthole to our left exploded. "Good job, everyone. Focus it on this piece of crap. One... two..."

He turned and ran into the tunnel, the darkness receding with him. In less than three seconds, he and the mysterious tunnel had vanished.

I let out a gasped breath. "I think I speak for everyone when I say, what—"

"He was taking energy from me," Bickley said, his chest heaving. "I could feel him draining something from my body."

"Then let's get the hell out of here." I was still staring at the place where the tunnel had been. "Torres, now, if you please."

Forget the *Taft*. The situation was simple: I'd never seen anything like that on the *Saint Catherine*, so back to the ghost ship I was going.

Torres pulled us into a huddle, and within the blink of an eye, we were back at the scene of the tragedy, where the wind still blew silently and salt spray blew everywhere but didn't touch me.

Rollins broke out of the huddle and flew upward. "This is where I leave you," he said sadly. "I'll be here." He gave me a thin smile. "I really am grateful for you trying to save me, Rach. I'm sorry that we weren't able to be friends." He saluted us, then floated up and away through the ceiling.

Torres gulped. "It's his choice. Let's go back now."

There was another sensation of falling, falling, falling as the world turned back, and this time I was cognizant of pressure on me—like I was traveling through something. The well-like opening of the *Saint Catherine*'s world neared, and then we were there.

A bomb exploded.

## 5

The world was ending.

I pushed myself up from the deck, my vision spinning. *What the...?* I gasped and shrank back into the corner of the hanger bay with my friends.

The sky was alight with sparks and embers, and so many planes. Some of them flew far overhead, shooting at something unseen to me on the other side of the *Saint Catherine*, their fronts lighting up with tiny orange-and-yellow bursts of light that contrasted sharply with the choking smoke.

Men sprinted back and forth across the deck, shouting to each other and hauling buckets of water, hoses, and flight gear.

"Move, move, move!"

"Stanholtzer, go!"

"Get more ordnance!"

A high whistle from above ended—and then the ship shuddered under the force of an explosion. I landed roughly on my knees next to my friends. Shards of white-hot metal and glass cut my hands and face, but I mentally shook them off. We were already dead, and no matter how scary...

I paused mid-thought and stared at my hands.

The cuts weren't healing themselves.

I struggled to control my breathing as I shook my hands, the blood flowing freely from several serious lacerations. The others did the same, smearing their blood all over their skin as they tapped and rubbed their wounds.

Bickley pulled Torres and me into a protective hug and shuffled us along toward the door that led into the bowels of the ship. "Let's go," he said, panting and casting a fearful look toward the skyward battle. "We need to get away. This is different."

My teeth began to chatter as I realized the truth: yet again, everything I thought I knew about this godforsaken water world had been thrown for a loop. The bullet hadn't hurt Commander Hollander, but the shrapnel was dangerous. Okay. What was the logic to this place? Why did a ballistic bullet not hurt a ghost, but jagged metal from a bomb did?

Someone slammed into us, shoving us into an unused flight deck control room. It was Commander Hollander. He opened up a closet, and we all crammed inside.

"Don't speak," Commander Hollander said, putting his hands over Bickley's and my mouth. "Just listen. I've been looking everywhere for you guys. There's a flotilla of... of *strange* beings on the starboard side. We can use the battle as a diversion to escape."

*A flotilla?* "How?" I asked into his hand.

He slowly uncovered our mouths and pulled a cord, turning on a lone ceiling bulb. "There's a small cargo plane out there that's not being used. On my order, get in the plane. I'll fly us out. I got one of the sailors to tell me where the nearest port is. It's not far. We can fly there."

Discomfort shivered to life. This was not a smart plan. "No," I said. "We have no idea where we are, nor do you know for sure if you can fly the plane. We could easily crash into the sea." I shivered at the memory of recent events. "And if those strange creatures are what I think they are, then I'd rather stay on a warship than risk getting captured."

And if I were being really honest, I didn't want to go anywhere with Commander Hollander.

Another bomb exploded, rocking us and knocking dust off shelves. Men shouted even more, calling for aid and ordnance. In the midst of the voices, Dot and Peggy shouted for someone to bring them more bandages.

"I don't think this warship is going to be sailing much longer," Commander Hollander said. "And I don't think we're going to get another chance."

As much as I wanted to stay on the ship, I didn't want to stay on the ship alone if the others were leaving. The light went out, causing all of us to huddle together. After a second, I opened the door, allowing in a narrow shaft of light. "Fine."

Commander Hollander peeked out, then beckoned for us to follow. "Everyone, hurry. Don't look around, just get onto that plane there." He pointed to a smallish cargo plane, the one I'd seen people unloading ordnance from earlier. "Three, two, one... go."

We all sprinted to the olive drab plane, which had seemingly been forgotten in the chaos of the attack. As predicted, the sailors rushed around us, never stopping as we wrenched open the side door and hopped into the cramped, musty cargo compartment. For once, being a nuke, and therefore virtually forgotten by everyone, was working in our favor.

When we were in, Commander Hollander slammed the door shut and all but jumped into the pilot's seat, his hands flying over the controls. The engine roared to life. "Everyone, sit down and hold onto something," he said loudly, barely audible over the din. He glanced over his shoulder at me. "Goldstein, what's in those crates?" We began to taxi toward the runway.

I was sitting on unmarked wooden crates, and I hastily got off and opened one. "Ordnance, I think."

"The hell is that stuff?" Torres said, kneeling next to me, the urgency of the moment forgotten. "Those aren't bombs."

The crate was filled with beautiful crystal spheres, about four inches in diameter. Each sphere contained a viscous, silvery liquid that shimmered as it moved, showing shades of blue, green, and yellow in the low light. Sparkles floated in the liquid, glittering like tiny bits of treasure adrift in a silver sea.

And the sphere was *humming*. Though the sounds of battle and the plane engine were all around us, the sphere was emitting a soft, almost musical hum. Multiple tones were perfectly audible, creating a chorus of gentle sounds in my head. Almost like... like *voices*.

"Can you hear that?" I asked Torres, carefully passing her the sphere. "It sounds like music."

Torres held up the sphere to her ear. "Yeah, I can. Bick, are you hearing this?"

Bickley was staring at the crate, the glow from the spheres lighting up his face. He nodded slowly, then took the sphere from me and placed it back in the sawdust-lined crate. "Yes, I can hear it. Let's leave this stuff alone. I don't trust inanimate objects that have a voice."

Commander Hollander looked over his shoulder again. "I can't hear anything. Hold on to something, because we're about to get airborne."

I shut the crate, then grabbed hold of an anchored shelf that held more crates.

Commander Hollander accelerated. The end of the runway neared, then disappeared—and then we were facing the smokey sky. The crates all moved back an inch as we ascended. Planes whizzed past us, the drone of their propellers coming in and out as we flew by them.

"Turning," Captain Hollander said, moving the controls to the right. "Let's take a look at... whoa." He'd turned the plane to fly over the battle.

The flotilla, at least six ships strong, flanked the entire starboard side of the *Saint Catherine*. Two of the biggest ships were firing glowing projectiles at the carrier. They exploded upon impact—yet the ship was unharmed. Whenever the explosive detonated, a silvery screen appeared, like a forcefield over the vessel.

However, as I watched, one of the bombs flew toward the ship and hit it directly, blowing a huge hole in the hull. Tiny sailors at mounted guns aimed their weapons toward the ship and started blasting the enemy, but that ship also had a forcefield. Two tiny people in white dresses dashed around, stopping at other tiny people lying on the deck.

I swallowed the lump in my throat. We were cowards for leaving in the middle of a battle. Dot and Peggy needed help.

*Rachel.* The breathy voice from Gorman's conference room stirred in the center of my mind.

"What?" I said aloud.

*I need you.*

Torres and Bickley had stiffened, their eyes unfocusing. "Can anyone else hear that?" Torres said. "I think it's her. I think it's the *Saint Catherine*."

Commander Hollander had maneuvered us around the battle, and already the sounds of war were growing dim.

*Come back.*

I stood partially. "Commander. Turn around."

"No!" Bickley shouted. "We don't take orders from the ship!"

I gave a stricken look to Torres, whose eyes were darting back and forth as she argued with herself. "No, I think we should keep going," she said. "This isn't our battle, and it isn't our ship."

"Turn around!" I shouted at Commander Hollander. "We shouldn't have left!"

"Why not?" he protested.

*"Because it's selfish!"*

We were being selfish, greedy, ungrateful people who'd been offered safety and security on the ship, and what had we done? We'd run as soon as we could. We were pathetic and deserved to be shot out of the sky.

Bickley jumped up and placed his hands on my shoulders. "Rach, this has nothing to do with selfishness, okay? We're protecting ourselves. We don't belong on that ship. Let's all just—"

Another plane nearly hit us, the drone canceling out Bickley's words. Commander Hollander banked sharply, tossing us off of our feet. The crate we'd opened tipped over, and several of the glowing spheres tumbled out. One flashed brilliant gold, like a flashlight turning on and off.

I picked it up, and it flashed again, and then again. It was hotter to the touch than before, and the humming was louder.

It flashed three times. Now it was uncomfortably hot.

I swore in Yiddish. "Open the door," I said loudly. "Now."

Nobody moved. "Why?" Bickley said.

"Now!" I shoved him aside, struggling to keep the sphere in my hands; I had to keep tossing it back and forth. My fingers were blistering, surely. I shoved the sphere in my pocket and grabbed the handle of the door. Now I could feel something seeping from the sphere into my body.

Their shouts of alarm were drowned out by the endless roar of the wind. We were at least two thousand feet in the air, and flying along at a brilliant speed, the battle already far behind. The ships looked like toy models in an endless gray-green bathtub.

I threw the sphere with all my might. The tiny glistening glass ball fell through the air, flashed once more, and then—

My vision went white as a wall of sound exploded outwards, like every foghorn on earth had gone off at once. The sonic blast knocked me backward and slammed the door shut.

Commander Hollander's hands scrambled on the control panel as the plane was buffeted up and down on the wave. We began to zigzag in the sky, and the rest of the crates fell off the shelf and tipped over. The flashing of the sonic bombs lit up the tiny space like the Las Vegas strip.

I looked up from my supine position on the metal floor and simply stared at the dozens of bombs that had begun their detonation sequences. *Well... this sucks.*

"*Now* would be nice!" Commander Hollander screamed over his shoulder. The plane tilted again, and this time I could see that we'd turned around and were heading toward the battle.

I jumped to my feet, wrenched open the door, and then began kicking the flashing bombs out of the plane directly into the slipstream. Commander Hollander was bellowing obscenities while he tried to control the plane. Torres and Bickley were screaming at the top of their lungs, chucking the bombs through the open door. I finally began tossing whole crates out. I moved like a madwoman, desperate to rid the plane of the otherworldly ordnance.

The sonic blasts obliterated all sounds, deafening me to even the rushing of my heart in my ears. There was no onomatopoeia in existence that could capture the sheer force of the sound. Nothing could possibly still exist, at all, anywhere, beyond the scope of the explosions.

Yet, a moment later, we were flying over tiny bits of wood and metal where, formerly, a fully-armed flotilla had been. Nothing else was there: not bodies, not furniture, not desperate survivors waving for aid. It had all been disintegrated.

By us. By me.

Weirdly, the *Saint Catherine* was fine except for the holes in the hull that had been blasted open by the flotilla. Dot and Peggy, tiny figures in white that were clear against the gray steel, darted around from person to person.

Commander Hollander tilted the controls, his chest heaving. "Oh my God. Oh my God. I'm landing," he said with gasping breaths. "Hold on."

The three of us in the back clung to each other. Torres hid her face in my shoulder, and Bickley wrapped his muscular arms around the two of us. The flight deck filled the windshield, growing nearer every second. Finally, we touched down, bounced, and then ground to a halt next to a few other planes.

Nobody said anything for a few seconds.

Bickley slowly released us from his tight embrace. "Okay," he whispered. "Let's get out."

Commander Hollander turned around in his chair. "Um... I don't know how to say this, but... the Master at Arms is on his way here right now, and all his men are holding hand cuffs."

# 6

The Master at Arms slammed my cell door shut. The metallic bang echoed around the brig, hammering home just how utterly pathetic I was. I slouched against the tiled wall, my hands in my pockets.

He crossed his arms. "I don't want to hear a peep out of you. Just sit there and worry about what you'll do when we dump your sorry ass in Port des Morts."

I gave him a sidelong stare, then mimed zipping my lips and throwing away the key.

He tutted and marched away, up the stairs, and then through the heavy steel door to the brig. The final slam of the brig door made me wince, and then sigh as I slid down the bulkhead. I banged my head against the wall repeatedly. *You're an idiot. You're an idiot. You're an idiot.*

The pain from banging my head distracted from the pain in my hands, which had burned ever since I'd picked up the glass spheres. I looked at them, studying the palms and backs for the millionth time, but could see no difference. The cuts and lacerations looked the same as before, and the pain felt much deeper than skin wounds.

A whistle sounded, high and long. Over the speakers, a tinny voice said: "Man overboard! Not a drill!"

Some things never changed.

"It could be worse," Torres said from across the small hallway and down two cells. "They could've put us in isolation."

"Oh, shut up!" I shouted back. "I didn't want to get on the plane in the first place!"

I slammed my head into the wall again. Maybe I'd knock myself out, floating away into oblivion and being freed from my new reality.

The *brig*. Of all places to end up after I'd died, I'd ended up in the brig of a ghost ship on the buttcrack of the universe. If my parents knew that I'd gotten tossed into friggin' jail in the afterlife, they would've stopped sitting shiva for me.

"Let's not fight," Commander Hollander said, his voice floating from the far end of the hallway. "This is the time to work together."

I glared in the direction of his cell. "Arthur, I still haven't decided just what I'm going to do to you for killing us, so put a cork in it."

Bickley, who was directly across from me, walked up to the bars. He gave me a look of exasperation. "He's right, you know."

I flipped him off. My patience with everything and everyone had just run out.

He sighed. "Let's look at this another way. We now have time to figure out what we'll do in Port des Morts, though of course, any plan will be tentative until we know where that place is and what the situation is there."

The pain in my palms flared. The burning was spreading up into my wrists. "Does it matter?" I shot back. "No matter what it is, it's—"

"Port des Morts is where the dead go to die."

I slowly raised my head and got to my feet. Who was in here with us?

The speaker, a young man judging from the sound of his voice, laughed quietly. "What on earth did you all *do*? You all are the fresh meat, right?"

I peered through the bars. "Who are you? Show yourself."

A handsome man in his mid-twenties, with rich brown hair and eyes, appeared and lazily draped his arms through the cell bars. "Seaman Wayne, at your service."

Bickley gripped his bars, an expression of pure hate suddenly marring his features. "You're the guy who was throwing chem lights into the water the night we died!" He shook his bars, then punched one. "You are so lucky you're in there, and not in my cell."

Wayne just stared at Bickley, bored, and then turned back to me and pointed at Bickley with his thumb. "What's his problem?"

"If you hadn't thrown the chem light overboard, most of us wouldn't be dead, that's what!" Torres shouted. She retreated deeper into her cell and began to sob.

Wayne's face fell. "Well, damn. Did I kill you all?"

I pointed toward Commander Hollander's cell. "No, the flyboy killed us all, but we were all in that compartment because *you* threw a chem light in the water. It made the lookout team think someone had fallen into the water, and we were at muster for the man-overboard alert." I took a shaky breath. "If you hadn't done that, Torres and Bickley would almost certainly be alive." I rested my forehead against the bars. "But I'd still be dead, I suppose." My voice had dropped to a whisper.

Wayne swallowed. "I... I didn't know that's what those things were. I thought they were toys. I'm so sorry."

"Toys?" Bickley gripped the bars again. "Why the hell would there be toys on a US Navy vessel, moron?"

Wayne threw up his hands. "I don't know! There's tons of other weird stuff on ships now, so why not toys? There's nuclear reactors, computers, women who aren't nurses, and planes that can go faster than sound! How was I supposed to know that little sticks that glow in the dark weren't toys?"

"And was that you who drew the little cartoon on the classroom board?" I asked through gritted teeth.

Wayne looked down. "I kept having visions of it. I didn't realize that it was going to..." He trailed off, true shame taking hold. "It seemed funny at the time."

I'd never wanted to throttle someone so much. "Yeah, that's just hilarious," I spat. "Moving around chairs and leaving ominous warnings? Surely you have an actual *job* on this stupid ship. Or are you just a waste of space?"

Wayne's head dropped and he sighed. "I'm in the engine room. It's just me. The rest of us died." He sighed again. "Everything just seemed so... so pointless after that day. I just wanted to laugh again, you know?"

I didn't know what I'd expected him to say, but it wasn't that. "What do you mean, they died?" I asked slowly. "We're all ghosts."

"We're not ghosts," he said, glum. "At least, not the way you think of them. We're not the leftover bits of people." His large brown eyes flickered up at me, and this time I just rested my forehead against the bars. "You probably think of humanity as bodies who have souls. It's the other way around. You *are* a soul. You *had* a body. When you can't stay in your body anymore, that's when you go to your eternal rest. Except not us. We were sucked into this realm."

"Is it Hell?" Torres asked. "Or Purgatory?"

"No. You're in the world of the Oceanus."

BICKLEY BLEW OUT A LONG BREATH. "Say that again?"

I racked my brains, recalling the unit on Greek Mythology I'd taken in World Literature class in high school. "Do you mean the *okeanos*, the great river that surrounds the world?"

Wayne looked at me, a small smile on his face for the first time. "Hey, you know it. Good job. Yeah, the Oceanus. That's how the Romans said it, and that's how we say it here on the *Saint Catherine*. But it's not a river. It's a vast ocean that covers most of this earth."

"And the *Saint Catherine* sails the Oceanus?" Commander Hollander asked.

"Obviously, Arthur!" I shouted down the hall.

Torres appeared at her door, her eyes red-rimmed and watery. "What's the point of it all, though? What's the ship do, and why are we here?"

"Rollins said there's a war on," Bickley said. He looked sideways at Wayne. "And to answer your earlier question, we stole a plane filled with glass bombs that were singing, accidentally detonated all of them, and obliterated an entire fleet of enemy ships."

Wayne paused, then nodded, clearly impressed. "And on your first day? Wow."

"The *war*," I said, glaring at Wayne. "Tell us about the war, since we won a battle for the ship."

He sighed. "There's a ton of realms, okay? Humans are from the human one, fairies are from the fairy one, et cetera. The Oceanus is the home of water creatures, mostly. Mermaids and stuff. But there's some land, and this world has a lot of weak spots into the other realms. It's become a hub for the chaff of all the other worlds. The entire fairy realm has been embroiled in a nasty war for decades. Refugees and deserters have been just pouring in, and they bring the war with them. This ship's original mission was to sail the ocean blue and stop monsters from getting into the world of the living. Nowadays, though, we're just as busy directing refugees to the bits of land, stopping the bands of pirates, stuff like that."

Monsters. Magic. Fairies. Pirates.

I wasn't in the Navy anymore—I was in a children's storybook. Except nothing about this was the stuff of children's stories. I'd come here though a violent death, and since then I'd seen an officer shoot Commander Hollander, and then I'd been attacked by a... wait, what *was* that guy?

"Wayne?"

"Yes?"

"What kind of creature has white skin and eyes, and hair the color of seaweed? One attacked me in the *Taft*."

He made a face. "Fairy pirates. Fairies can change their appearance, and they imprint on the inhabitants of other realms when they leave their own. The fairy pirates imprinted on mermaids when they came here. Too bad they didn't take the tails, though. It might make them easier to kill," he muttered. He sighed. "Unfortunately, the fairies are tricky bastards. They can cloak themselves in the world of the living and appear and disappear at will. Half the stuff you know about fairies from the old stories are true."

"They didn't seem so hard to kill a bit ago," I said, smiling despite myself. "Those were fairy pirates, weren't they?"

"I don't know. I was down here. Were there a bunch of ships lobbing bombs at us?"

"There *were*."

"Yeah, that was pirates." He smirked. "I suppose dropping an entire payload of magic on them would do the job."

The painful heat in my wrists was snaking up my arms. I bit my lip and rubbed my forearms. "Magic, huh?"

"Yeah, it's what this whole world runs on. The world of the living runs on solar energy. This place runs on magic. It's what the pirates are always looking for. They prey on ghost ships because ghosts are almost entirely magic. It's a limited resource, you see."

"Ghost ships? In the plural?" Bickley asked. "How many are there?"

"There's a ghost ship for every active navy in the living world. The sailors are people who died through accident or injury. Never met someone who died in combat on one of these ships. Even the nurses died like that. Dot blew up when someone accidentally dropped a missile next to her, and Peggy caught typhoid or something. I fell off my cruiser and drowned."

"Even Gorman and Muree?" Commander Hollander asked.

"I said shut up, Arthur!" The pain in my arms was making me short-tempered.

"Gorman and Muree died from the flu in the same night. They replaced the old skipper and executive officer, who were taken by the fog. You know how it goes."

Torres tutted. "Wayne, you gotta remember that we were born into this world literally today."

Wayne nodded. "Okay, well, the fog is—"

The pain was in my shoulders now. "Guys, be quiet. Please." I sank to my knees, shaking. The heat was beginning to tighten in my chest. "Something's wrong. Something's really, really wrong."

Bickley kneeled and held his hands out helplessly. "What is it?"

"It's heat!" If I'd thought that pulling my clothes off would've cooled me down, I would've. Instead, I wrapped my arms around myself and choked back sobs. *Hashem, take this pain from me.*

Bickley gripped the bars. "Hey! Can anyone hear this? We've got a medical emergency!"

It was Wayne's turn to punch the bars in frustration. "We're dead, pal. That doesn't work here. Believe me, I've tried. Not my first night in the brig."

Yet, the door at the top of the stairs opened with a clang.

"*Help!*" My shrill scream echoed in the small brig.

A burly Seaman rushed down the stairs, a key in his hand. "Out you go. Follow me."

"Hey, who are you?" Wayne demanded. "I've never seen you onboard before."

But I was already halfway up the stairs, just a step behind the Seaman, who wore no name tag. He sprinted down a passageway, then another, and then down a ladder-like staircase.

I slid down the rails, the friction producing less heat than what was burning brightly in my chest. It was spreading downwards into my legs now, and up into my neck.

At the bottom of the stairs, he pointed. "Go to the engine room. You'll know what to do."

And I did. Like the north end of a magnet pulled to a south end, I ran like the wind down the passageway. Invisible hands were the wind in my sails—my legs moved faster than they'd ever been able to in life. I could literally feel the heat spark into energy in my muscles, making them move like they never had before.

Silver, sparkly tendrils of light began to seep from my fingers.

I shoved the door open, surging into the engine room. Ahead of me, the engines and generators roared away, churning power into the electrical systems of the ship and propelling the enormous vessel through the water.

*Power.*

That's what was in me. Pure, undiluted power. I slammed my hands onto the largest generator, closed my eyes, and willed the power to flow out of me.

A flood—no, an avalanche—coursed out of my hands and into the main power lines of the ship. The lights overhead brightened to eye-watering levels, and beads of light danced in the exposed wires overhead. A musical hum of a million voices sang in happiness as they flew through the lines, finally where they needed to be.

I rested my head against the generator, that beautiful, beautiful machine. The pain was gone. A tear escaped my eye, and then I was wheezing from laughter that mixed with my tears.

Rachel Goldstein, naval nuclear electrician, had just powered an aircraft carrier once more.

The Master at Arms shut my cell's door again, though this time without slamming it. "Just stay here, okay?"

"Yeah," I murmured. "Nothing to unload anymore. Keep the light on, though."

"Okay, but we turn the lights off at Taps so people in here can sleep. That's in about five minutes."

"Fine."

I sat on the thin mattress of the small bed, then laid back and stared up at the cracked ceiling of the isolation cell.

The Master at Arms—Master Chief Buntin, I'd been told—hadn't said much when he'd hurried into the engine room, his drones hot on his heels. He hadn't pointed a gun at me or threatened me with dismemberment. He'd simply stared at me in shock. When I asked what was up, he'd blurted the reason: nobody had ever survived absorbing that much magic. Raw magic ripped ghosts apart.

Wayne had said that I'd dropped a payload of magic onto the flotilla, but the full meaning of that hadn't registered with me when he'd said it. Yet, unbeknownst to me, I'd held the sphere in my hand and had somehow absorbed some into my body.

And my body had converted it into power. Not "captain of a ghost ship power" power. Not "I'm a superhero, hear me roar" power. But engine power. Generator power. Rachel-Goldstein's-professional-specialty power.

Pouring all the power into the generator had felt right. Familiar. As regular and normal as the other routines that had made up my life. I was made for it, though I couldn't begin to guess who had made me this way, and for what purpose.

Hashem, maybe?

Now, there was an idea. Perhaps Hashem had elected to keep me out of paradise because my job, as it were, was not over. My earthly job was, but my spiritual purpose stretched beyond that. He'd given me a calling that I'd followed, and it had taken me here.

The intercom whistled. "Taps, taps, lights out. Maintain silence about the decks. The smoking lamp is out. Now, Taps."

The lights dimmed.

Now that I was in my quiet isolation cell, away from my friends, I was clear-headed enough to push all the emotion aside and truly ponder my new paradigm.

The ship had said that she needed me. Was this the reason? Did she need a nuclear electrician—or three? Wayne had said that the engineers had been depleted, and he was obviously not up to snuff if he was spending half his days in the brig.

The door to the isolation wing opened, and masculine footsteps came toward my cell, followed by the tip-taps of high-heeled shoes on steel. The lights turned on again.

I sat up as my door was opened by none other than Captain Gorman. Nurse Dot, the brunette, stood behind him. He was holding a thick leather-bound book.

# 7

"Captain Gorman."

"Petty Officer Goldstein. May we come in?"

"Please." I stood, and the pair came in, arranging themselves on the other side of the small cell. "How can I help you?"

Captain Gorman surveyed me with his usual calm. "You've had a busy day, Petty Officer. First you escaped onto the *Taft* and fought a fairy, and then you stole one of my cargo planes and detonated several dozen class-a storage spheres, thereby destroying a small fleet of pirates. All within..." He removed a gold pocket watch from his pocket and flipped it open. "...six hours."

Dot lifted a slim finger to her lips and demurely coughed, but I saw the mirth in her eyes. She was a good ole' Southern rebel, no doubt about it.

Captain Gorman put his fob back in his pocket. "I'm sure you're wondering why we're here."

"To yell at me, right?"

To my surprise, Captain Gorman sat on my bed and patted the spot next to him. Dot settled on the small stool and straightened her roomy white skirt.

"Actually, Petty Officer, I'm here to talk to you about what happened in the engine room earlier. I'd suspected as much before, but now I firmly believe it's why you came to this ship. Can you describe the sailor who freed you from your cell in the brig?"

Slightly startled by his casual demeanor, I gave real thought to the question. "Um... tall, I guess. Muscular. A Seaman."

"But what were his features? His coloring?"

"He was... um..." I faltered. Now that it was put to me, I couldn't remember what the Seaman had looked like. Not his skin color, eyes, hair, anything. It was as though someone had gently erased that part of my memory from my brain.

Dot smiled at me. "When I died, all those years ago, I woke up in a ship even older than this. It was the USS *Shadow* back then. There was a Seaman in the room with me who told me that I was going to be the first real, proper nurse on board. But I can't really remember what he looked like... because he wasn't really there, you see."

I rubbed my forehead. "What do you mean?"

Dot leaned forward and took my hands in hers. "It was the ship, sweetheart. It speaks to you. It speaks to me. It's in our heads. It's alive, an ancient vessel that takes new forms as needed. I brought the *Shadow* into the new world with me, and it turned into the *Saint Catherine*. I was born on Saint Catherine's Island in Georgia—it took that little piece of my heart and built an aircraft carrier out of it. And today the ship freed you and led you to the engine room. That's where you're supposed to be. You and all the others are meant to bring the new ship into a new age. The nuclear age."

I pulled my hands out of hers. "What does this mean?" My eyes flickered to Captain Gorman. "And what's the book for?"

"The book is the official roster of all sailors stationed on the *Saint Catherine*. I'll be completely honest with you: the ship can't upgrade unless you sign it. The others have already, and they're getting settled in their berthing spaces right now. But the ship still hasn't upgraded. We're waiting on you."

I studied him. "There's a 'but,' isn't there?"

"But, if you sign it, it means that you're going to be on board for a long time. Dot and I have been with the *Saint Catherine* for a lifetime, and time works a little funny here. It can feel longer when you don't actually age."

I raised an eyebrow. "And I'm not in trouble because of the bomb thing?"

There was hint of a smirk on his face. "Not unless you want to be. We are en route to fight a large sea dragon, and punishing you all is more trouble than you're worth, right now."

Sea dragons. I wasn't even shocked anymore.

I considered that, and thought back to all that Wayne had said. I'd interrupted him during a crucial moment, and I had the sense to not make any decisions without all the information.

"What's the fog?" I asked, looking back and forth between them. "Context being, what happened to the last skipper?"

Captain Gorman blinked quickly. "You've already heard about that?"

"Uh huh. Explain."

Even Dot looked uncomfortable. "We don't fully understand it. It's... well... a fog that appears and disappears in the night. Sometimes sailors say they can hear someone calling for them, and..." She put a hand to her throat.

"They disappear and never return," Captain Gorman finished. "We don't know what happens to them."

*Interesting.* Even we, the dead ones, had a death of sorts to look forward to.

"So that it's, then? If we stay on the ship, we can renovate it and make it a nuclear aircraft carrier, and then we'll sail around the Oceanus until possibly the end of time."

"Not the end of time," Captain Gorman said. "Everyone goes into the fog, in the end. Or they die in battle, but even then, we don't know if that's true death."

"Will I ever see my family again?" The question came out before I could stop it, but I meant it all the same. I could put up with almost anything as long as I knew I'd see my family some day. It was the naked hope of reconciliation that brought me through the dark nights of deployment. If I could just know that I'd hug my mother again in the afterlife, I could fight any war they pointed me at.

Captain Gorman paused, and then said, "There is an island, at the edge of the known world. We call it the Far Island. It is said that it's the portal to the... the beyond. It's shrouded in fog, probably the same fog that takes sailors. If you go there, you may one day be reunited with your family. But nobody ever comes back from there, either."

"Whoa, whoa, whoa. Hold the phone. There's a place I can go to *now*? I don't have to wait for the fog to take me?"

"Yes, but—"

"I'm not signing that book. I'll help you fight the dragon, but I'm not staying on the ship. I'm going home."

And that was that. I would not spend untold decades, or even centuries, on a ship when I could go to the real afterlife. This was my hard limit. My life had ended on a sour note with my parents, and I had to make it right. This was the first step.

They both exchanged a sad glance, then nodded. "Fine," Captain Gorman said. "Then you get off at Port des Morts in two days."

## 8

"Okay," Bickley said. "Let's try this again, and this time I want Torres to direct the magic into the generator."

It had been a day since we'd been freed from the brig. Bickley, Torres, and I were standing in the engine room by the main generator. We'd asked for a lone glass sphere of magic to practice with; it was now in a spindly metal perch that allowed us to touch it without jostling it too much.

Wayne had been condemned to the laundry when it became clear that his services were no longer required in the engine room. The other engineers had perfected a complicated process that involved placing the magic spheres inside a special machine, but without the old team, it had been left to Wayne to do it all, and he was... well, not the most responsible.

Cue the ship shanghaiing us.

Torres took my hand in her right one, while I slipped my free hand into Bickley's. Torres touched a finger to the sphere.

"I love the humming," she murmured. "It's like music."

The jolt of magic from the sphere coursed through us—but this time, with the concentration of three nukes to contain it, we were able to control it. Like a solid rope, we were yoked together by the raw magic. Though it begged to be unleashed, we were the masters, not the other way around.

"I can feel it changing," Bickley said. "It's subtle, but it's definitely taking a different form."

I could feel it, too. It was almost as if the magic were leveling up, growing bigger and badder, but still definitely a version of itself. I was listening to instincts I did not know I had, and those instincts told me to be very, very gentle as I manipulated the magic inside me.

"I'm about to direct it into the generator," Torres said. "Careful... careful... okay, let it go."

I released the magic and pushed it into her. She touched the generator, and it hummed a little louder than before. But this time, the lights didn't brighten, and there were no curious luminescent beads moving along in the wires. As amusing as that had been, I suspected that I'd nearly overloaded the system and made the ship go dark.

Bit by bit, the magic swirled out of me and into Torres, like a bath-tub-full of water circling a small drain. It was peaceful, almost. Relaxing. We were the power people, just doing what we were made for.

"Goldstein, you're next," Bickley said.

I placed my hand on a sphere and let the magic pool in my stomach. I was about to redirect it into my coworkers when I felt the magic slip into my legs and arms. Once again, my limbs felt amped up, like I could run a marathon in an hour. I'd felt that way when I'd been freed from the brig by the ship's avatar.

"Hey, I want to experiment with something," I said, bouncing on my heels a little. "Stand back."

Bickley shook his head. "Let's not—"

I shot a blast of magic into my legs at the same that I jumped. Instead of going up six inches, I blasted into the air several feet, banged my head on a pipe, hit a generator on the way down, and landed with a thud on the floor.

*Ouch.*

Torres and Bickley burst into laughter. Torres helped me up, still laughing, and cuffed my ear. "You looked like someone had placed a trampoline beneath you."

I rubbed the throbbing spot on my scalp. "Well, now I can say that I survived something Rollins didn't."

They laughed harder. "Dark, Goldstein. That was dark," Bickley said, handing me a sphere. "No more experiments, if you please."

We all grinned and shook our heads at the funny moment, and I stepped up to the dais. Time to be serious. I took Torres' hand in my own and opened up the connection.

"Hey, everyone!" Commander Hollander called from the doorway.

Moment over.

Cursing, I severed the connection to Torres and whipped around. "We're a little busy here, Commander, as you can see."

Commander Hollander cocked his head. "What are you doing? It looks like a kumbayah circle."

Bickley placed a firm hand on my shoulder and steered me behind him. "We're practicing converting magic into useable energy for the ship. We're the only ones who can do it."

Commander Hollander walked up to the generator and patted it appreciatively. "I never got to see the engine room on the *Taft*, being in the air wing and everything. We always wondered what you nerds got up to down there." Immediately, his eyes widened. "I—I'm sorry, that came out wrong. That was unkind."

"We were refining uranium," I said, rolling my eyes.

Commander Hollander looked stunned. "Really?"

"No. We *nerds* were completing a series of highly-complicated procedures designed to ensure that the uranium within the two nuclear reactors was bombarded with the correct amount of neutrons, thereby making sure that we didn't kill everyone within five hundred miles. When we weren't doing that, we were studying how to do that better, so your butt had the power to fly planes. What were *you* doing?"

Ugh, this guy. Every single thing about him was sticking in my craw. He'd killed me, refused to accept agency for that act, and now he was trying to get us to warm up to him like nothing had happened. Here I was, dead and still somehow in an engine room, listening to the man who'd killed me call me a nerd. In my space. In my domain. That was like me going up to the air wing office and calling all of them "jocks in flight suits," which is definitely how much of the *Taft* had felt about the air wing. You weren't supposed to actually say how you felt about other rates.

Commander Hollander sighed. "Remember to call me 'sir.' I was providing air support for operations overseas, Petty Officer. Let's not play this game. I came down to get to know you all a little better, since we're spiritually connected." He patted the generator again. "Like this. This is important to you, so I want to know more about it. This engine has, what, eighty thousand horsepower?"

"That's a generator, sir."

He held his hands up. "Are you still angry about the accident? Is this what this is about?"

"You *killed* me, you dickhead!"

Torres grabbed my hand and dragged me behind another generator, a reproving look on her face. "Don't talk, just walk." She didn't stop until we were on the other side of the room, where she turned around and faced me. "Rach, for the love of God. He's an officer. You gotta be respectful." She frowned and shook her head. "Why are you being like this? You've never had a problem with military bearing before."

I crossed my arms. My friend was not this daft. "He killed us. As far as I'm concerned, he's bupkis to me."

Torres's chagrin morphed into surprise. "It was an accident. Don't do this."

"Do *what*?"

"Hold on to hatred. You might as well hate the storm from that night. I'm surprised to hear this from you."

I wasn't going to be chastened by her. "I'm on my way to Port des Morts, and there I'm going to catch a boat to go to an island where I may or may not ever reunite with my parents. Don't you see how messed up this is? It's his fault. He killed me. He's why—"

"You're being selfish."

Horror coursed through me, molten and electric. "No. No, I'm not being selfish."

"Yes, you are. You're selfishly focusing on your own feelings instead of forgiving him for screwing up. He died too, you know. He's been punished as much as a person can. Now you're just slinging mud in the afterlife. You're the bad guy in this situation, Rach. Face it."

She turned and left me in the corner, my mouth open, unable to even blink.

"I'm not selfish," I whispered. "I'm not."

I'd died. I'd literally *died* because of Commander Hollander's mistake. If he'd only maimed me, nobody would've questioned my anger at him. He was supposed to know how to land a stupid plane on the flight deck, for crying out loud. Yeah, I was sure it was a tricky maneuver, but nobody would've just la-de-da forgiven *me* for incorrectly handling the uranium in the reactor, especially if someone had died.

"Or if twenty-five people had died," I hissed to myself. Heat crept up my collar. He was a flyboy, a jock in a flight suit, so of course he got a pass. He'd killed more than a score of sailors, all proudly wearing our country's cloth. He needed to own up to that before I could even begin to move past it.

But stewing about it in the engine room wasn't doing me any good. I shoved my hands into the pockets of my coveralls and wandered back to the group. Bickley was explaining the basics of marine engines to Hollander, who was nodding along politely. I joined Torres and elbowed her hard in the ribs. I was still mad about what she'd said.

And it wasn't true. *I wasn't selfish.*

Without warning, the tinny whistle of the captain's com went off, and we all jerked our heads up to look at the intercom.

"This is your captain speaking. We're approaching the location of the Belles Échelles dragon. Aviators, report to the hangar bay. All other sailors, man your stations."

The whistle sounded again, and he cut the line.

"Belles Échelles dragon?" Torres repeated. "And Port des Mortes. Why is everything around here French?"

"I asked another aviator that yesterday," Commander Hollander said. "Our location roughly corresponds with the Mediterranean. These are considered the safe waters, too. Beyond this world's Gibraltar, it's nothing but wild sea. Apparently it's pretty hairy out there." He stepped through the doorframe, then turned and nodded at us. "See you all. First mission."

He disappeared down the passageway, but was immediately replaced by Seaman Wayne. "Guys, you're going to want to see this."

Bickley raised an eyebrow. "Captain just said to man your

stations, which means we're staying down here, and you're going back to the laundry, bucko."

Wayne waved his hand dismissively. "Nah, ignore that. Come with me and check out the dragon. All the guys are up there." He winked at me. "You know you want to."

Torres and I exchanged a glance, and I knew she was thinking the same thing as me: on one hand, Wayne was trouble. On the other hand, a *dragon*.

Like there was any question.

"Come back here!" Bickley shouted. "Goldstein! Torres! You're smarter than this!"

"We won't be five minutes!" Torres shouted over her shoulder as we ran down the passageway after Wayne. "We'll tell you all about the dragon!"

I stifled a giggle and flew up the stairs. The thuds of our boots joined dozens of others as the entire crew, it seemed, congregated in the hangar bay to catch site of the Belles Échelles dragon.

Could it fly? What could I expect? What were the aviators going to do?

A small crowd converged in the corner of the hangar bay, comprising mostly supply guys and other rates that weren't strictly necessary in battle. Torres and I stood on our tiptoes to get a better look until one of the taller men noticed me and hissed at the others to let the ladies through. We were gently pushed to the front, and...

"Wow." Torres and I breathed the word at the same time.

Far out in the water, at least a quarter mile, swam the most fearsome creature I'd ever beheld. Turquoise blue on its back, but iridescently white-gold on its belly, the dragon slithered in the air as it dodged the volley of bullets from no less than five Helldivers.

As it moved, it flitted in and out of the sunlight that streamed down through broken clouds. Whenever it did, the sun scattered off the dragon's scales in marvelous bursts of rainbows. No gem in the living world could compare to the fire in the scales of this magnificent beast.

I was dazzled.

A yeoman leaned over and whispered, "Its name means 'beautiful scales.' I've always thought it was pretty swell, too."

I grinned. "Were my thoughts that obvious?"

"Your eyes were sparkling more than the scales."

I looked up at him, and couldn't help but notice that he was cute, in a dashing, James Dean-kind of way. In fact, he was the kind sailor who'd stopped me in my flight from the conference room on my first day. He'd been concerned for me. What a sweetheart.

I stuck out my hand. "EMN2 Rachel Goldstein." At his confused look, I added, "I'm an electrician."

He shook my hand. "Yeoman Third Class Hanson. John Hanson."

*More like John Handsome.*

The silly thought brought me up short. How very unlike me to think like that...but goodness, he *was* handsome. Blond hair, dark green eyes, a lantern jaw—my mother would've squawked in horror if she'd seen such a man hanging around me. Men were "distractions."

But now that I thought about it, it was about time I let myself be distracted. I was an adult with nothing to lose. Besides, I was still angry about Commander Hollander, and I wanted to feel good again. A tall blond with a winning smile was conducive to that.

He handed me a pair of small, brass binoculars. "Here, why don't you take a peek? Your friend can use them, too, if she likes."

Blushing, I peered through the binoculars, focusing them until the dragon's features were brought into sharp clarity. It was at once familiar and alien, the living embodiment of an idea—a fantasy in thrashing, snarling three dimensions. Its lizard-like face was surrounded by a midnight-blue fan, and with the binoculars I could see that even the fan had tiny sparkling scales.

I lowered the binoculars. "It's a shame that they're going to kill it. It's so pretty."

"Oh, don't worry! If you look carefully, you can see that they're mostly just strafing it to drive it away from one of the weak spots. Look, right there," he said, pointing. "I bet you can almost see it. Sometimes the sky is a little different."

I peered through the binoculars again, following his finger. Behind the dragon's head was a disc-shaped... something. Like a smudge on a mirror, it was hard to focus on, but it was definitely there.

The clouds in the disc didn't match the clouds around it. That was it.

My mouth fell open. "That's the living world?"

"Possibly, or maybe an opening to the fairy realm, or any of the others. We patrol to keep all the worlds safe, though there are more openings to the world of the living than any other. The living world used to be like a motel for these kinds of monsters until the ships started patrolling."

I handed him his binoculars. "How many ships are there?"

He flashed me his movie-star smile. "Would you like to have dinner with me in the galley tonight? I'd be happy to tell you all about your new life. I know you have a ton of questions. I sure did."

A smile tugged at my lips, but I didn't want to seem too eager. I nodded. "I'd love that. Can Torres come, too?"

Torres glanced at me, absorbed in her own conversation with three good-looking sailors. "I've already got my galley invite, thanks."

We were still sharing a naughty smirk when a klaxon began to blare, ear-shattering and everywhere.

*"General quarters! General quarters! All hands man your battle stations! This is not a drill!"*

Commander Muree's voice, amplified over the intercom, contained a vein of fear. Hanson and I looked at each other, then hurried away from the entrance of the hangar bay. What on earth was going on?

The ship lurched. Something had hit it—from *underneath*.

Sailors near the edge of the flight deck waved frantically for us to go inside. "It's her!" one man screamed. "It's her! *Run!*"

Torres and I grabbed hands and turned to flee together, but the rush of people flooding through the open bay doors tore us apart. "Torres! Torres!"

"Rach! Where are you?"

A large body shoved me aside into a large coil of rope. Inspired, I settled down into the rope, piling it up and crouching down as low as I could. I risked a single peek over the edge of the coil, searching the skyline for incoming planes, ships, or anything else that would warrant such panic.

There was a hiss, a large splash, and then...

"Hashem help us," I whispered, covering my mouth with a trembling hand.

A woman rose up from the sea, at least one hundred feet tall. Her immense, nude torso loomed over the ship, so starkly white that it hurt to look at her. Her snarled black hair appeared to slither around her neck and shoulders, and then I realized that it *was* slithering. Her hair was snakes. I could see the eyes now, and their thin, forked tongues.

But it was her face that nearly made me pee myself. Her bulbous eyes never stopped moving, practically spinning in their sockets as the planes turned away from the dragon and began shooting at her instead. Her toothy grin only widened, and a long, pointed red tongue darted in and out as she hissed.

A Helldiver arced in the air and turned toward the massive woman, little bullets bouncing off her shoulders as though she were made of marble.

She caught the plane in midair and rent it into halves, plucking the flailing aviator out of the cockpit. He struggled against her fingers, but she just opened her mouth and swallowed him. There was a burst of light from behind her teeth.

I knew the truth immediately: she'd killed a ghost.

Hanson grabbed my shoulders and hauled me out of the rope, shoving me toward the doorway. "Now! Go now!"

The woman's bestial eyes flickered toward us, and her hand shot into the hangar bay.

Hanson pushed me into the passageway. My hand was still in his as the enormous white grasp of the woman closed around his torso.

"*No!*" My high scream was drowned out by his cries of fear. She began to pull him toward her, but but I didn't let go. "Let go of him! Let go! *Let go!*" My shrieks grew increasingly shrill as I was dragged along the hangar bay, never letting go of Hanson's hand. Bullets tore through the air, bouncing off the concrete. Around us, men ran to the mounted guns and aimed at her.

But I still didn't let go.

She lifted her arm, and then we were airborne. Torres was screaming from the edge of the flight deck, and from the corner of my eye I could see someone grab her and pull her away.

Hanson's hand was slippery, but I tightened my grip. I'd never let go. I'd never let go. I would be brave. I would—

The woman lifted us up to her eye level, laughed, and shook me off like a fly.

The last thing I saw before I hit the churning, frothy water was a burst of light.

---

Down, down, down.

The watery darkness enveloped me like a cool blanket. It was quiet in the depths, and the pressing silence was a welcome counterpoint to the carnage above. Frankly, I didn't want to go back up there. And since I was dead and didn't strictly *need* to breathe, I had no particular reason to go back.

Except Bickley and Torres. And the other nice sailors. And the fact that horrible ghost-killing monsters inhabited this ocean and I was increasingly convinced that the ship was the only moderately-safe place for me to be. I could still feel the knot of raw power inside me, since we'd been interrupted during our engine room practice. My very body contained a valuable resource.

I began to swim toward the ship.

Well, sort of. I'd never been one for swimming in life, and now I regretted it. Apparently there was more to it than "move your arms and legs," because I was doing an elaborate underwater dance and going nowhere. After a few minutes of buffeting up and down in the water, I looked around.

The woman's legs were clear to see by the ship. She was moving them back and forth in a gentle scissor-like motion. I copied her, and lo and behold, I moved upward a little. Angling my body, I began to move toward the ship, swimming in little frog-like motions through the dark blue water.

Something moving by the woman's legs caught my eye. I paused, then swam a little closer to her. Was it a shark? I could just make out a long fish tail. No... not a shark. The tail was too long and thin, and had too many fins.

I swam even closer, then stopped moving altogether, hardly believing what I was seeing.

It was a merman.

He was chained to her leg like a sad little pet, a metal collar around his neck. He strained and struggled against the collar, but to no avail. His long tail thrashed mightily as he fought for freedom, catching the weak light in the water and shimmering various shades of green and blue. Like the fairy who'd imprinted on merfolk, his skin was also quite pale, and his loose, long hair was like seaweed.

However, there were differences. The fairy had been thin and underfed, but this merman was muscular, and a circlet dotted with pearls adorned his head. His face betrayed no malice, just fear and consternation.

My heart swelled with pity for him. I frog-swam over to him and held out my hands, hoping the gesture of peace crossed the inter-species divide. He stopped, his white eyes widening, then reached out and touched my hands.

I laced my fingers with his and gave his hand a reassuring squeeze, then broke away and touched the collar. It was metal, and very solid. There was no breaking it. The chain it was attached to, however, was much thinner.

I held a finger up to my lips, and the merman copied the gesture. Grasping the chain, I focused the rest of the latent power inside me and shot it into my hands.

Both of us were blasted backward several feet—but the chain was broken.

The merman swam a fluid victory lap around me, naked joy clear on his face. I waved, pointed to myself, then pointed up to the ship while mouthing, "I have to go." I began to kick my legs back and forth, moving slowly upward.

He swam up to me, so close that our noses were almost touching. After a second, he wrapped his arms around my torso, then leaned in and gently kissed me on the lips.

I was too bemused by my first kiss to react at all.

When we were done, he gingerly pulled me to him as if he were hugging me, then began to swim away from the woman, his undulating tale propelling us at a shocking speed. He circled around the keel of the *Saint Catherine*, to comparatively safe water. When we were on the far side, he moved us upward, toward the light.

Our heads broke the surface at the same time, the silence immediately punctured by the whizzing of planes, shouts of men, and small explosions. I couldn't see the woman beyond the ship, but I could hear her—every shriek, hiss, and roar. The battle was still raging, but I could do nothing more.

I hugged my gentleman friend and pointed toward the sound. "What is she?" I shouted.

His face darkened. "Scylla." His voice was surprisingly deep.

I gasped, memories of yet more Greek mythology washing over me. "Is the dragon Charybdis?"

He shook his head and pointed to the east. "Charybdis." He kissed my forehead, then tapped his heart. "Tank...ooh." Slowly and carefully, he directed me to spread out my arms on the water, and he wiggled his index and middle fingers while looking at my legs.

I kicked my legs as he'd directed, and then tapped my heart in turn. "You're welcome." I laced my fingers with his again. "Friends."

He nodded, and I was satisfied that he understood. After one last tender look, he let me go, and disappeared under the water, zipping away in seconds.

A throaty scream from the woman made me flinch, but smile at the same time. Surely that was a scream of pain and defeat. Indeed, there was a massive splash that rocked the ship, and then her dark shape moved under me, swimming away in a different direction than the merman had gone.

Cheers erupted from above, on the flight deck. Tiny heads appeared over the edge. "There's someone in the water! Get a ladder!" More heads appeared, and some kind soul threw down a life preserver, though I was treading water well and wasn't in danger of ever drowning.

I slipped under the life preserver and chugged over to the rope ladder that had been lowered, then began to climb up, shivering from the cold and adrenaline. Sailors crowded the edge as I climbed, all extending their hands even if there was no hope of me reaching them.

Suddenly, one pointed beyond me toward the water. "Look! It's an aviator!"

I looked over my shoulder, and sure enough, an aviator was floating facedown in the water by the stern. Blood colored the water around him. I put a hand to my heart, moved. *That poor man.*

And for once, I could do something about it. I turned back, gave my heartiest grin to the sailors, and pushed myself away from the ship as I let go of the ladder with my life preserver in hand.

Down again I went, landing in the water with more grace than before. I frog-swam all the way over to the aviator, kept afloat by the raucous cheers from above. When I was by the unconscious aviator, I angled myself so I could flip him over. "Hey there, shipmate," I whispered. "You're going to be okay." All my former antipathy toward aviators had evaporated. They really were okay, generally smart and very brave. It was just one aviator I didn't like, since he was an asshat who refused to apologize.

He turned over, and I cursed. It was the one aviator I didn't like. Naturally.

But as my eyes combed over his body, my ire cooled, then morphed into concern. Commander Hollander's chest bore deep parallel gouges that oozed a silver-greenish pus that stank strongly of sulfur. His face was slack, though his eyelids fluttered as I maneuvered him into the life preserver. Torres could never accuse me of selfishness again. I was saving him, and I would've done so even if the entire crew of the *Saint Catherine* hadn't been watching.

Several sailors lowered a wooden lifeboat over the side, with two of them in it. They hoisted Commander Hollander inside, and then helped me clamber aboard. When the boat had stopped rocking, one put two fingers in his mouth and whistled. "Take us up!"

Up we went. Bit by bit the flight deck crew winched us up, the boat banging against the hull, until we were level with the deck. Dot and Peggy, ever present, fluttered and fussed over Commander Hollander as they placed him on a stretcher. They carried him away into the ship. His arm was hanging limp over the side of the stretcher.

I was now shivering uncontrollably. An ensign threw a blanket around my shoulders, and Stanholtzer handed me a steaming mug of the most disgusting drink I'd ever tasted in both of my lives.

"We don't have coffee here," he said by way of apology after I'd choked on my first sip.

A huddle of men escorted me back into the hangar bay. We passed the planes, many of which were riddled with bullet holes and large cracks. Aviators were sitting up against bulkheads, their eyes dulls with fatigue, or heartbreak. There were fewer planes now than before, and I could suddenly see how very few planes there truly were for an aircraft carrier of this size. The *Saint Catherine* was dying by degrees thanks to beings like Scylla.

"Goldstein? Goldstein? Where are you?" Bickley's booming yell made me look up from the drink I was daring myself to sip again.

"I'm here!" I shouted.

He shoved aside two sailors and pulled me into a huge bear hug. "Torres said you'd been whisked off the ship by a monster," he said into my hair. "I thought I'd never see you again." He looked down at me, tears in his eyes, and our connection revealed the source: I was one of two people who'd known him in life, and I'd run off toward trouble without a thought.

That *had* been selfish of me.

"I'm sorry," I said quietly. "I won't do that again."

He put his hand around my shoulder and ushered me into the ship. We passed the coil of rope where I'd hidden. I looked over my shoulder at the ocean, where Scylla had come from, and to where she'd fled again. She'd robbed the *Saint Catherine* of at least two brave, true sailors—and me of John Hanson. I'd known him for just a moment, but already a future was gone. It was the second future of mine that had been snatched from my hands.

I narrowed my eyes and turned back toward the door.

Scylla and I had unfinished business.

## 9

"Well, you know how the saying goes, right? If the *Saint Catherine* had wanted you to have a boyfriend, it would've put him in your seabag."

I paused in the middle of rolling my coveralls and looked over at Torres, who was eating a sandwich. "The only reason I'm not punching you right now for that tasteless joke is because we've been friends for so long. John was really nice, okay? And that *schtik drek* literally ate him. Have some respect."

She grimaced. "Sorry. What's a *schtik drek*?"

"Context clues, Mar. Use them."

I wrinkled my nose and resumed putting my few possessions into my seabag. They'd appeared on one of the spare racks in the tiny female berthing compartment, opposite Dot and Peggy's and above Torres's. My material possessions in this life comprised spare coveralls, the world's ugliest underwear, extra boots, socks, an amulet bearing the Traveler's Prayer, and a Star of David necklace.

I had to put them away, because whether I liked it or not, they were mine, and we were almost to Port des Morts. In a few hours, I'd sling my seabag over my shoulder and get off the ship, never to set foot on it again.

I was going to do this. I *had* to do this—for my parents. I wasn't selfish. I wasn't going to hang around on a boat when I had a chance to see them again. I'd taken myself away from them by joining the Navy, but now that was over. I had to go be with my people, whatever that meant, and prepare a place for the man and woman who had loved me more than anything else.

I idly rubbed my necklace, then reached out a hand to Torres. "Let's try again." Anything to take away the sting of John's death.

Torres touched her fingers to mine, and I passed her the bit of magic I'd taken from a glass sphere earlier. The more we worked with it, the easier it became to manipulate. She and Bickley needed to be on their toes after I left.

*After I left.* It sounded so dismal.

The captain's whistle sounded, heralding an announcement. "This is your captain speaking. We're coming up on the *Krasnoye Morye* on our starboard side in about ten minutes." The whistle sounded again, and he cut off the intercom.

*Krasnoye Morye? Must be Russian.*

She chewed thoughtfully. "Where do you think ghosts go when they die again?"

"Heck if I know."

"This place is so weird. I wonder why it wasn't ever mentioned in any of our holy books. Like, not even some rando's scribbles from a thousand years ago. Are you *sure* it's not in the Jewish apocrypha?" She reached out her hand. "Again."

I snorted. "I promise you." I accepted the power back into my body, and this time I neatly tucked it into my stomach. I'd take it with me when I disembarked as a backup weapon. Just in case. Who knew what was out there?

Scylla. Scylla was out there. And I'd kick her ass yet.

She sighed. "The hardest part is still feeling alive, you know? I still feel like I'm just Marisol, and that I'll return home soon. It felt so natural to chat up those guys back on the flight deck. We're all still interested in romance." She sat up. "Hey, do you think we can have kids?"

I eyed her sandwich. "No, probably not. The only reason the galley exists is because food and eating are comforting, not because we actually need it. I didn't need to breathe underwater. I doubt our reproductive systems are still functional."

"Well, hey, no periods. That's something."

"Ever the optimist," I murmured as I placed my overalls into my seabag. I latched the top, then pushed it into the corner of my narrow rack. "That's everything. Now we just wait until we sail into port, then I'm getting off."

Torres finished her sandwich and threw the wrapper into the little trash bin. "Is there anything I can say to keep you on board?"

"No. I'm really going to the Far Island. I can't go back and comfort my parents, so the next best thing is to be there when they die."

"You don't even know what's there, though. It could be something awful. There are others like Scylla, you know. Mythology is full of horrid stuff. I was happy to sign the book."

"The Far Island is more likely to be paradise than the ship is, Mar."

"But what about fighting Scylla again? You said you were going to."

"And what am I going to do, exactly? Sit around here and wait for her to attack?"

"Yeah, I think you should, actually. Better sitting here in relative

safety than twiddling your thumbs in Port des Morts. Wayne told us a little bit about the place when you were off having your little adventure in the engine room. It's like the Mos Eisley of the afterlife."

I crossed my arms. "You mean it's a wretched hive of—"

"—scum and villainy. Worst of the worst."

There was a beat. I smiled despite myself.

"I miss Star Wars," I admitted, my heart throbbing in my chest. "And movies in general. Going to the theater…"

Virginia Beach had had an enormous movie complex, a lovely centerpiece to Lynnhaven Mall. My mother and I had always loved to take in a film after a long day of shopping. After the movie, we'd go out to dinner somewhere nearby and chat about the movie, gabbing for hours about the plot and performances.

I'd never do that again.

I sank down onto the chair and covered my eyes with my hands, trying to keep back the tears.

I couldn't stay on the ship. I had to get off and secure passage to my one chance to be at peace. I'd be there when my parents passed away and entered paradise. I'd run and hug them, and our argument would be nothing more than a distant memory.

"Oh dear. Are you thinking about Yeoman Hanson?"

Dot's rich southern accent cut right through my tears, and I looked up and sniffed. She was standing in the doorway with a galley tray in her hands, smiling with such sweetness that I dried up a bit.

"No. Come on in, Dot."

She handed me the tray. "Peggy told me all about it. He was your beau, right? I thought maybe a good hot meal would help you. This was the best the galley had today."

I balanced the tray on my knees and took a deep breath. She'd brought me a ham and cheese sandwich, green beans and bacon, and lime jello.

Torres smirked and raised an eyebrow at me, clearly communicating her thoughts. *What are you going to do, Rach?*

I carefully placed the tray on my bed. "I'll eat a little later, Dot. I'm not really hungry right now."

Dot sat on her rack and smoothed her white cotton skirt. "I know it can seem impossible, but you do really move on as the years go by. I've been here for a long time and I don't feel sad when I think about all the people I've said goodbye to. Most of the sailors I've met here are gone, and I left behind parents and six siblings. I'm sure they're all dead now."

"I'm sorry to hear that," I said. "I don't know what to say."

Dot held up a hand. "*I'm* sorry that you're leaving. I'd hoped to get to know you more. Both of you, actually. I've been waiting for female sailors to join the ship since I'd heard that the Navy was accepting them." Her eyes took on a distant look. "I think I would've liked to serve in the modern Navy."

"I don't think your job would've been that different," Torres said. "We've still got nurses."

Dot shook her head. "I wanted to be a doctor. My parents felt that going to medical school would've hurt my marriage prospects, though, so they didn't allow me to go."

I laughed for the first time since Scylla's attack. "My parents were mad at me for joining the Navy *because* they wanted me to be a doctor. Funnily enough, it probably would've helped my marriage prospects."

Dot grinned. "It's a different world out there. I would've loved to experience it, or at least have a granddaughter who experienced it. But I died without issue. I doubt anyone even remembers me."

Well, that had turned dark real fast.

Dot bolted to her feet and ran to the porthole. "Ladies, you need to get outside. You'll want to see this."

*KRASNOYE MORYE.* Red Sea. At least, that's what Dot had explained.

The USSR's own private ghost ship was now, in a way, a true ghost ship. Even larger than the *Saint Catherine*, it floated in the mild current of the Oceanus, dead in the water and unlit inside and out. In the quiet moonlight that reflected off the still water, it looked like a monument to aircraft carriers of the past. Broken-down planes littered the flight deck, and through the shattered portholes I could see rooms in shambles. A red hammer-and-sickle logo, faded and peeling, was the lone decoration of the ship—the flags were long gone.

It felt like a warning...though of what, I could not say.

As the *Saint Catherine* slid past the derelict, I detected movement in one of the portholes. "Is there someone aboard it?" I asked Stanholtzer, who'd joined the small crowd of people with me in the hangar bay.

"One or two sailors, probably," he said quietly. "The USSR ceased to be, so its navy ceased to be. Russia has a different ship. The sailors on the *Krasnoye Morye* are just remnants. The fog will come for them soon, and then the ship will be claimed by the Oceanus for good."

"How sad," I said, my voice soft with true pity. The *Krasnoye Morye* was like an old soldier, silently fading away long after the war was over.

Stanholtzer frowned. "It's what will happen to the *Saint Catherine* if sailors keep getting claimed by Scylla...or leaving." He turned to face me directly. "This ship is a key force protecting your loved ones from monsters. Something to think about, Petty Officer. Good night."

He strode off, leaving me to mouth wordlessly after him.

A few minutes later, when the *Krasnoye Morye* was shrinking in the distance, I walked along the edge of the flight deck, too keyed up by what Stanholtzer had said to consider sleep just then.

A lone sailor stood on the edge at the aft end of the ship, his binoculars up to his eyes. He lowered them as I approached, and gave me a polite nod of greeting. "Good evening, Petty Officer. We haven't met. I'm Seaman Dartsch."

"Are you part of the lookout team?"

I couldn't read his expression. "I am the lookout team. Hanson was the other member." He swallowed. "He was a good friend."

I held out my hand for the binoculars. "Hanson died to keep me safe. If I may, I'd like to take over his duties while I'm still on the ship."

He handed me the binoculars. I peered through them, scanning the horizon for anything unusual or suspicious. "What are we looking for?"

"Pirates, mostly. Pirates can swoop in unbelievably fast, since they exploit the weak points and sail in and out of worlds. They've been our bane for years, far more than Scylla and her ilk."

"And they want magic?"

"Yes. Unfortunately for us, each monster and pirate attack wears down our defenses just a little more. We may look ferocious, Petty Officer, but the truth is that we're one good attack away from total loss. There are fifty-five souls aboard this ship. We're barely running."

I looked up at him. "What happens, really, if the ship stops patrolling?"

"Not to sound dramatic, but the forces of good will lose a major player in the fight to keep the forces of evil firmly stuck in this world. They're constantly trying to get into the world of the living. We cycle endlessly around the weak spots, warning anyone who nears that we'll attack."

"And what happens if the forces of evil get through?"

"You know those old myths and legends about monsters eating maidens, destroying cities, and generally oppressing mankind?"

"Yeah."

"Where do you think they came from?"

He took back the binoculars, and we stood there on the stern, silently watching the dark ocean together.

---

I SHOVED my shoulder against the exterior door, trying to get it to stick in its jam. This ship was seriously falling apart. After a few attempts, I gave up and left the door ajar. A cold wind blew down the hall after me, making me shiver. It wasn't often that a rack sounded comfortable, but right then, I wanted nothing more than to curl up under my blanket.

The sick bay's door was open when I passed it, allowing me to hear two voices in conversation. I walked quickly past the door, but not quickly enough.

"Petty Officer Goldstein." Commander Hollander's voice grated against my ears.

*Hashem, have mercy.* What could he possibly want now?

I stepped into the sick bay. "Yes, *sir*?"

He was propped up on pillows in one of the real racks, the same that he and Torres had been in when we'd woken up. Peggy had put him in a white T-shirt and roomy cotton pants, both of which were stained with blood and the stinky pus.

He leveled a glare at me. "You don't have to make it sound like a foul word."

"Sir, I was on my way to my berthing. Did you need something...*sir*?"

The old "sir sandwich." They'd told us to do it to officers when I was in basic training. Turns out, they didn't like it much.

"Bickley said you weren't like this on the *Taft*. What happened?"

"Well, sir, you flew an aircraft into the side of the ship and killed me. I guess you could say I'm bent out of shape about it. Sir."

"Stop it. Stop saying it like that."

"You can't have it both ways, sir."

"*Stop it*! It was an accident, for God's sake! I died too!"

To hell with self-control. "I don't care if you died! You cocked it up and killed me! Why on earth does that not matter just because you didn't mean it? Why should I forgive you?" A small medical device was suddenly in my hand—and then flying across the room toward Commander Hollander. He ducked just in time.

Peggy flew out of the nurses' office. "Petty Officer! What are earth are you doing to my patient?"

I didn't care if he was an officer. I didn't care if I could land back in the brig for this. I wasn't even officially part of the crew, damn it, so who the hell was he to demand that I call him 'sir,' like he was important? Like he was something? He was nothing. He'd messed everything up when he'd said...

I took a step back. No, he hadn't *said* anything. He'd done something. He'd killed me.

What was going on in my brain?

I swallowed the lump in my throat and pointed at Commander Hollander, whose mouth was open. "He wanted to speak to me, but he wouldn't get to the point. What did you want to tell me, *sir*?" It was miraculous that I hadn't cracked my teeth from how hard I was gritting them.

He crossed his arms, incredulous. "I wanted to thank you for saving me in the water. They said one of the new women aboard pulled me out, and the description was clearly of you."

There was a short silence.

"Torres did that," I snapped. Peggy raised an eyebrow, but I glared at her. "No, it *was* Torres." I dragged my eyes back to Commander Hollander. "Would I save you? Really?"

Hurt flitted across his eyes, and then his expression darkened. "No, you wouldn't. My mistake, *Petty* Officer."

My jaw tightened. He thought he was so slick, didn't he? "That's not even my title anymore, Arthur. I'm not part of this crew. Tomorrow, I'm getting off in Port des Morts. If you have anything you want to throw at me, now is the time to do it." I crossed my arms and jutted out my hip. "Lay it on me."

But both Peggy and he startled. "You're leaving? Why?" Commander Hollander's surprise sounded genuine.

"You can't leave," Peggy said. "The ship chose you. It's your des—"

"If you say it's my destiny to be on this clunker, I'm going to overload the power supply so you're all dead in the water, do a backflip off this ship, and swim to Port des Morts. I swear I will." I looked at Commander Hollander. "I'm leaving because you stole me away from my parents. I'm making it right by going to the Far Island. I don't owe you anything. Not time, energy, respect, manners, and certainly not my afterlife."

I tossed my hair and stormed out, but limping footsteps behind me made me turn around, then roll my eyes. Commander Hollander was bracing himself on the bulkhead as he lurched out of the sick bay. "Wait," he wheezed. "Don't... don't..."

"Dude, go back to bed," I said, lowering my voice. "Don't die just to boss me around. Peggy! Come get him!"

He came to rest a few feet in front of me, a hand on his injuries. "You have to stay," he said, breathing hard. "There's a weak point right by Virginia Beach. It's where they were sailing from when they hooked up to the *Taft*. Something's going to happen in my hometown."

*His* hometown?

But...

But...

But Virginia Beach was *my* hometown.

"You're from Virginia Beach?" I asked.

"Yes. And I know I don't have any right to ask, but please stay onboard and help the ship upgrade. Please join the crew. My family could be in danger."

I gulped, unable to meet his eyes. "What's your alma mater?"

Maybe he was lying. This would be a quick acid test.

"I went to high school at Norfolk Collegiate, and then graduated through Old Dominion University's NJROTC program eight years ago."

Several sailors walked past us in the passageway, only sparing a glance at the injured officer and the nuke.

"Norfolk Collegiate." I let out a long breath, carefully choosing my words, laying my trap. "Did you have Mr. Stern for math? He was cool."

He straightened, not even wincing. "Did you go there, too? Mr. Stern taught World Lit when I attended."

He wasn't lying. *Well, I'll be.*

I nodded. "No, you're right. He taught World Lit, not math. I graduated two years ago. Salutatorian. I was in the prom queen's court, too. President of the Jewish Student Association in my senior year. Did that partnership program with Eastern Virginia Medical School, you know the one, where students can shadow a doctor for a day?"

"My best friend's little brother did that! His brother's name was Daniel Levinson. He might've gone there when you did."

Talk about a small world.

"Danny was the president of the JSA when I was a freshman. I thought he was cute. I don't think he ever knew I was alive." Though he definitely would've heard I was dead. We'd attended the same synagogue.

We stared at each other. I hugged myself, then said, "I bet you looked up at the jets whenever they flew over when you were a kid, didn't you? And you said, that's gonna be me one day."

His large eyes were wet. "And you looked out at the ocean and said, I'm going to go out there one day."

"We ran in the same social circle, even. We're the same. Same high school, same friends, same call to the sea."

"Yes, and—"

"So you're not better than me, sir." A sob escaped my chest as I said it.

He gasped. "Rachel, I don't think I'm better than you."

"Then *why* won't you apologize?"

We were two Virginia Beach natives, born and raised under the same sky. We'd gone to the same high school. We'd known the same people. We'd walked the same halls, studied under the same instructors, breathed the same air. I was him, and he was me. It was only a quirk of fate that he was an officer and I was enlisted, and that quirk was that I'd been so desperate to stick it to my parents that I'd driven to the recruiter's office at eight in the morning on my eighteenth birthday.

I could've been an officer. I could've been a Navy doctor. I could've been in command of a ship one day. And had I been all of these things, I never would've strode around an engine room and called the engineers nerds, and I never would've been so lofty in my thinking that it never occurred to me to take ownership of a mistake that had killed twenty-five people.

Because he never had. He'd simply insisted that it was all an accident, that he hadn't meant to—as if that somehow excused the damage he'd wreaked in a single second. Drunk drivers never meant to kill their victims, but somehow they ended up in jail all the same.

My father had probably forgotten his terrible parting words to me the second he'd said them...but I never would. I couldn't. They were a part of me, as much as my curly hair and overbite. They'd sunk into my soul, and now my soul was all that I had. Was all that I *was*.

Commander Hollander placed a hand on my shoulder, his breath coming in little puffs from the pain he was in. "I'm sorry," he said, so softly I could barely hear him. "I'm really sorry. I don't know what I did, but I must've done something wrong, because the rest of the guys in the air landed. I'm so sorry, Petty Officer. It was my mistake. I just wish I knew what it was."

The pain in my chest shattered, shards of regret and anger flying everywhere inside—but the resentment began to drain away. I'd just wanted an apology, an acknowledgment that he'd harmed me.

I rubbed my eyes and looked at him, and though I was still unhappy that I was dead, seeing his face did not make me want to dropkick him anymore.

He gave me a sad half-smile. "Will you sign the book? We need all the nukes we can get, and the ship does need an upgrade. It's hardly ocean-worthy anymore."

I sniffed and shook my head. "I'm going to wait for my family. I'm their only child. I'm all they have."

He sighed, then nodded. "I understand." His leg wobbled, and he fell to one knee.

I helped him to his feet, and he staggered as his leg gave way again. I caught him and threw his arm over my shoulder. "Did Peggy explain why some things injure us, but Commander Muree's bullet didn't hurt you?" I began to help him into the sick bay.

He placed a hand to his chest and sucked in a shaking breath.

"Magical weapons, and magical attacks, can't hurt the people who create them, or their allies. Scylla is a beast of untold power, and she's definitely not my friend. Peggy and Dot are doing the best they can, but the ship isn't fitted for this kind of wound."

I helped him into bed again, a new lump forming in my throat.

"But if it were to upgrade, it might be," Peggy said from the doorway. "You're being very selfish for not signing the book."

I ran from the room, slamming the door behind me. I leaned against the bulkhead, pain pulsing in my temples as if Peggy had struck me.

I was not selfish. I was not selfish. I was not selfish. I was going to meet my parents, and nobody had any right to shame me for making the choice.

When I'd gotten my heart under control, I hurried down the passageway toward the female berthing. When I was inside, I slipped underneath my scratchy wool blanket and squeezed my eyes shut.

*I'm not selfish.*

## 10

"And you're really not going to join the crew?"

I resisted the urge to step on Dot's foot. This was all beginning to border on harassment. "Yes, for the millionth time, I'm sure."

We were idling in the hangar bay while other sailors set up the covered gangplank, which obscured our view of the landing area of the port. Only the wings of the beach, far to each side, were visible. Any additional view was blocked by a neighboring ship in the next pull-in spot at the port. The Royal Canadian Navy's ghost ship, the HMCS *Sérendipité* was a large battleship, and if the waving sailors were any indication, they were very friendly. It was impossible to miss how run-down the ship was, though. Parts of it had been patched up with wooden boards.

She fiddled with the cuff of her sleeve, her eyebrows drawn together in deep concern. "But... Port des Morts is dangerous, Petty Officer. And I'm sure you're very courageous, but it takes more than bravery when you're dealing with the people who live there." She pointed a slim finger toward a remote area on the shore.

The place she indicated looked like a campground. Tents dotted the small hill, about fifty in all, and small campfires were burning even though it was daytime. Tiny people milled around the area, though I couldn't tell if they were men or women. Children were dashing here and there, though, so there were probably a few families.

"What is that place?"

"A refugee camp. Please promise me you'll stay away from the fairies. Most of them are fine, but there's always a few malcontents from the war, and you have no way to discern who is whom."

I watched the children run around a little more, then turned to Dot. "I promise."

"And don't fall in love with one just because he's good looking. They're all just trouble."

Real laughter bubbled out of me. "I *promise*, no fairies, no ill-advised romance."

"Liberty call!" One of the chiefs waved a clipboard around in the air. "Sign out on this sheet! Everyone has to be on board by eighteen hundred, no exceptions!"

"Except me," I said, slinging my seabag over my shoulder. "Thanks for everything, Dot." I gave her my firmest handshake, then joined Bickley and Torres in the line.

"Name and rank," the chief said when I reached the gangplank.

"Rachel Goldstein, no rank. I'm getting off."

He looked up from his clipboard. "You're disembarking for good?"

"Yes."

He looked at Bickley and Torres, his eyes darting back and forth between them worriedly. "Are you two going with her?"

"Only for liberty," Bickley said. "But we're part of the crew. We'll be back tonight."

The chief stared at me for another second, then dug around in his pocket for a few seconds before removing three silver coins. "Take these," he said, placing them in my hand and folding my fingers over them. "And stay away from the fairies, okay?"

*Stay away from the fairies.* If it was worth repeating, it was worth remembering.

"I will, thanks," I said softly. I put them in my pocket and hurried down the gangplank, determinedly not looking back at the ship that had been my home for a few days.

I walked off the gangplank, taking my first hesitant step onto the land of the undead. It was an underwhelming moment—land felt the same here—but as soon as I truly focused on what was around me, I forgot all comparisons.

Port des Morts was unlike any port city I'd ever seen. Marseilles, Palma, Rhodes, Lisbon, Dubai, Naples, Southhampton, Bahrain... I'd seen them all. But none of them had anything on Port des Morts, the "port of the dead people."

I walked around with my mouth open, agog at the endless rows of booths and stands. People crowded around them, swapping silver coins for fruits unlike any I'd ever seen, in odd shapes, with bizarre little bits sticking off of them. Some of the fruits were even moving. An old man was peeling purple paisley bananas and feeding slices to a parrot-like bird. The bird swallowed, and its feathers became purple paisley, too.

An old lady caught my eye and held up a beautiful necklace, the lapis lazuli pendant glinting in the sunlight. "Pretty bauble for the pretty girl?"

I rubbed my Star of David and shook my head, moving on before she should argue. I hadn't taken more than three steps before I ran into a small stand selling the loveliest dresses I'd ever seen, all cut from a material that shimmered with rainbow fire, like opal cloth.

"Did you see that?" Torres asked suddenly. "Someone was watching us from behind that kiosk."

I looked, but there was nobody there.

"It's crowded," Bickley said. "Let's keep moving."

The farther end of the market dealt in living, breathing goods, such as squawking birds in cages, cats with multiple tails, snakes with diamond-encrusted scales, and lizards that blew fire from their nostrils.

Another kiosk offered tiny blown glass balls with moving lights inside them. Upon examination, I realized that they were alive—tiny little winged creatures, darting around with gauze-like wings and emanating a light from their insides as fireflies did. I reached out to touch one, but a gnarled hand on mine stopped me. It was an old lady with emerald-green hair and eyes. "Don't touch," she said, her voice raw and rough.

I backed away.

The final part of the market was foodstuffs, and I had to remind myself that I didn't need to eat. Dripping meats on spits were being sliced off and stuffed into bread, and fresh fruits were being squeezed into pewter tankards. Delicate, spindly candies were as tempting to me as they were to the throngs of small children looking at them with big eyes.

Such delights for a sailor such as myself. Alas, I had only the three coins. Common sense dictated that I move on.

I walked beyond the port market into the city proper...and saw at once why it was the Mos Eisley of this world.

Rowdy bars filled with young men lined much of the street, their drunken inhabitants fighting outside them, sleeping in corners, or stumbling around. Every few doors, young women in shocking outfits beckoned to passerby, cooing at them and fluttering their eyelashes.

The few businesses that weren't bars or houses of ill repute were shuttered and dimly lit, their true purposes left to my imagination.

Only one such business had a sign above the entrance: The House of the Setting Sun. From the doorway, a handsome man about my age, hooded and cloaked, pointed a gloved finger at me. "Sailor. You wish to go to the Far Island." A shaft of light fell across his face, causing sparkles around his eyes to reveal themselves.

I stopped in the middle of the road, foot traffic flowing all around me. I had no particular destination in the city, though I needed to find some kind of shelter, and this guy seemed to have answers.

But I wasn't stupid. Guys in hoods who knew stuff I hadn't told them were trouble. Always.

I held up a hand. "No thanks. Just passing through."

He smiled enigmatically. "I'll be here when you return."

Another hooded man brushed past me, stopped in the doorway, and spoke inaudibly to the man who'd spoken to me. They both nodded once, and then the second man hurried inside.

The first man looked back to me. "You should leave, sailor."

I backed up. *Yeah, okay. Doing that now.*

Bickley and Torres caught up with me and pulled me away. "Don't talk to anyone," Bickley ordered. "I just saw a guy with a revolver. Let's assume everyone's armed and none of them are your friends."

Torres pointed ahead. "There. I see a restaurant, I think. It doesn't look too creepy. Let's go there."

Bickley put his arms around the both of us, and we hustled along the busy street until we were at the doorway of "Aurora's."

Aurora's was a small pub, quiet compared to the other establishments on the street. Through the gabled windows, people sat in huddles around rough-hewn wooden tables, eating food from pewter plates and drinking from large flagons. A roaring fire lent it a distinct cheer that the rest of the street lacked.

My hand was on the wooden door when I noticed three more men in cloaks down the street, watching us without any pretense of looking occupied.

I wanted to go back to the ship.

But I pushed open the door, and we went inside. A few patrons looked up from their food, but nobody greeted us or otherwise acknowledged that we were there. We sat at a corner table.

Torres leaned forward, her hands on her head. "Rach, *please*. You can't stay here."

Yeah... I had already come to that conclusion myself, but what option did I have? I'd told everyone I was leaving, and I wasn't going to waltz back on the ship and be like, "Psych! Changed my mind!"

It wasn't a simple pride issue, either. It was a core value issue. The US Navy's Sailor's Creed demanded that I "represent the fighting spirit of the Navy"—and what kind of sailor ran from a rowdy port? US sailors lived and breathed rowdy ports. I was self-evidently a spirit, and now it was time to prove that I had fight left in me.

On the other hand, I had a rack waiting for me on the *Saint Catherine*, and I was reasonably sure nobody would rob me in the middle of the night there. I was brave, but I wasn't a moron—I knew that a lone woman out of her element was an easy target. The men in cloaks were probably part of a local organized crime outfit, and they'd made me their next mark. I'd have to watch myself, and my seabag, *very* carefully.

A middle-aged woman in a shimmery dress and a leather apron came up to us. She was plump, and her eyes bore the same sparkles that I'd seen on the hooded man's face. Her raven-black hair fell to her waist. The whole effect was that of someone trying to be human and failing miserably.

"Are you Aurora?" I asked.

"Yes, this is my tavern. What can I get you?"

I held up one of the silver coins. "What can this get me?"

Her sharp eyes locked onto the coin. "Drinks for you and your friends, and a place to stay for the night."

I placed the coin in her outstretched hand, and she wandered into a back room. Through the door, I could see her speaking to two men. She shot several furtive looks our way.

I looped the strap of my seabag around my leg.

Torres leaned forward. "What do you think they eat here? I wouldn't mind testing out the food just for curiosity's sake."

"I don't know," Bickley said, "But earlier I saw some fruit that looked like it could bite me back. Let's just eat in the galley."

The door opened again, and this time two men in black pants and blue shirts came in. They spoke briefly with the man behind the bar, who nodded and slid two flagons of a foamy, amber-colored liquid at them.

Torres stood partially. "Those men are in the Royal Canadian Navy. Check out their flag insignia."

Bickley caught their eye and waved, and the men came over with their drinks. "Hey, what do you know?" the taller one said. "Haven't had a drink with the US Navy in an age. How are you guys doing?"

We all shook hands, and they sat down with us. The taller one was named Pierre, and the shorter one was Hal.

I eyed their drinks. "What's on tap? We're waiting for our drinks."

Hal took a long swig. "You must be new deadies. It's this world's beer. Instead of making you drunk, though, it's infused with fairy magic. It's a nice tingle. Been drinking it since the 80's."

Was there anything magic couldn't do or be? I could feel the raw magic I'd squirreled away in my insides before leaving the ship, gently humming with life. I mentally patted it and turned my attention back to Pierre and Hal.

Pierre traced the rim of his flagon with a finger, clearly thinking. "You've got a seabag. You leaving the *Saint Catherine*?"

"Yes. I'm looking for passage to the Far Island, and hopefully another chance to kill Scylla. She attacked the carrier a few days ago. We lost some good people."

Hal and Pierre looked at each other. "Scylla's been unusually active," Pierre said. He spoke with a French purr, but his words were laced with unignorable warning. "She came after the *Sérendipité* last month. We lost thirty men, plus our captain." He inclined his head to me. "You're invited to join our crew. We're not picky. We need all the help we can get these days. If you want to fight Scylla, our ship is a good bet."

"We can do that?" Torres said. "Just join another country's ghost Navy?"

"You can switch allegiances in life, so why not in death, too? We've got a few fairies, even. The war has caused a lot of displaced young people from their world who need a job and a purpose."

"No offense, guys, but your ship doesn't even look seaworthy anymore," Bickley said.

"It's not," they said at the same time.

Hal heaved a sigh. "Yeah, okay, it was worth a shot. But I gotta be honest: we're on our last legs. Between Scylla's attacks and the constant skirmishes with pirates, we're not much more than a floating bathtub. Now we're under Commander Gagnon, too. Heaven help us."

Pierre snorted. "Don't you mean *Captain* Gagnon?" He gave us a significant look. "She loses her mind if you don't call her that, even though she's still officially a Commander. I'll be the first person to give someone the respect they deserve, but this woman is something else."

"It sounds like I'd better off staying away from your ship," I said.

"Sorry, guys. I'm not looking to join another Navy. I'm actually trying to figure out how to get to the Far Island."

Another man in a cloak entered the tavern. He strode into the backroom where Aurora was, never sparing anyone a single look.

"You need to go to the House of the Setting Sun," Pierre said. "They can take you anywhere, if you're willing to pay their prices. I don't know the details, but they don't want money, or so I've heard. Frankly, I'd stay away from them. Stay away from fairies in general."

Stay away from the fairies. Stay away from the House of the Setting Sun. There were a lot of things to stay away from in this place.

Bickley leaned back in his seat. "So, what are you going to do, Rach? You're a free woman. You've got an invite to be in Canada's navy, or you can stay here for three nights before you have to find other lodging."

Aurora saved me from having to answer. She bustled over to our table with our drinks, and set them down in front of us with a winsome smile. "Here you go, loves." She placed a small brass key in front of me. "You're in room two. I'll have my daughter bring you fresh sheets later. It's up the stairs over there."

I picked up the heavy vessel and inhaled the effervescence. The heady, hoppy smell seeped into my brain and made strange colors swirl behind my eyes, strange visions of people I'd never seen, dancing women in flouncy skirts, and eyes... red eyes that bore right through me.

Scylla's eyes.

I took a sip and nearly choked. Lightning coursed through my insides, spreading into the tips of my fingers and toes. Warmth followed it, and I was beset by the sudden desire to lie down.

"I'm checking out my room," I said, giving my head a little shake. "You can all come with me if you want. I don't... I don't feel so good." Bickley and Torres's eyes were also droopy.

Pierre frowned. "Man, you all are lightweights. They give this stuff to kids around here."

Hal dipped a finger into my drink and licked it, then choked. "What is this? Here, try," he said to Pierre.

Pierre copied him, his eyes widening. "Whoa. That's not the normal ale. I've never had anything like that."

I was too sleepy to care. Instead, I dragged my feet toward the stairs, the doors blurring together. My seabag felt like a load of bricks.

I stumbled into my room. Hal picked me up and placed me on the bed. My head touched a pillow. Bickley and Torres laid down next to me, while Pierre and Hal were speaking to us, their plaintive voices simultaneously loud and incredibly far away.

I blinked. Pierre had shoved a chair underneath the doorknob, and Hal had a pocket knife in his hand.

Time melted into nothing, each second dragging on like an hour, and each minute just the blink of an eye.

And in the distance, there was screaming.

## 11

"Rach! Rach, wake up! Come on, wake up!"

Someone propped me up in bed. The room swam, a mural of colors and shapes moving back and forth. My head felt full of rocks, and the inside of my mouth was more like a desert than anything.

And the air...it smelled of smoke and ash.

The image in front of my eyes stilled. Hal and Pierre were by the door, knives in hand. The chair had been replaced by a solid-looking dresser. Bickley was standing by the window, which was covered by a thin curtain. He was watching the street below, unblinking.

Torres helped me to my feet. "Rach, how are you feeling? I've been trying to wake you up for five minutes."

"They meant to rob you all," Hal said, turning to look at me. His mouth was a grim line. "Aurora must've been paid to drug your drinks. However, they may have actually done us all a favor by giving us a room."

"There's at least three bands down there," Bickley said. "They're looting. They have weapons."

"Not much to loot in a tavern," Pierre said. "I don't think they'll come up here."

"What happened?" I asked, taking a hesitant step to test the strength of my legs. They felt like jelly.

"Pirates attacked shortly after you all crashed from whatever she put in your drink," Hal said. "It sounded like they attacked anyone and everything they could. They were taking people, too." He patted the dresser. "We barred the door. They messed up the place downstairs, but they didn't come up here."

I gasped. "Guys, the ship! We need to get back on board!"

Torres shook her head. "We're not leaving until nightfall, when we can sneak around."

I held up my hands. "I've got some power left inside me. If anyone tries anything, I'll blast them. But we gotta get back to the ship."

Bickley stepped away from the window. "Well, if that's the case. The bands moved over to the next street, so maybe now is as good as any other time. And she's right," he said to Hal and Pierre. "We all need to get back on our ships. Goldstein's not a member of the crew, but we are."

Hal and Pierre had a silent exchange, and then they shoved the dresser aside. I picked up my seabag and slung it over my shoulder. Bickley broke the hatstand over his knee and gave one of the ends to Torres, while he took the other. Hal and Pierre whipped out their pocket knives.

"All right," Pierre said, cracking open the door. "Don't even blink."

---

PORT DES MORTS was in shambles. We'd planned to sprint for the port, but there was to be no running of any kind in the dark streets. The setting sun was low on the horizon, but the remaining fires cast enough glow to see the carnage I'd slept through.

Every building now lacked windows or doors. Furniture had been tossed through them, spreading broken glass all over the cobblestones. Dead people lay here and there in pools of blood, their throats slit. It took me a moment to see that all of the deceased had the tell-tale sparkles around their eyes.

"Fairies?" I whispered as we passed a dead mother still holding her baby.

"Most of the permanent residents of this city are fairies," Hal whispered. He held his hand up, then hastily beckoned for us to follow him into the dark doorway of the House of the Setting Sun. It was the only building in sight that didn't have a scratch.

The door swung open, revealing the same cloaked, hooded man as before. He smiled mildly, and held his arm out behind him. "Please, come in."

Bickley held up his half of the broken hatstand. "We're just passing through. You can shut the door."

But the man merely cocked his head and studied Bickley. "Your father is waiting for you, Jack. And the little child. Your heart broke when Tanya lost the baby. Isn't it time you go and join them? The baby needs a daddy."

Bickley froze, then lowered his weapon. "How... how do you know that? How do you know my name?"

The man looked to Torres. "Marisol, your grandmother still thinks of you fondly, but she regrets that she couldn't speak English and tell you that she loved you. Why don't you go to her now?"

Torres's eye twitched. "Everyone, get away from this guy. He's a psychic like me. It's a cheap trick. C'mon, let's go."

She grabbed my shoulder, but he was looking at me. His dark

eyes were like tunnels, pulling me in deeper and deeper until all other sound fell away.

"Rachel Miriam Goldstein. Your middle name means 'sea of sorrows.' How appropriate, don't you think?" He held out a gloved hand to me. "Take my hand, child. Your sorrows are almost over. I will take you to your people. They are waiting."

"They're waiting?" I whispered. *If they're waiting... it would be... rude to delay...*

Someone was shouting at me, but I disregarded them. His eyes were so velvety and dark, enveloping me, like nightfall after a long day in the reactor. Encasing me in—

Bickley hit him with the hatstand. The spell was broken, and I shook my head to clear my thoughts. "Wha...?"

Torres, Hal, and Pierre wrenched me away from the door and spun me around. "That guy is the creepiest person in all of Port des Morts," Hal hissed, shoving us inside another broken doorway. "People go through the door and never come out. They're always the ones looking for a way to get to the Far Island, or the land of the living, or wherever. I don't know what he does, but he's a predator. Stay the hell away from him."

"Noted," I said, gulping. "Quick, let's run to the corner. Nobody's watching."

We all dashed for the corner, around which would be the final leg of the journey to the market that had been filled with so many stalls. Bickley held up his hatstand again, and gestured for us to stay low. "Okay, let me just check to s..."

He'd peeked around the corner.

Torres hurried to see what he'd seen. "Oh. Oh... *dear.*"

I joined them, equally lost for words.

Across a battlefield of destroyed kiosks and stands, the USS *Saint Catherine* was half-sunk in the water, listing heavily and completely, utterly without hope. A few dozen sailors were camped out on the pier next to her. A lone blonde figure in white attended to a line of injured sailors.

The blonde was Peggy. Where was Dot?

Beside it, the HMCS *Sérendipité* was in equal disrepair, partially sunk and taking on water. Canada's finest hurried around the pier, their own nurses attending to everyone. Around both camps, armed guards patrolled the perimeters.

"Let's go," Bickley said. "Hal, Pierre, this is where we part ways."

We all shook hands and wished each other the best, then began the long walks toward our destroyed ships.

---

THEY'D COME FOR PEOPLE, not goods or weapons. That much was obvious. Captain Gorman had been taken, along with Commander Muree, a dozen sailors of various ranks, and Dot. The pirate fleet had come around the coast, sweeping up to the side of the ships in their cutters and easily overwhelming the skeleton crew. Most of the sailors hadn't been on board, but out and about in town.

Peggy's victory rolls were limp and unkempt as she worked diligently on the injured sailors, which were many. She wound bandages, dabbed at burns, and pulled shrapnel out with tweezers, never letting her despair appear on her face.

But I knew. I knew how shock and sadness sat in a heart, and I could see it in the trembling of her hands and the glaze in her eye. "Do you need medical attention, Petty Officer?" she asked as she passed me on the pier. Her accent had somehow lost the midwestern smile.

"No, and I'm not a Petty Officer any more. Do *you* need medical attention?" I reached for the gash on her cheek, but she batted my hand away.

"I'm fine. It could be a lot worse."

"What happened?"

Her eyes filled with tears. "We were in our berthing when they came. Dot had stuffed me into a linen locker before I knew what was happening. I heard them come and get her. She was screaming so..."

Peggy broke down, and Torres hurried over to comfort her.

I silently picked up Peggy's kit and began attending to the injured in her stead. The first person I went to was Commander Hollander.

He was lying down with his eyes closed on a blanket next to two other injured officers, and his chest still bore the bloody, stinking wounds Scylla had inflicted on him. I kneeled next to him and made to change his bandages, but he put a hand on mine. "Don't."

A rod slammed down my spine, forcing my hand to retract. Captain Gorman had used the same voice on us in our first hour onboard the ship.

What in the *hell*?

"How did you do that?" I demanded. "That voice—that was the bossy voice like Captain Gorman's."

He propped himself up on his elbows, wincing the whole way. "I didn't do anything."

"Stop lying. You made my hand move away."

"No, I didn't."

I threw down the bandages. "I don't have time for this. Why won't you let me take care of your injuries?"

"I shouldn't be here," he muttered. "They took all the other aviators. I should be with them, not here."

If I'd rolled my eyes any harder, I would've been able to see my brain. "Not now, Arthur. Be dramatic later." My mom had said that to me several times in my teens. I finally understood. He made to reply, but I held up a hand. "I didn't save you before just to have you bleed out or whatever right now. And if you use your Hashem-voice on me, I'm going to smack you all the way back to the living world."

His lips twisted as he thought, and then he settled back and let me begin removing the bandages. "What's Hashem?"

"It's what some Jews call, you know..." I pointed at the sky.

"You're an interesting friend to have, I gotta say."

"We're not friends, sir. That's fraternizing."

He scoffed. "There are two problems with that."

"And I'm sure you're about to tell me. I can't wait to hear this."

He grinned. "One, you're not part of the crew, so it's not fraternizing."

I ripped off a piece of tape and placed it on his new bandage. "And two, you're a smartass, so—"

"And two, you just admitted to saving me after Scylla's attack, so I have to be your friend whether you like it or not. Whether I like it or not, as a matter of fact. I don't make the rules."

I paused, then looked up from his wounds and rested my arm on my knee. "Fine, you got me. I pulled you from the water. Happy?"

"Goldstein! Torres! I need you!" Bickley's shout made me turn my head. He was standing by one of the large holes in the hull. The ship was tilted in such a way that access via the hangar bay was impossible. However, a person could climb up onto the hull via the gangplank and fall into the hole.

I made a face at Commander Hollander, then rushed over to Bickley. "What's up?"

"We've been asked by a few members of the crew to go into the ship and find the remaining stores of raw magic, and if they're still there, to secure it. I say we split up to cover as much ground as possible in the shortest amount of time. Torres, you go up to the hangar bay and check there. I'll search the weapons locker where the

Master at Arms stored his firepower. Goldstein, you're in the engine room."

"Got it," Torres and I said together. Torres clambered up the gangplank, then carefully slid onto the hull and into the gaping wound in the hull. She held my hand while I maneuvered into place, and then dropped me down into the compartment below. A minute later, Bickley joined me. He caught Torres, and then we all took stock of the damage.

And holy cannoli, there was a lot of damage.

The pirates had ransacked the place, throwing furniture and paperwork everywhere. We were in what appeared to be a destroyed yeoman's office, but it was impossible to know for sure—there was just too much mess.

"At least they didn't set the place on fire," Bickley said. "Come on, you two. Keep sharp."

The bowels of the ship were almost pitch-black. We didn't have flashlights, and the sun was almost out of sight. I wasn't familiar enough with the ship to know the layout by memory, but there was something I could do.

I placed my hand on an exposed wire and whisked a tiny amount of power into the system. *Bing, bing, bing*, the lights popped on, then off, creating a silent-but-bright chain of illumination down the passageways.

"I'll do that periodically," I said. "I've only got enough power for about five more times, so memorize what you can, and run when possible."

They nodded, then sprinted off in the opposite direction of the engine room. I walked purposefully toward the stairwell at the far end of the passageway. When I reached the top, I stared down into the vast nothingness at the bottom.

Was there water down there? I couldn't say, because I couldn't see. I touched another wire and lit up the ship for a few seconds.

No water.

I awkwardly descended the crooked stairs down and walked with equal awkwardness down the passageway, past berthings, storage rooms, and offices. All had been rummaged through by pirates.

Another stairwell, another passageway. I was getting close. I lit up the ship once more, and this time I could feel how low on power I was getting. I'd have to save it for the engine room, the most important part of my journey. Hopefully the others had made good use of their light.

I pushed open the door to the engine room.

Silence.

*Engine rooms should never be silent.* Engines and generators—the stuff of life, so to speak. They should've been roaring like the beautiful machines they were, taking in fuel and churning out power that pushed the ship through the water, armed the catapults that launched the planes, heated our water, cooked our unnecessary food. All of it was because of the lifeblood pumped into the ship's arteries by its beating heart.

Its broken heart.

My final pulse of power had revealed the terrible damage. The machines were sideways, the parts scattered everywhere, busted and bent. The tiny lights on the machine were dark. The magic was gone. The USS *Saint Catherine* was well and truly dead in the water.

I looked up at the softly glowing lightbulbs above me. Why were they still on?

As soon as the question passed through my mind, a soft melody caught my attention, a young woman's pleasant humming. I knew the tune from somewhere, far away in my mind. A lullaby? A child's playground song?

"Hello? Is someone there?" I stepped over a broken piston and peered around the main body of the engine. "Dot, is that you?" *Please be Dot. Please tell me she hid in here.*

The humming grew louder as I approached the dead center of the engine room. I steadied myself, then turned the corner that led to the nerve center of the ship.

A young woman, no older than me, was crouching by an access panel in one of the generators. She wore the familiar blue coveralls that nukes wore when working, and her long dark hair had been pulled back into a sensible ponytail. She tinkered around in the generator, her brow knit in concentration.

"Who are you?" I asked. "Are you from the HMCS *Sérendipité*? If you are, I can escort you off the ship. Your chain of command is probably looking for you."

But she just stood, smiling, and brushed a lock of hair behind her ear. "You're very kind, but I'm not the *Sérendipité*." Her mid-Atlantic accent perfectly matched my own.

"Oh. Then... who are you?" I looked her up and down. "If you're a new nuke, you may want to sit down, because I've got some bad news." How was I supposed to explain to this woman what had happened to her?

But she just laughed. "I'm not a nuke, Rachel. I'm used to appearing as a Seaman, but I thought you'd maybe be more comfortable if I looked more like you."

My mouth fell open a little. I was talking to the ship. I would *never* be used to this. "You're the *Saint Catherine*."

She shrugged. "That's what some people call me."

"What do you call yourself? You must be very old." My guess was that her name was something complicated and unsayable, perhaps in Etruscan or even Proto-Indo-European.

She shook her head and smiled. "I have no name. I am older than the ocean. Older, even, than the mountains and the firmaments of the earth. I was wished into existence before memory, born from the utterance of a single word. I am *so* old."

I took a step back, a wild thought of taking off my boots flitting across my brain. I was in the presence of something much bigger than me, and I needed to act like it. "What do you want from me?" I asked, as respectfully as I could.

"I want your heart, Rachel. I've been trying to grow, but I can't without your heart. Why have you been running away from me?"

My lips shook as they silently repeated formed the words she'd said, but I couldn't give them voice. Did she want a human sacrifice? What was she talking about?"

She laughed. "No, I don't want your physical heart. I want you. Your physical heart is long gone, but you remain. Your soul."

"What does that mean?" I took another step back.

"It means you'll sail in me and provide power to me. It means you'll be a part of the eternal chain of sailors that have called me home. It means you'll live again, free, as the sailor you have always been." She placed a gentle hand on my chest. "You heard my call. That's why you're here."

Tears were dripping down my chin. "Did you kill me? Did you take me away from the *Taft*?"

She pulled me into a tender hug and rubbed my back. "Never. I don't have that power, and even if I did, I wouldn't. I merely made you take a detour on your trip to the final place. There are many evil beings here, and many more who are indifferent. But I am on your side. That's a promise."

I wiped my nose with my sleeve. "I want to go there, to the final place. My family is comforting themselves with the knowledge that I'm waiting for them. I need to make it true."

She assessed me, thinking. "I'll make you a deal, Rachel. If you stay with me, I will send the fog for you when your parents pass on."

"*You* make the fog?"

"I call it. It, too, is alive. You needn't fear it."

Such sweet words from a being whose entire existence I did not understand. But for all of her promises, I still didn't want to stay on the ship. I wanted to go home. *Home is where the heart is,* I thought to myself. And my heart was with my family, not there on the *Saint Catherine.*

She tilted her head, still smiling. "They're not the only thing in your heart. Let's see. Where's Commander Hollander?"

Dust on the floor swirled in a silent breeze, traveling up and up, coloring and taking the form of Commander Hollander. Dust-Hollander patted the generator. "We always wondered what you nerds got up to down here."

Heat flooded into my cheeks. It stung just as much now as it did then. Maybe I was a nerd, but he'd had no right to say so.

The dust collapsed into a little pile on the floor. "Respect," she said. "You want it. You want it from your family. You want it from your superiors. You want it from the entire Navy. Nobody respects the reactor division because you're not as exciting as the aviators and SEALs, correct?"

I gulped. "Yeah. They're think we're bookish and weird."

She drummed her fingers on the generator. "Admiral Rickover would be proud of you. I never knew him, but I know his work. He labored long and hard to turn the Navy into a nuclear force. I think it's time that evil-doers and monsters become familiar with his name, don't you?"

Where was she going with this? "I'd like that," I said slowly. "But again, what do you want from me?"

"You, right up until your parents pass away. No more, no less. At that time, you will be gathered to your people. You'll be beyond my reach there."

Now wasn't the time to pretend I wasn't scared. "Will it be dangerous?"

"Incredibly so."

"What happens when ghosts die again?"

"I have no idea."

"Is there anything good for me in this deal?"

A gleam appeared in her eye. "Adventure. Endless and awesome."

My heart began to beat a little faster. "How can I have adventures in a derelict ship like this?"

She held out her hands, and the name book appeared, already open. A pen materialized in the air in front of me. "Sign the book, and you'll see."

I hesitated, then plucked the pen out of the air. The tip hovered over the paper for a second as I read my coworker's names, neat and formal at the end of a long line of signatures. The pen met paper, and I wrote:

*EMN2 Goldstein, Rachel Miriam*

She grinned, excitement lighting up her face. "Oh, thank you, Rachel!"

She melted into the floor, making me shout in alarm.

The ship began to tremble, then shake with earthquake force. Overhead, lightbulbs exploded, throwing little shards of glass everywhere, all over myself and the floor. I dashed to a spot far away from a bulb and crouched.

Then I gasped.

The ship righted itself, lurching up, listing no more. Deck plates flipped over, revealing newer, stronger steel that was polished to within an inch of its life. They flipped up one by one, traveling out of the engine room. Every time they changed, a puff of gold dust flew into the air.

I began to sprint after them, laughing all the while. Flip, flip, flip —the deck plates, the bulk heads, even a few panels on the ceiling, all changing into something new at a breathtaking speed. Light danced along the wires and pipes, snaking around, changing its avenue as it went.

Each room I passed was clean, neat, and organized. The signs pointing the way around the ship were sleek and modern, and there were no anti-smoking signs anywhere. I flew up the stairs toward the flight deck. Could it be...?

I banged the door open just as the transforming magic reached the few remaining planes. They shimmered—and then suddenly they were brand-new F-18s. Twenty in all, they were lined up like new cars in a showroom. Lights blew into being, blinding me, but I kept running around the flight deck, the decks flipping up just one step ahead of me. I sprinted to the edge—and the ship began to grow. The flight deck expanded out, shifting, growing, elongating the *Saint Catherine* into something bigger and more beautiful.

There was a metallic groan from above. I turned, happy tears streaming down my cheeks. The eagle's nest was stretching higher and higher, reaching toward the midnight blue sky, lit up by lights. And the name, there for all to see...

I was now aboard the USS *Rickover*. True to her word, the ship made sure that everyone would know his name.

Cheers erupted from the pier. I ran to the side of the ship and peered down at the assembled sailors. They were climbing to their feet, hale and whole. Two tiny figures were waving their arms and facing me.

It seemed that I was thudding down the gangplank in just

seconds, the world blurring in my haste to get to my friends. Torres ran up to me, now in sharp green camo, the latest working uniform of the Navy. "You did it! You helped the ship upgrade!" Though she was tiny, she lifted me up in her excitement and spun me around.

Bickley ran over. Since I was eye-level with his chest, I saw straightaway his biggest change. "You're a chief now! Chief Bickley!"

Torres and I jumped up and down, shrieking with excitement and pointing at his rank insignia on the front of his uniform. Other sailors were admiring their own new, higher ranks. All were dressed in green camo; they were striking poses for each other and laughing with abandon.

Peggy ran over, also in camo. "I'm not in that dress anymore! Look, I'm a real sailor now!" She twirled in place, and her brand-new bob fluttered. She patted her hair. "I've been wanting to update my look for a while. Maybe I should start going by Meg now? That's a little more modern, I believe."

"Naw, stay Peggy," Torres said. "It's cute."

Bickley pulled us into a huge bear hug. "Congratulations, Petty Officers First Class Goldstein and Torres. And since I'm a chief now, feel free to go get me some coffee. A good chief always has a coffee in hand. I should probably work on my chief face, too." He rubbed his face, and schooled his expression into an overdone frown. "Just like Chief Swanson."

Torres and I broke into peals of giggles, but Torres stopped suddenly and peered around Peggy. "Aw, he went up two ranks. Come *on*."

I craned my neck to see who she meant, then sighed. *Go figure.*

Lieutenant Commander Hollander was no more. Instead, Captain Hollander cut a sharp figure as he walked toward us in his somber dress blues, the light from the ship glinting on his gold buttons and braiding. His hat was so white, it appeared to glow.

I put my hands on my hips and held my chin up as he approached. "That's not even kind of fair, sir."

He tugged on his sleeves and looked away. "Um, well, I guess it's because the commander of an aircraft carrier is always an aviator, and I *was* the highest-ranked officer left."

"The *Rickover* healed you right up, huh?"

"Yeah. Never felt anything like that."

"Are we going to go after the others?"

He blinked in surprise. "Of course. I don't know how to command a vessel like this, but we're honor-bound to follow and mount a rescue."

Beyond his shoulder, I could see the sad remnants of the crew of the *Sérendipité*, still trying to salvage what was left of their poor battleship. The ship's magic only went as far as its hull and its crew, apparently—leaving the Canadians hopelessly out of luck.

I gave Captain Hollander a sad half-smile. "You know, we're down to a handful of crew now. We need more enlisted, and a ship can't run with... how many officers are there now?"

"Five," he said with a sigh. "The other four are ensigns. They've never been on the bridge."

"Then why don't you go and ask our northern neighbors if they'd to come along, too? The great American-Canadian alliance."

He gave that thought. "Well, there's an idea. I'll do that. Thanks for suggesting it." A soft happiness lit up his eyes, and he gave me the same half-smile. "In the meantime, why don't you grab the other two and go turn on my ship?"

"Your ship? It's my ship. It's the USS *Rickover*, not the USS *Top Gun*."

"*My* ship. I am the captain. I was promoted five whole minutes ago."

I scoffed. "Well, if that's so, there's only one thing left to do." With self-control I did not know I had, I dropped my smirk, snapped to attention, and rendered a sharp salute.

He returned the salute, then offered his hand, which I took. "Thank you," he said. "For helping the ship become what it needs to be. We'll protect our home together."

We shared a winning grin, then ran off. As I ascended the gang-plank, Torres and Bickley joined me. We ran into the ship, down the many flights of stairs, and straight into the new engine room.

There was a new place for us, a circular platform surrounding the central generator. Every few feet around the generator, small spindles stood, awaiting the crystal spheres from which we'd draw out magic and convert it into power. Three spheres were already there, waiting for us.

We stood in our places, placed our fingers on the spheres, and began the slow process of absorption and refinement. Bickley took Torres's hand, and she joined hands with me. The magic hummed inside us, coursing through our bodies, and finally I placed my hand on the special panel on the generator with a handprint on it.

The machine roared to life. Nearby, pistons began to pump up and down, and the entire ship shook as its mechanism and systems came online.

I smiled. The Oceanus had never seen anything like the USS *Rickover*.

*My* ship.

# 12

The clamor of the one thousand new sailors aboard the *Rickover* got old real quick.

I was already being jostled in the passageways by sailors far larger than myself, making me realize how much I'd come to enjoy the comparative roominess of an almost-empty carrier. While none of the new sailors seemed hostile, there was a definite frostiness between the factions that had emerged in the space of a few hours.

By the second day of sailing, we were a ship of three separate crews.

I was a member of the "old" faction, the original sailors who'd been aboard the *Saint Catherine*. Unfortunately, we were also the smallest group, and therefore had to make nice whether we wanted to or not. Though I had no qualms with our new coworkers, I'd overheard one fight already as I'd passed a men's berthing. A chief had shoved me aside in his haste to break it up.

The second faction was much larger: our new Canadian friends. Their uniforms had automatically changed upon signing the captain's book, but they stuck to themselves and their old chain of command, leading to people butting heads over who was in charge in, say, the supply room. I had no idea what the climate of the eagle's nest was like now that it was half American, half Canadian, but I was sure Captain Hollander could handle it.

One of the three new women in my berthing was Canadian. Rielle was blonde, gregarious, and a galley cook, though she'd been a quartermaster on the *Sérendipité*.

The third group was the quietest, and to me the most interesting: the fairies. Neither American nor Canadian, my pale, withdrawn shipmates comprised perhaps one hundred people in all, and it didn't escape my notice that there were no officers among their number. The fairies were healthier-looking than the pirates, and evenly distributed between male and female. Their naming conventions were odd, to say the least. The fairies in my berthing had introduced themselves as "Frost of Night" and "Mother's Sigh."

"You're kidding," Torres had said. "We can't call you that."

"You're the one with the weird name," Mother's Sigh had insisted. "A name for your family *and* yourself? What are you, a queen? And why do you have a girl's name when you look like a boy?"

I'd stepped in and tried to get them to make nice, but all that I'd really accomplished was making sure they glared at each other instead of trading insults. As a result, by dinner time of the second day, I was good and ready to steal a lifeboat and go after the kidnapped people myself. Since I couldn't do that, I opted to enjoy some food.

I served myself a small plate from the kosher section and sat in the corner. However, the tension of the ship settled on my shoulders, and I pushed the plate away and rested my head on my arms, focusing on the way my water rippled in my glass from the constant thrum of the engines below. Almost at once, self-pity kicked in.

*Don't wallow. Don't wallow. Don't you dare wallow, Goldstein.*

Okay, no wallowing allowed. But I could still worry.

Where on *earth* were the pirates? They'd come and gone like phantoms, disappearing into weak points and shaking us off without any apparent effort. Of course, nobody had told me this, but I was good at eavesdropping on officers.

And if we ever actually found the pirate fleet, what could we expect once we'd recovered our shipmates? What did they want from them? Certainly not ransom, or we would've been contacted already. Perhaps skills? They'd taken Dot, and the whole of the navigation team. In fact, they'd taken nearly everyone on the ship. The only people who'd been left behind had been in the city, like myself, or had hidden, like Peggy. They'd probably meant to take the entire crew, regardless of usefulness.

But why?

Someone else sat across from me, interrupting my thoughts with a plate loaded with a hot dog, fries, and apple slices. I looked up. It was Wayne.

"They let you out of the dungeon, did they?" I said, laying my head back down.

"Naw, the brig is the dungeon. The laundry is more interesting than you'd think. I charge people money for extra favors. Silver gets you express service. Gold gets your clothes folded and brought straight to your rack."

I snorted and brushed my bangs out of my face. "You're such a... such a..."

"Enterprising businessman, ma'am. That's the term you're looking for."

"Try 'layabout,' Wayne."

"You're the one actually laying down right now." He poked my arms.

"I've got a lot on my mind. Go bug someone else."

"Are you worried about crossing the straits? If you are, you should be. Captain Harebrained wouldn't know how to navigate the wild sea if his life depended on it, and it most certainly does right now."

I sat up. "What?"

"Oh, you haven't heard?"

"Wayne, if you don't cut to the chase, I'm going to take that hot dog and—"

He held up his hands. "Okay, okay. Sheesh. I overheard some of the other officers talking a few minutes ago. Apparently, the good captain thinks the pirates have gone beyond Gibraltar. He wants to follow, but he's never sailed in those waters. Basically, we're screwed."

"Why?" I asked sharply. "What's out there?"

"Pfft, what isn't out there? Scylla, the kraken, the triangle, everything." He lowered his head and leaned toward me. "Even the old ones."

I leaned toward him. "The who?"

"We're not supposed to talk about them by name," he whispered. "It summons them. We probably even shouldn't talk like this."

"Describe them," I whispered. "Quick."

"I won't describe them, but I will say one name, just once." Wayne looked around, then beckoned me closer. He held up a hand to cup his whisper. "Poseidon."

The word lingered between us as I pulled away, almost as if it had substance beyond that of an idea in my head. My memory flickered back to my previous life in Virginia Beach, which had erected a massive statue of King Neptune—Poseidon by another name—that reigned over the boardwalk. Massive and austere, the majestic god of the ocean commanded respect even as a statue.

Could he truly exist?

"Hey, knock it off!"

The shout came from the dinner line. One of the human sailors shoved a fairy, who crashed to the ground. His tray clattered loudly to the side.

I jumped out of my seat and rushed to the fairy's aid, putting my arm around his shoulder and hoisting him up. When we were both up, I glared at the offending sailor, a third-class petty officer named Fox. "Back off," I said, sizing him up. "If you're so stupid that all you can do is get physical, then you're too stupid to be on this ship."

Fox and his buddies were crowding around, while other fairies had come and were standing behind me. The fairy who'd been shoved, Mountain Echo, was dusting himself off.

"He grabbed food with his hands," Fox said. "That's disgusting. That's how diseases spread."

"You're already dead, dumbass."

"And you're going to get messed up if you keep befriending their kind," Fox said, pointing to the fairies behind me.

Well, this conversation had gone straight out the window. Time to pull out the long toms.

"Did everyone else just hear Petty Officer Fox threaten me?" I said, raising my voice to near-yelling. "If you did, say 'aye.'"

Half a dozen fairies, and a few humans, said 'aye.' Fox's scowl faltered a bit.

"Let's see," I said, tapping my foot. "You started a fight in the galley, and now you've threatened your superior. That's not a good way to end the day, Fox. So what are you going to do?" I leaned in. "Are you going to sit down and shut up, or are you going to find out what the next step is for me?"

There was a beat.

"I don't have time for this," Fox muttered. "Come on, guys." He retreated to the other side of the galley with his friends, all of them throwing me furious looks occasionally.

I kept my stony expression in place, but inside, my dead heart was beating wildly. I was going to have to be very careful when I walked around the ship for a while. Maybe I'd ask Bickley to escort me from the engine room to my berthing after my shift.

Mountain Echo placed a gentle hand on my shoulder. "Thank you. You are very kind."

I turned around and took in his appearance. He looked like every other fairy I'd seen, all pale skin, greenish hair, and sparkles around the eyes. "Sorry you have to deal with this. I know what it's like to be the different person in the lunch line."

He cocked his head. "What do you mean?"

"When I was alive, I was... well, there are different kinds of humans, I guess. I was in the minority at my school."

He stifled a laugh. "That's ludicrous. Your differences mean nothing, you know. You all look the same to me."

I raised an eyebrow. "What side of the war were you on?" I didn't even know what the fairy war was over, but I knew he'd have a side.

"The General's side, of course."

"And who were the others?"

"Those who sided with the northern tribes."

"Are there any northern sympathizers on this ship?"

His face darkened. "They work on the flight deck. Don't talk to them. They can't be trusted."

I rocked back on my heels. "Really? Your differences mean nothing, you know. You all look the same to me."

He paused. "Oh. Well... I see your point."

I clapped him on the shoulder and went back to my table, which Wayne had vacated. My food was cold, yet I appreciated my dinner all the more for the conversation I'd just had. I took a bite, then reached for my glass of water.

I froze mid-chew. The water wasn't vibrating anymore.

The engines were off.

I stood, looking all around. People were eating as normally as ever... but an officer had just sprinted down a passageway.

Three more followed her, hushed and frantic.

I leapt up and ran out of the galley, toward the engine room. Had there been an accident? Had someone attacked Bickley or Torres? Was I too late?

The captain's whistle rang throughout the ship, followed by the click of the intercom turning on.

"This is Captain Hollander. All hands report to berthing immediately. Do not speak to each other. Not even one word."

The intercom switched off, and the whistle rang again.

I exchanged a what-the-hell glance with another sailor in the passageway. "Battle stations" meant we were under attack. "Power hour" meant we needed to start cleaning the ship bow to stern. But our berthing? We were being sent to our rooms, and on top of it, we'd been told to shut up. Something very serious was going on.

Still, what was I going to do about it? I tried to edge down the passageway against the crowds of sailors who were trooping past, since my berthing was on the other end of the ship. After a minute of going nowhere, I sighed and opted to cut through the flight deck. He'd never said I couldn't do that.

I ran down a side passageway and pushed open the door to the outside. I froze. There was no way I was seeing what I thought I was seeing.

I rubbed my eyes.

No, I was seeing this.

The ship was stationary *in the air*. Something had lifted up the ship out of the ocean without anyone in the galley noticing.

I slowly walked out onto the flight deck, my feet numb. What were we dealing with now? What could possibly overtake an aircraft carrier like this?

I looked up, and suddenly I was back in Virginia Beach again, standing on the boardwalk and holding my mother's hand, looking up at the massive statue. Looking at King Neptune.

Looking at Poseidon.

---

POSEIDON WAS A BEING of unfathomable size. Made up of the sea, all swirling water and leaping fish, he rose up out of the ocean in a clear male figure. However, he wasn't all water—the crown on his head glistened as the setting sun caught the jewels there, and his trident was very real, possibly of gold.

He stood at least two hundred feet high, and around him the sea bowed away from his form, as if he were emanating an invisible force. Near his waist, which was at ocean level, mermaids and mermen swam around him, calling to each other in their language.

From my position on the flight deck, I could see Captain Hollander run out onto the bow of the ship. He took off his cover, revealing his disheveled brown hair.

"WHO DARES SUMMON ME?"

I pressed myself against the steel bulkhead, too scared to breathe. The voice of Poseidon was scarier than his image. His words had cut right through me, a knife in the center of my being. Such authority.

Captain Hollander's voice was too far away to hear.

"A MORTAL ABOARD YOUR VESSEL UTTERED MY NAME."

"Oh, crap," I breathed to myself. "That was me and Wayne. Oh crap. Oh, *so much* crap." Wayne had warned me, and I'd insisted. I was just as culpable as he was. More so even, because I was supposed to be smart.

Captain Hollander replied.

"First you sail through my sea intent on war, and now you lie to me. A woman summoned me. I will not suffer your disrespect." His trident lit up with electricity, far more than was necessary to "smite" Captain Hollander.

*No!* "It was me!" I shouted, running toward the bow and waving my arms like I was on the Jumbotron at a Norfolk Tides game. "Don't smite him! It was me!" *Don't smite him. Yeesh.* I wasn't so scared that I couldn't feel stupid for my word choice.

Poseidon drew back slightly, clearly surprised that a tiny little mortal was making such a fuss. "Who are you that commands me to withhold judgment?"

I ran straight to the tip of the bow and stared directly up at him. "I'm EMN1 Rachel Goldstein! I was the one who said your name! Don't kill Captain Hollander!"

He sighed. "You are not the one who said my name."

"I made the guy tell me, so it's my responsibility! You hear me? I'm taking responsibility!" I wasn't selfish. I wasn't going to throw Wayne under the bus—ship?—and get him in trouble.

Captain Hollander grabbed my hand and jerked me away from the bow. "Petty Officer, get. Inside. Now."

Boy, he sounded *pissed.* If I made it through the next five minutes without dying again, I'd skip going to my berthing and just head directly to the brig.

"Be silent, mortal. The woman is speaking to me." A hand made of water came toward me, then encompassed me gently. He picked me up and raised me to eye level. "Why did you summon me, woman?"

"I didn't mean to. I was speaking with another sailor and he was telling me about the old ones. He was warning me about the wild sea."

"He should've warned your captain. I do not allow ships to sail through my waters with hostile intent."

"Forgive him, please. We're all new to this, including him. We're sailing to catch pirates. They kidnapped half the original crew."

"I do not care about the trifling of lesser beings. I should destroy your ship for breaking my law."

"No!" The shout left my mouth before I gave it thought. I lowered my voice. "Your Majesty, do you consider yourself a good ruler? A being of justice?"

"I am the benevolent king of my domain. All will know justice within my realm."

"Well, if you let the pirates free, but destroy the *Rickover*, you're colluding with pirates in act, if not in intent. Every being in your domain will know, because the actions of the leaders are always known." I narrowed my eyes. "I dare you to put that to the test." *For I am Rachel Goldstein, righteously stupid and stupidly righteous.*

He tutted. "Your arrogance is——"

One of the mermen swam up Poseidon's torso just then, spiraling in long arcs along with the water. He wiggled along the arm, then popped out of his wrist and gave his long hair a good shake.

My mouth dropped open. It was my merman friend, and his collar was gone, replaced by a jeweled necklace bearing a pendant of breathtaking beauty. The pendant was a crystal ball that contained a glowing, ethereal substance that produced tiny lightning strikes within the ball.

"My son, go back to your siblings."

Son! Merboy was Poseidon's son. That explained the circlet on his head—I'd saved a prince. My, my. Who was his mother? Gaia? Was there a Gaia in this world?

But the merman just reached for me and pulled me into his embrace, giving me a long hug that I returned. When he was done, he looked up at his father and said something in a language I did not recognize.

His father replied, his tone arching to make me think it was a question.

The merman turned back to me and tapped his chest. "I am Jordan."

"Hello, Jordan," I said, breaking into a wide grin. "I am Rachel."

Two mermaids swam up Poseidon and joined Jordan. They popped out of the water and shook their long hair just as he had; all of them were wearing circlets. They both beamed at me.

"I am Potomac," one said, her voice lilting and lovely.

"I am Mersey," the other said. "You save our brother."

Their brother was still holding me. "You come to palace," Jordan said, a hopeful glint in his eyes. "Live with us. We make you mermaid."

"Son..."

"Rachel save me from Scylla!" Jordan shouted. "We are friends!"

I'd never felt so relieved to have done a good deed in my entire existence. I cupped Jordan's cheek, and he leaned into the gesture, smiling with true affection. "I can't go. I'm sorry. I have to stay here and rescue my shipmates, and I promised the ship I'd sail on her for a long while more."

His large eyes grew wide with sadness, but he nodded. "Still friends."

"Oh, yes. We'll always be friends."

"Friends," Mersey and Rhine said together. They both swam up and pecked my cheeks. "Tank-oo for save our brother."

With a flip of their long, green-blue tails, they dove back into their father's arm. They disappeared back into the sea via their father's torso. Jordan, on the other hand, lingered and stroked my hair. After a few seconds, he carefully removed his necklace and placed it over my head. "Keep. Gift."

The pendant was remarkably heavy. I rubbed my fingers over it, enjoying its warmth. "Thank you. I'll treasure this."

Jordan rubbed his nose against mine, then gave me a long kiss that I returned.

Poseidon cleared his throat.

Jordan shot a naughty smirk at his father, then backflipped into his arm and swam away. I was still in Poseidon's grasp, seawater whirling around me like a jacuzzi. Poseidon brought me back up to his eye level.

"My son interceded for you. I will let your ship sail through my waters unharmed."

I inclined my head. "Thank you. That's very generous of you."

"Take warning, Rachel Goldstein. There are forces at work that even I do not understand. The walls of the worlds are thinning under the stress of the fairy war. I cannot watch all that happens in my domain."

"I understand. Can you put me down now, please?"

Poseidon lowered me down onto the flight deck again, where he let me go with a gush of water that knocked me down. Other officers from the bridge had joined Captain Hollander there, and some rushed forward to help me up.

Poseidon sank beneath the waves without so much as making sea foam rise up. After a second, the ship shivered to life as the engines turned on.

I put a hand on my chest to steady my heart. Captain Hollander parted the crowd around me, staring at me in blank shock.

I swallowed. "I'll, uh... I'll see myself into the brig. No need to call Chief Buntin." My ego couldn't handle another tour of the ship while in handcuffs.

"Petty Officer, what in the name of *hell* just happened? How did you know that merman?"

I was excruciatingly aware that I was surrounded by people who outranked me by about thirty-seven thousand ranks. I shrank back. "I saved him from Scylla, sir," I muttered through stiff lips. "Right before I saved you."

Maybe I'd been sassy with Captain Hollander before, and maybe we had a personal connection where we grew up, but he was now surrounded by his command team. The very least I could do was make him look better by showing due deference. I stood at attention —though with weak knees—and said, "Sir, I'm very sorry for disobeying your order to go to berthing. I was on my way there when I overheard him talk about the person who'd summoned him. I... I hadn't meant to—"

"Oh, at ease, Petty Officer," Commander Tremblay said, shaking his head and smiling. "Captain, he *was* going to kill you. This sailor just saved your ass, and probably the entire ship. Let her go. It seems like she's good at saving people, so you might want to keep her around."

The group laughed, though Captain Hollander was still looking at me like he couldn't quite figure out what I was made of. "What did you talk about up there?"

I could feel my blush. "Prince Jordan asked me to move in with him. He said he could make me a mermaid."

A lieutenant junior grade crossed her arms, nodding. "Well, if we ever need a liaison when we're dealing with merfolk, we know who to call. We could've had a mermaid princess on our hands."

They all laughed harder, making me feel ever smaller.

Captain Hollander glared at them, then said, "You can go now, Goldstein."

I turned, but another officer said, "Wait, Petty Officer. What's that around your neck?" She grabbed my shoulder and spun me around, then dragged me toward her by the pendant. Her name plate gleamed, and I saw the word Gagnon neatly printed on it.

"Hey!" I protested. "It was a gift!"

"Sir, this is a magic cradle," she said to Captain Hollander, as if she hadn't heard me. "This is—ow!" She let go of the pendant and shook her hand. "What? How did it do that?"

The "magic cradle" wasn't flashing, however, so I tucked it beneath my collar. "It was a gift," I repeated, my voice soft with anger. "And I don't appreciate being manhandled, ma'am. I don't care who you are, Commander."

The pendant had hurt her. Though I understood little of magic, I knew one thing from my adventures here: the magic of the enemy could hurt you. The necklace was mine, and it had hurt her.

That was simple enough.

Commander Gagnon blinked, then straightened. "My apologies, Petty Officer. I got away from myself."

She and I shared a hard stare, and behind her eyes I could see ugly emotions swimming there. I stepped back, nodded politely at Captain Hollander, then turned and ran into the hangar bay.

When I was inside the ship, I sprinted down the empty passageways, sliding down the rails on the stairs as usual, my frenzied thoughts crashing around my skull. I'd just smart-mouthed a god. I'd kissed a merman named Jordan—again! I'd received a gift of untold power. Commander Gagnon was my enemy, in the martial sense. I'd never even met the woman before now.

What a day.

I pushed open the door to my berthing and was immediately assailed by Torres. She jumped to her feet. "Where the blazes have you been? I've been worried sick!"

"Relax, mom," I said, taking a huge breath. "I got, um, distracted on my way back to berthing." I pulled out my new pendant. It filled the small berthing space with whiteish light.

Rielle pulled back the curtain on her rack. "Your face is red as a tomato, girl. Were you making out with someone? Was he cute?"

I looked at Torres, who shrugged with exaggeration. "You know, we just got to talking, and..."

Frost of Night and Mother's Sigh were playing dominoes at the small table in the corner. Mother's Sigh stood partially. "Goldstein, where did you get a magic cradle?"

Frost of Night's head whipped around. "Holy—"

"Shhh," I said, holding a finger to my lips. "Ladies, this has already drawn the attention of Commander Gagnon, so I want it kept secret." I kneeled next to the fairies while Rielle slid out of her rack. Torres pulled up a chair and leaned in. I turned to the fairies. "What's a magic cradle?"

Mother's Sigh stroked the pendant with a shaking finger. "It's like a bucket you pour magic into. It can hold an unimaginable amount of power. I've heard of cradles that could bend reality and rewrite the story of life."

Frost of Night nodded emphatically. "You know those stories humans tell about genies? Genies are just fairies who have cradles. They're really hard to make, and incredibly rare." She looked at me, awed respect evident on her face. "Where did you get one?"

"When Scylla attacked the ship a few days ago, I fell into the water," I said in hushed tones. "And there, I saved a merman from captivity. Well, anyway, he was a prince of the ocean, and we were stopped by his father, the sea king, just now. Prince Jordan gave me this as a gift. He kissed me, too." I put my fingertips to my lips. "So yes, I guess you could say I was making out with someone."

Rielle snorted. "'Well, anyway, he was a prince...'" she mimicked.

"If I'd kissed a guy who turned out to be royalty, I'd be crowing about it."

The captain's whistle sounded. "All hands, return to your stations." The whistle sounded again.

Rielle waved dismissively. "Whatever, I'm staying in bed. So, now, Rachel... tell us about this Prince Jordan. Details, please."

I tucked a lock of hair behind my ear, overcome with the urge to giggle. I quickly shucked my sopping clothes and pulled on my clean, dry coveralls, then sat on an empty chair. "He's... well... I mean, he's a merman, right? So he—"

A knock on the door cut me short, and I stuffed the magic cradle down my collar again. "Come in," we all said in unison.

Bickley stepped into the room, a formal Navy folder with an embossed seal in his hands. "Goldstein, Torres, I gotta show you something in the engine room. *Now.*"

There was no arguing with that tone. She and I hurried out of the berthing and into the passageway. "What's up?" Torres said.

Bickley looked both ways down the passageway, then pulled us in. "Nothing," he said in a low voice. "I was told by the captain to send Goldstein up to his conference room, but to let nobody know she was going there. Here, take this." He handed me the folder. "It's empty, but it'll make you look like you're delivering something. Torres, let's get to the engine room to make the cover story stick." He put a hand on my shoulder. "I won't ask what's going on, but tread lightly. Hollander is agitated about something."

I nodded once, then hurried down the passageway. What was waiting for me?

# 13
---

I hurried down the passageway that led to Captain Hollander's conference room, my sweaty palms making marks on the paper folder. Why the subterfuge? I wasn't a SEAL, I was a nuke-slash-magic-wielder, and this was way above my pay grade. Still, there was something very James Bond-ish about it all. I stood up a little straighter.

When I arrived at the conference room, I saw that the placard had changed. It now read:

*Captain Arthur Hollander, USN*
*Commanding Officer*

The door next to the conference room bore a similar placard, except this one said:

*Commander Holly Gagnon, USN*
*Executive Officer*

A chill ran down my neck. So Commander Gagnon was the second-highest officer on the ship. That did not bode well for me. Officers that high had the power to make my life *very* difficult.

I knocked on Captain Hollander's door. It opened, and I saw the familiar mahogany table, nautical map, ship's wheel, and chairs—in one of which Commander Gagnon was sitting.

Captain Hollander ushered me inside. "Thank you for coming so quickly, Petty Officer. Please take a seat. We'll get right down to business." I sat down, and Captain Hollander pulled up a chair next to me. "I'd like to talk to you about that necklace of yours."

"I assume you mean the magic cradle and not the Star of David."

"Right. I'll be blunt: what will it take for you to part with it?"

Part with it? He was asking me if I wanted to *sell* it? This was unusual, to say the least. What was so special about the magic cradle? It held a lot of magic, sure, but I had a whole cage of magic spheres in the engine room. Though magic was a limited resource in the Oceanus, we did not lack for it.

"Why do you want it so badly?" I hedged, pulling it out of my collar. Commander Gagnon tapped her pen on a pad of paper as I talked, staring fixedly at the pendant.

"Because we think we can weaponize it," Captain Hollander said. "The bands of pirates have grown in number and strength, and we need all the firepower we can get, if we ever find them." As soon as he said the final words, a sheepish expression overtook him.

"You don't know where they are, sir?"

"It's... well, it's..." He faltered. "Don't worry about it."

"We should talk about it," Commander Gagnon said, her tone dark. "Your captain doesn't know how to read nautical charts, so it's slow going." She spat the words "your captain."

I narrowed my eyes. "Our captain." A weird sense of protectiveness surged to life in me. Nobody was allowed to disrespect him in front of me. That was one of my new rules.

"What?"

I rested my arm on the table and drummed my fingers. "Our captain, ma'am. He's your captain, too." I turned back to Captain Hollander. "The navigation team is gone, right? That's why you want the cradle—it's a warhead while we're sailing blind."

"Yes," he said with a sigh. "Anybody of real use to me was taken, and the only thing we know for sure is that we're not near any weak points. Not for a thousand miles. I have no idea how the pirates are sailing the way they are. We should've overtaken them by now." He looked at me with such emotion that I was taken aback. "So, what will it take for you to give me the necklace? Do you want a commission? I can do that."

I sat back in my chair, at a loss for words.

My little present from a cute boy had turned into quite the asset. On one hand, I wanted it simply because it was one of the few things I could call *mine*. It was a memento of my first kiss, a reminder of the moment when I'd been ready to die to save someone else's life— proving that I wasn't selfish—and, honestly, it was just really pretty. I was as normal as any other young woman in my desire to own pretty things.

On the other hand, Captain Hollander needed all the help he could get. We had no idea what was waiting for us in the wild sea, and while I didn't know for sure how the necklace could be weaponized, it held untold power and might. On top of it, he was offering me the officership. With a simple trade, I could be Ensign Goldstein, in charge of the engine room. A bigger berthing. Better food. People would salute me.

So what to do?

My eyes flickered up, and again Commander Gagnon was staring, unblinking, at my necklace. I'd seen dogs stare at cooked chicken with less desire.

I tucked the magic cradle back into my shirt. "I'm sorry, sir," I said quietly. "This is a precious gift from a friend. It's beyond price."

"You are unbelievable," Commander Gagnon hissed. "Sir, artifacts like that have no business being in the hands of junior sailors. In fact—"

"I'm E-6, ma'am."

She sputtered. "So?"

"So I'm not a junior sailor. I'm a first class petty officer."

She took me in, sizing me up, and I realized my error immediately: I never should've corrected her. If she thought I was just some little junior sailor, then more power to me in her mistake. I'd defeated my opponents on the lacrosse field many a time because they felt that five-foot-two Rachel Goldstein couldn't possibly be a threat to them.

"Enough," Captain Hollander said. "She said no, Commander. I can't take it from her, especially considering who gave it to her."

"Thank you, sir," I said. "Am I excused?"

"Yes, have a good night." He sighed. "How is everyone down in the engine room?"

I smiled. "The nerds are still alive, sir. In a matter of speaking, of course."

He gave me a half-smile, and then gestured at the door. "I'm glad to hear it."

I left as quickly as I'd come in, then sprinted down the passageway—but not in the direction from where I'd come. No matter what, I wasn't going to return to my berthing. That's where *she'd* be looking for me. No berthing, no kosher counter in the galley, no engine room unless it was my shift. In fact, I needed to stay away from the engine room the most. It's the one place someone could count on me being alone.

I needed to stay away from Commander Gagnon. More than fairy pirates, more than Scylla, more than every cutthroat in Port des Morts, that woman was bad news. I had no idea why she wanted the cradle so badly, but I wasn't in a great position to fight with her.

There was much to unpack in the short meeting I'd just had. Commander Gagnon obviously had no respect for Captain Hollander. Her disrespect had stretched as far as to reveal a weakness of his in front of a subordinate. She'd wanted me to know. And if she wanted me to know, she wanted the whole crew to know.

But she wasn't so crafty. I would tell no one.

A whistle sounded. I slipped into a vent space, a small section of the ship where we could check on the ventilation systems for maintenance. On the *Taft*, people usually used them for making out without being interrupted. I pulled out the cradle again, and held it up in front of my face.

What had Prince Jordan inflicted on me?

———

AFTER A FEW MINUTES OF REFLECTION, and several prayers for safety, the whistle sounded again, signaling a shift change.

I slipped back out of the vent space and hurried up to the hangar bay. Seaman Dartsch was the leader of the new, expanded lookout team, and he was handing out binoculars to the night crew. I got in line.

"Petty Officer, you're not on the lookout team," he said when I got to the front of line. "Engineers are needed below deck."

"For Hanson," I reminded him. "And come on, an extra pair of eyes is a boon to you. You know that. It's not my shift."

He shrugged and handed me the binoculars and a phone set.

"Fine. Stern, port side. You're looking for pirates more than people, but look for chem lights, too."

I grinned and began the short journey to my lookout spot. Seaman Dartsch had been correct; engineers were typically expected to be below deck, not up here. Commander Gagnon would have a heck of a time finding me if she wanted to.

When I was at the stern, I fixed the headphones from the set on my head, adjusted the mouthpiece, then straightened the little breast plate. I planted my foot on the rail and lifted the binoculars to my face, scanning the dark horizon. Storm clouds were gathering there, looming tall and foreboding. Yet, they were far enough away that the muggy night air was undisturbed for me, and all I could hear was the crashing of waves as the ship coursed through the water.

Though I was possibly being preyed on by Commander Gagnon, my thoughts began to wander all the same as I continually scanned the water. Chem lights had appeared in the hangar bay when the ship had upgraded, and everyone who worked on the flight deck had been given one. I didn't have one, since I mostly worked in the bottom of the ship. It had been that way on the *Taft*, too.

While I kept lookout, planes were flying on and off the flight deck, their exercises identical to those I'd watched on the night I'd died. My position allowed me to see the white-hot fire at the back of each one, the result of magic instead of jet fuel. Though I didn't understand this new fuel that I could manipulate, I respected what it could do.

After looking near the ship for chem lights for the tenth time, I returned to scanning the horizon.

*Wait... what's that?* I squinted against the darkness, not sure what I was looking at. I wiped the lenses on my sleeve, then looked again. Just as I'd seen before, the lightning in the storm clouds lit up the sky, but there was a patch of clouds untouched by the light. It was as if

Hashem had used a huge hole punch and removed a portion of the sky where it touched the horizon.

A weak spot.

I slowly lowered the binoculars. Captain Hollander had said we weren't in a thousand miles of a weak spot, so what was I looking at? Where had he gotten his information? It was obviously not correct.

I peered through the binoculars again. The lightning lit up the sky again—and threw the silhouettes of three large ships in the distance into sharp relief. From what I could tell, they were coming toward us.

Couldn't have a still night on the high seas of the Oceanus, could we?

Still, no need to panic. Surely this world had merchant ships. If not, maybe it was another ghost navy's fleet. I pulled up the mouthpiece and pressed the call button. "Bridge, port stern watch. Three contacts sighted, two hundred degrees, range ten klicks."

A muffled voice in my headphones replied, "Port stern watch, bridge. Three contacts sighted, two hundred degrees, range ten klicks. Bridge, aye."

I couldn't do anything further, but it was still my job to monitor the three ships. I looked through the binoculars again.

The ships were coming closer, but in the darkness I couldn't see much beyond the fact that they were ships. The bridge crew was certainly trying to hail the ships over the communication channels, and if that failed, they'd resort to using lights because it was night.

I watched them, idly thinking about what was coming. Maybe they weren't ghost ships. What other creatures sailed the Oceanus? Elves? Leprechauns?

The huge spotlight near the eagle's nest began to flash in bright patterns. So, they'd failed to connect with the ships. That was... not promising. I looked through the binoculars just as a tiny burst of orange light appeared from one of the ships, followed by a high whine.

The missile missed the ship by mere yards, exploding in the water and throwing sea spray everywhere.

I sprinted back to the hangar bay, pressing the call button as I ran. "Pirates! It's pirates!"

All around, people began running and shouting to each other.

"We're under attack!"

"Three enemy ships! Port side!"

"Get to the guns!"

The familiar klaxon rang out, followed by, "*General quarters! General quarters! All hands to battle stations!*"

A jet soared off the flight deck into the midnight blue sky. A few seconds later, a second followed. One by one the entire squadron flew into the night, breaking off into small formations and heading straight toward the ships.

I stood to the side while sailors ran to the guns and mounted them, waiting for the blessed moment when they could unload a carrier-load of ordnance into the enemy. Brought into the 21st century, the USS *Rickover* was simultaneously an airport, a city, and a military base, capable of wreaking absolute destruction on anyone stupid enough to attack.

As I watched, one of the jets launched two missiles at a ship. It was a direct hit. The jubilant cheers of my shipmates filled me with joy, and I cheered along with them. This was going to be a short battle.

The planes swooped in low and unloaded bomb after bomb onto the pirates. These ships lacked shields, so they blasted to pieces in marvelous displays of wood and metal that were visible in the reddish light of fire.

The ships were quickly overcome by the flames, and I could see tiny individuals abandon ship, diving off one after another. The living US Navy would've rescued them, per the Geneva Convention. What would the *Rickover* do?

One by one, the jets returned to the flight deck, filling my chest with the wonderfully deep vibrations I'd come to love about carrier life. Sailors still ran around the deck, ignoring me where I stood next to the entrance to the hangar bay.

There was a high whine of cord being let go through a pulley, and then a splash from somewhere unseen. A boat's motor turned on, and then another. Two small motorboats zipped away from the ship, racing toward the sinking pirate ships. They were rigid-hulled inflatable boats, or RHIBs, and armed to the teeth with both mounted weapons and highly-trained security forces who surely had no problem denting someone's face with the butt of a rifle.

I leaned on the rail and watched them, smiling despite the violence. Hashem knew, I *loved* the Navy. I loved ship life, the tight structures and flawless logistics that kept thousands of people afloat on a craft built for intimidation. I'd loved it from the second I'd stepped on the *Taft* and inhaled the metal, oil, and salty air. I loved the camaraderie that came with being in a profession as old as time. I loved the silly traditions and somber lore, the call of sea birds and the creaking of the ship. I loved it all. It made sense that I'd wound up on a ghost ship. The navy was in my soul.

But my soul was not at peace as long as Commander Gagnon was angling for my necklace. Strange and evil things were afoot on my ship. There was little I could do in the light, since I was not high enough to command anyone or anything. I was enlisted, and not even the highest enlisted in my department. There was a reason why the greatest pieces of nautical literature—heck, even stuff like *Star Trek*— were about the captains and commanders, all bedecked in gold and braid. They were the natural choices for main characters.

If I could not operate in the light of the bridge, then I would operate in the shadows of the engine room. I was more comfortable there, anyway. I was a nuke.

I pushed away from the rail. It was time to slip back into the shadows.

## 14

I shook Rielle awake. "Psst. Hey, wake up. I need you."

Rielle lifted her head from her thin pillow and blinked at me several times. "Are we under attack again?"

"No. But it's important. Get dressed." I looked at the rest of our sleeping berthing mates. "I'll tell you the rest when we're alone."

It had been a few hours since the security forces had returned in their RHIBs with a handful of pirates in custody. Rumor had it that the rest of the pirates had refused to return, instead opting to stay afloat on bits of flotsam. Since the Oceanus had no Geneva Convention, they'd been left there.

Rielle slipped into her trousers and thick sweater, the quartermaster office's answer to coveralls, and pulled back her long blonde hair into a ponytail. When she was done, I opened the door and beckoned her to follow me.

She yawned. "I take it this is urgent."

"It is. Quick, get in the head." I opened a women's restroom door. They were completely unnecessary for us, and therefore one of the few places I could rely on us not being overheard. It was a wonder that the ship even had them. When she was in, I shut the door. "I'll be blunt: can you get me the paper nautical charts from the quartermaster's office? He has them, right?"

Rielle startled. "Uh, yeah. I don't think I'm really supposed to, but I guess he never said I couldn't." She eyed me suspiciously. "Why?"

"Captain Hollander told me directly that we weren't in a thousand miles of a weak spot, but I saw one with my own eyes a few hours ago. He also said that nobody on board can read the charts, so we're sailing blind. I'm going to take a whack at it."

She stared at me, raising an eyebrow. "He told you that nobody on board can read nautical charts?"

"Yes."

"That's total crap. I'm a quartermaster. *I* can read nautical charts. It's part of my job."

"*What?*" My exclamation echoed around the tiny room. I cleared my throat. "I mean, what? Then where did he get the idea that nobody can?"

"Probably the same place he heard that there's no weak spot for a thousand miles, don't you think?" Her eyes glazed a bit as she thought. "I wonder if... wow. I should've been more suspicious."

"What happened?"

"I was assigned to the galley when we came onto the *Rickover*. All the quartermasters were assigned somewhere else, but the other rates got to stay in their job. I thought it was unfair, but I didn't question it. But yeah, there's a half dozen of us, and we all know how to read nautical charts."

I digested that. "You think someone's been feeding lies to the captain, taking advantage of his ignorance?"

"Either that, or he's pulling it all out of his ass. Is he the kind of person who'd do that?"

"No. At least, not that I've seen." There was a tense silence. "So basically, we're sailing around the wild ocean, with no idea where we actually are, unable to chase down pirates, and not taking advantage of the weak spots."

"Sounds like."

"You know what I think?"

"What?"

I cracked open the door and peered out. "I think it's time to take a look at those charts."

---

I UNROLLED the largest of the charts on the table, smoothing out the edges. Rielle held a small flashlight, the only illumination in the dark spare office we were in.

"Okay, what can you see?" I whispered.

She sighed. "Without knowing our location, it's just another map. It might as well be a map of Yukon Territory for all the use it is to us."

"Okay, well, how about this," I said, pointing to a narrow strait on the east end of the map. "Is that Gibraltar?"

She stared intently at the map, her eyebrows drawn together. "Yes."

"Since we're traveling at about, oh, thirty knots, where might we have gone in the last three days? If you can't calculate our position, then try to figure out the outer limit of where we could plausibly be."

She handed my the flashlight. She dragged her finger back and forth across the map, humming in concentration. She traced a long line north to south. "Here. My educated guess is that we haven't gone past this longitude, and if that's so, then we're near one of these three weak spots." She indicated three points marked in red ink, each with a number next to it and a coordinate. "See these numbers? They correspond with these three points here."

She pointed to three other points in the ocean, each with a matching number and the coordinates of the first three. "The first weak spot of the three connects to a point in the Indian Ocean. The second—" She pointed to the edge of the map. "—pops out in this part of the ocean, which roughly corresponds with Ohio, I think. There's no North America in the Oceanus. And the third one pops out here, where the Chesapeake Bay is."

I stared at her finger, which was hovering over a small notation on the map: *Hampton Roads*.

Ice shot down my spine.

"Hampton Roads," I whispered. "Rielle, that's my home. That's what the region is called, Hampton Roads. The 'roads' refer to all the waterways there." I took in several deep breaths. "Back on the *Saint Catherine*, Captain Hollander told me that the pirates were planning an attack on Virginia Beach." I gulped. "I bet you anything we're near the third weak spot. They're patrolling these waters because they're gearing up for a major operation."

She looked at me, nodding. "Okay, I believe you. But why? What would pirates want from Hampton Roads?"

"What do pirates always want? In the living world, they want money, ships, all that."

"Pirates here want magic."

"Is there any source of magic in the living world? Anything substantial, worth mounting an attack for?"

She thought. "Well... sort of. It's us. People. We die, and sometimes we become ghosts here. Sailors aren't the only ghosts. There are islands all over the Oceanus where people end up seemingly at random. And it's easy enough to make a ghost." She gave me a knowing look.

"You kill the person." My voice was barely audible. "Hashem help them."

She quickly rolled up the map. "How many people are in Hampton Roads?"

"Over a million," I said, leaning against the wall to catch my breath. "It's a huge population center."

"And you said that there are lots of waterways, right?"

"Yes. That has to be why they chose that weak spot. They'll pop out in their ships and set sail up the bay and into the rivers. There's tons of watercraft on the water there at any given time. Docks, moors, everything. People on the beaches..."

My family's wealth was derived from beach-front real estate. Goldstein Group owned half of the Virginia Beach boardwalk. My parents were in the line of sight of brigands.

My fists clenched, and I took another steadying breath, then stood up and looked at Rielle. "Someone is hiding this from Captain Hollander, and I'll bet my magic cradle it's Commander Gagnon."

Rielle pondered that. "That's... not exactly hard to believe." She sat down in the folding chair, and I sat next to her. "Listen, I don't want to fan any recent flames by speaking ill of my officers—"

"Rielle, I get it. Just tell me."

"Commander Gagnon was the captain of our ship for about a month before the attack in Port des Morts. She was the XO before that, but Captain Kellerman was killed in Scylla's attack. In fact, a ton of people were lost. Our defenses were down, and nobody has been able to figure out why. We were slammed with pirates every month for nearly a year, too."

"Commander Gagnon was the one who told you to report to the galley, wasn't she?"

"Yes."

"Was your navigation team taken, like ours was?"

"The main navigation team, a ton of the officers, and a lot of the security forces. And we were already low on manpower."

"Just like the *Saint Catherine*. I think both ships have been fighting a war of attrition, and I screwed it up by suggesting that the ships combine forces." I pounded a fist into my other hand. "Maybe that's why the ship needed us. It needed to upgrade into a proper, modern warship."

Rielle slid the map back into its tube. "We're duty-bound to report this to the captain. I say we forget the chain of command and go straight to him. Hell, knock on his stateroom door and get him out of bed. Considering the substance of the report, you won't get reprimanded. I'll go with you, even."

I shook my head. "No. Commander Gagnon is circling. We need to approach him quietly without attracting *any* attention. Go back to bed, and I'll talk to Chief Bickley. He'll go to the captain, arrange a meeting sans Gagnon, and we'll get this squared away."

She looked doubtful, but nodded once. "Okay. We don't speak a word of this, yeah?"

"Right." We pounded fists. "Let's go." My hand was on the doorknob when I paused, an idea coming to me. "Hey, where are the pirates who were taken into custody? The brig?"

"I think so. Why?"

"If Gagnon is playing dirty, then maybe one of them knows about it. We can get them to snitch on her." I opened the door. "Act casual."

---

AFTER STOWING the nautical charts in Rielle's locker—we figured they were in danger of being tossed overboard—we strolled down the long passageways toward the brig. If the head Master at Arms was around, we'd say we were visiting Wayne, who was back in there for making moonshine in the laundry room.

However, the security officer wasn't at his post when we arrived at the enormous steel door, nor were any of the other security forces present. That was the first oddity.

The second was that the door was ajar.

"That's not suspicious," Rielle murmured. "Come on, let's say, eh, we heard your friend yelling for help."

"He's not... oh, who cares? Sure, we heard my friend yelling for help. Actually," I said, putting my hand on her shoulder. "Go back to berthing. You're not getting hurt on my account."

"But—"

"Please don't make me make that an order." She was a second class petty officer, so I could do that, if I wanted. She didn't really offer me any protection, so taking her with me wasn't worth the risk.

She heaved a sigh, and then hurried away toward berthing, throwing a chagrined look at me over her shoulder.

When she was out of sight, I cracked open the door and cupped a hand around my mouth. *Make this good, Rach.* "Wayne? Is that you? I heard someone yelling for help! I'm coming down there!"

I ran down the steps, my heart pounding away in my chest. Nutty as it was, I loved a good adventure, and this was—

Blood was spilling out of the cells. All of them.

I raced to the first cell and yelped, jumping back from the doorway. Three fairy pirates were lying on the floor, dead as doornails, their bodies leaking blood from multiple bullet wounds.

Each cell contained several very bloody, very dead fairies. They'd been shot in their heads and torsos, and all were leaning against the far bulkhead, as if they'd been cowering away from the shooter.

The final cell contained only Wayne's remains. My first guess would've been that he'd shot himself. He was lying on the tiny bunk, a single bullet hole in his temple and his hand limp over the side. The gun had clattered to the floor out of his hand—or so it appeared.

But I didn't believe that for a second. Not Wayne. Not the guy who'd sat with me over dinner. And how'd he even get one of the fairy's guns? Because it had to be the gun of an enemy, if the bullet had killed him. And if that was so, why hadn't the security forces properly searched the pirates?

None of this made *sense.*

The door to the brig opened, and heavy footsteps came down the stairs. Certainly that had to be Chief Buntin.

"There's been murders!" I shouted. "I heard a sound and I came down to check! I'm coming out with my hands up!"

I stepped out of the cell—and stared directly down the barrel of Commander Gagnon's gun.

She had just overtaken Scylla as the woman I hated the most.

"Who knows you're here?" she asked, her voice like ice.

"Everyone in my berthing," I lied, never taking my eyes off the gun. "And I told Torres to tell Chief Bickley that I'd heard a commotion." It took every ounce of self-control in my body to not rattle off the name of every sailor I knew.

"Then this will have to be the hard way. Give me the magic cradle, if you please, and as you do so, say aloud that it's mine."

"Okay. I'm going for the necklace now. No sudden moves, see?"

I removed the cradle, only able to absorb a tiny shock of magic before she brandished the gun and said, "Don't even think about it."

I moved my hand away from the glass and removed the chain from my neck. "It's yours now. Here you go."

Never taking her eyes off me, she placed it over her head and tucked it securely beneath her collar. "Thank you for seeing reason. Start walking up the stairs and head for the stern. If you so much as sneeze, I'll shoot you and say you attacked me. Keep your hands where I can see them at all times."

There was no reasoning with a maniac, especially a maniac with a gun. I squared my shoulders and climbed the stairs, my feet heavy but my chest airy with fear and adrenaline. *Please let someone see that I'm not okay. Please let someone ask me if I need help.*

But nobody did. It was night, and most people were in their berthings, offices, or attending duties, never sparing either of us a glance as we walked all the way to the stern of the ship.

I opened the door to the deck that led to the far back rail, and I could see a lookout standing at the same place I'd been when I had seen the pirates hours earlier. As soon as the door was shut behind us, she shoved me into a dark corner. "Stay here. Don't you dare breathe a word."

I was too scared to even nod. She stalked off toward the lookout. She caught his attention, then exchanged a few words with him. He nodded once and sprinted to another end of the ship.

She was getting rid of the potential witness.

I put a hand to my chest. "Okay, okay, think Rachel, think," I gasped. "Just run and tell Bickley. Run and—"

She turned and faced me, then beckoned. Trembling, I walked to her, bracing for the bullet I knew was coming any second. Of course she'd killed the pirates and Wayne, but why? What did she stand to gain from their deaths?

Her gun was low at her hip, unobtrusive but still dangerous. "Captain Hollander has been telling me about you," she said. "The pretty little nuke who lost it all when she died in the tragic accident."

How the hell was I supposed to reply to that?

"You weren't even going to stay on the ship. You were going to go directly to the Far Island. But you stayed, and now you're screwing everything up for me." Her voice had become a hiss.

"I... I..."

"Jump, Petty Officer. Jump or be shot. It's up to you."

"No!" I took a step back. "I'm not your enemy! The necklace thing wasn't personal!"

"You're my Jonah, Rachel Goldstein. You got on this ship and threatened everything. You know what happened to Jonah, don't you?"

She seized me and clamped her hand over my mouth while I thrashed wildly. But she was taller, wider, and stronger, leaving me hopelessly outclassed. I tried to grab her gun, but one good bang against the railing sent my senses spinning. I felt my body lifted up, and then—

Down.

Down.

Down.

I HIT the black water with brain-rattling force, immediately sucked under by the undertow of the ship. I kicked wildly, spun around in the ocean currents, madly scrambling for something, anything to orient myself.

My head broke the surface, and I screamed for all my life. I wasn't wearing a chem light. It was the witching hour. The ship was noisy and my screams were small.

Nobody knew I was out here. Nobody would ever know what had happened to me.

Above, and growing smaller, the small glow of the magic cradle flared, and then disappeared as Commander Gagnon turned and walked away from the stern of the ship.

My fear roared to life, morphing into such rage as I'd never felt. Jonah? Maybe if she'd read the Old Testament a bit closer, she would've remembered that Jonah survived. But no matter what, I wasn't Jonah. I was *Judith*, and I was going to cut off that woman's head with a damned ax, if I could find one. How dare she try to silence me? How dare that scumbag look me in the eye and threaten me?

I took several deep breaths. What did I have to fight right now? What would save me?

The answer came immediately: I had magic, and I wasn't in the engine room tonight. I already knew how to turn it into explosive fuel in my body.

The small bit of magic I'd squirreled away inside me flooded into my legs, allowing me to swim as fast as Jordan up to the ship, unperturbed by the waves the ship threw up. I needed to get to the ladder on the side.

When I was beneath the ladder, I blasted the last of my magic into the water, giving me enough lift to grab the bottom rung with both hands.

Now the hard part. My magic had run out.

With a cry of effort, I hoisted myself up and grabbed the next rung. I lifted my legs and looped one on the ladder, allowing myself to finally rest a bit and catch my breath. If I climbed up about a million more feet, I could clamber over onto the fantail.

Arm, up. Legs, up. Again and again and again, with the waves crashing below me and my fake heart beating inside like war drums, I lifted myself up toward the railing. Though I was a ghost, I'd never felt more alive.

After ten excruciating minutes, I reached the railing and climbed over, falling down flat onto the stern's deck and taking several deep breaths. Nobody was running over to see what wretched sea creature had climbed onto the ship—she obviously didn't want the lookout team anywhere near the railing.

I stood on shaking legs, but my shoulders were thrown back, and I lifted my chin high.

Commander Gagnon had just made a *big* mistake.

## 15

I punched through the glass of the fire box and wrenched out the ax, sending shards of glass all over the deck. My cuts healed on their own. I didn't even feel them.

The only thing I felt was the need for murder thrumming in my veins. And oh, I was going to murder Commander Gagnon. Her, and anyone foolish enough to try to stop me. I felt capable of anything, at that moment.

Another petty officer stopped in the passageway and balked. "What are you doing?"

I looked sidelong at him. "Go down into the engine room and tell Chief Bickley that he's needed in the galley."

"But—"

"Now!"

He ran off toward the stairs that led to the engine room. I gripped my ax and narrowed my eyes, feeling its solid weight in my hands. There were at least a dozen identical axes around the ship, and probably some knives somewhere. The quartermaster? Supply? Whatever. There were definitely guns in the armory, and plenty of magic running through the entire ship and its many systems. I could feed into it, if I really had to.

I stormed into the galley, where the late-night shift was eating dinner. All eyes turned to me: sopping wet, armed, and pissed off.

Stanholtzer stopped eating, his spoon halfway to his mouth. "Petty Officer? What's going on? Why do you have an ax?"

I stood on a table, almost high from the fury inside me. "Commander Gagnon just tried to kill me!" My furious shout made everyone flinch. "And I'm very certain she killed Seaman Wayne tonight! Now," I said, even louder, raising my ax, "Are we going to sit back and die as she kills us one by one, or are we going to *do something*?"

Stanholtzer bolted to his feet. "You mean a mutiny?"

I gulped. "Yes." Worried whispers ran through the crowd, and I lifted my chin up again. "She's been telling the captain that nobody on this ship can read nautical charts! Does anyone else thinks that's weird, considering that there's half a dozen quartermasters on this ship?"

One of the Canadian sailors stood up. "I'm a quartermaster! Gagnon told me that I was needed on the flight deck!" I thumped his chest. "I can read nautical charts! Why? What's she doing this for?"

The twenty-five or so sailors abandoned their table and crowded around me, and I hesitantly lowered my ax. "Prince Jordan, that merman I know you all know about, gave me a magical artifact. She stole it from me at gunpoint. I *think* she wants magic, and I *think* she's working with the pirates. We're sailing blind by her design, and I'm not sure, but she may have had something to do with Captain Kellerman's death." The systems had been mysteriously non-functional that dark day, according to Rielle. Everywhere Gagnon went, there was a stench of feces.

"You said she killed Wayne?" Stanholtzer said. "In the brig? But why would she do that?"

"The pirates were all shot, and then it looked like he'd shot himself," I said. "I'll bet you anything she wanted to shut up any pirate who knew that she's colluding with them. I found the bodies in there not even an hour ago, and then she pushed me off the ship. She said it was the water or a bullet." My voice cracked, and I blinked back tears. I'd never felt so violated in my entire existence. But now was not the time to fall apart.

Stanholtzer assessed me, and then he nodded. "That's enough for me," he said, facing everyone. "I won't serve under an officer like that. How about it, boys?"

The undercurrent of suspicion subtly shifted, and real anger appeared on faces. Hands reached out and patted me on my shoulders, and I gave them a wan little smile.

Stanholtzer held out his hands for the ax. "Petty Officer, go get the nukes. No offense, but you're not the scariest-looking sailor on the ship."

There was no laughter. Instead, they all murmured assent as I handed over the ax. "Remember, this is just against Gagnon," I said. "Captain Hollander is being lied to, and we have to assume that the rest of the officers are, too. I don't want this to turn into a massacre."

He nodded, and then turned and faced everyone else. "All of you! Go wake up everyone in berthing! Now! Go, go, go! Muster in the galley!"

His deep shout was all I needed—I fled down the passageway. I ran all the way to my berthing and burst inside, flipping on the light. "Up, now! Muster in the galley!" I shucked my wet clothes once again and pulled on dry coveralls and boots. "All of you! Up!"

All four of my berthing mates slid out of bed and hastily pulled on their clothes. "What is it?" Rielle asked. "Is it something to do with that thing we were dealing with earlier?"

I opened her locker and pulled out the damning nautical chart. "It's a mutiny against Commander Gagnon."

Everyone's eyes widened. Sailors were running in the passageway now, all of them heading toward the galley. Some of them were armed.

I turned to Torres. "Go get Bickley. Get as much magic inside you both as you can. Rielle, you're coming with me. I want you to tell Captain Hollander exactly what you told me about the quartermasters. You two," I said, looking at my fairy shipmates, "We're taking down Commander Gagnon for her crimes against the crew. Are you with us?"

They nodded. "We've never liked her anyway," Frost of Night said. "She's a jerk to fairies."

"It's time to air your grievances," I said. "Let's go."

We all ran out and went our different ways. With the chart tube in hand, Rielle and I pushed against the crowd toward the long officer's passageway a few decks up. Certainly they would've heard the commotion by now, but probably wouldn't have known it was a mutiny against Commander Gagnon.

The passageway was blessedly quiet, since there were no enlisted berthings near there. I ran straight to Captain Hollanders stateroom and banged my fist against it as hard as I could. "Captain! Captain, get up! You need to get up right now!"

A few officers poked their heads out of their staterooms. "Petty Officer, what are you doing?" one asked. "You can't just—"

Captain Hollander opened his stateroom door, bleary-eyed and confused. He was wearing shorts and a t-shirt. "What's going on?"

I took a step back and slid the nautical chart out of the tube. "Sir, this is Petty Officer Rielle Guyon. She's a quartermaster, and as such, she's trained to read nautical charts. Rielle, tell him."

Rielle unfurled the chart. "Sir, I calculated that we're near this coordinate," she said, pointing to the weak spot I'd identified earlier. "Was it Commander Gagnon who told you that nobody on board could read nautical charts?"

He stared at the chart for a long second, and then nodded. "Yes. Yes, it was. She said all of her quartermasters had been taken in the attack. I had no idea there was a quartermaster on board."

"There are six of us," Rielle said. "And we were all sent to other departments."

Other officers were gathering around. I stepped up and looked Captain Hollander square in the eye. "Not only has she lied to you and the rest of the chain of command, it appears that she killed the pirates in the brig along with Seaman Wayne. When I discovered the bodies, she tried to silence me by throwing me overboard. She also took the magic cradle at gunpoint." I leveled my coolest expression at him. "I also came to inform you that the crew is gathering in the galley as we speak. Sir, if you won't remove Commander Gagnon from her command immediately, we will. There is no direct threat to you or any of the officers right now, but we mean business."

I could appreciate the tight spot I'd put Captain Hollander in: his crew was spiraling into a mutiny against his XO, and now I'd told him we were going to do it whether or not he allowed it. In a way, he was no longer in command no matter what I said, and I was the one bringing the news to him. This was going to hurt our relationship, but at that moment, I had to care about removing Commander Gagnon more.

Captain Hollander inhaled deeply, then snapped his fingers and pointed at two ensigns. "Hilpisch, Dykstra, get dressed. Get Chief Buntin and arrest Commander Gagnon. You three," he said, indicating three other officers. "Wake up the entire chain. Petty Officer... Guyon, was it?"

"Yes, sir," Rielle said.

"Go get the other quartermasters, and report to my conference room. Bring that chart."

"Yes sir," she said again, before running down the passageway.

That left me with Captain Hollander. What could I say to him anymore? Decorum dictated some kind of apology, but... yeah, no, I wasn't apologizing for this one.

But he laid an expressionless, if cold, look at me. "Petty Officer, what is the name of the lead mutineer?"

"It's me, sir. I'm the lead mutineer."

Whatever he expected, it wasn't that. His coldness shattered, allowing me to see the hurt and shock. "You? This was your idea?"

"Yes, sir. I came up with the idea while I was in the water after your executive officer pushed me over the railing, and I solidified it when I was climbing back onto the ship."

He winced. "What did I do to deserve this?"

"What do you mean?"

"This lack of respect."

"Sir, I respect—"

"You never gave me a chance, Goldstein. That's not even a chain of command issue, that's personal." He drew back from me. "You never gave me a chance."

There was a beat as I realized that I'd broken my own rule. Nobody had disrespected Captain Hollander like I had just now.

My simmering fury quieted, and I swallowed. "So what would you like me to report back to the others in the galley?"

A muscle in his jaw flexed, but he took another deep breath and said, "I'm going to get dressed, and we're going to the galley together."

---

THE SEA of furious crewmen parted for Captain Hollander as he cut through them, his flashy dress blues a naked contrast to our grungy overalls, baggy sweaters, and smudged hands. Behind him, a line of ensigns and lieutenant commanders followed, their faces identical masks of consternation.

Bickley grabbed me and pulled me into the crowd, partially shielding me from the contingent of officers. "I thought you said you wouldn't do anything stupid," he whispered. "Declaring a mutiny is beyond stupid."

"We'll talk later, okay?" I whispered back.

Captain Hollander reached the middle of the crowd and surveyed us, his eyes all but sparking with anger. The low murmurs died down.

He threw back his shoulders. "I have spoken with Petty Officer Goldstein about the murder of Seaman Wayne, and the attempted murder of Petty Officer Goldstein. Let me assure you that Commander Gagnon will be dealt with, and punished according to the severity of her crimes."

"We've been sailing *blind!*" one sailor shouted from the back. "If you'd asked the crew—"

"This is a naval vessel, and I will run it how I see fit!" Captain Hollander shouted. "I speak with my officers, and yes, I trust them to tell me the truth! This is how it is on every ship any of you has ever served on!"

An angry ripple of whispers and mutterings moved around the crowd. Stanholtzer twirled his ax.

"Now," continued Captain Hollander, "Considering the extenuating circumstances of tonight's events, I will be lenient and show mercy on all of you despite every person here being guilty of mutiny and sedition." He unholstered a revolver. "You all have until the count of ten to disperse and go back to your stations, or you will find out why the ship placed me in command. One..."

Nobody moved. I thought I saw Captain Hollander sigh.

A gun's blast rocked us all backward. *"Go back to your stations!"*

It was the voice that would not be disobeyed. The imperative shot through me, forcing my legs to move, left, right, left, right, as they carried me out of the galley and to the passageway that led to the engine room.

Other sailors cursed and hissed about Captain Hollander, but just like that, the mutiny was over before it had really begun.

As I descended the stairs, I mulled over my course of action. I'd obviously irrevocably destroyed my good relationship with Captain Hollander, but at least now everyone knew Commander Gagnon was in bad faith. I'd get my magic cradle back, hopefully. We'd be able to chart a course and rescue our friends.

Sometimes victories were tainted with loss. That was the way of both worlds, it seemed.

Bickley, Torres, and I joined up in the final passageway and walked into the engine room together. When the door was shut behind us, Bickley rounded on me. "Rachel. We have to talk about this."

"I know," I said quietly. "I expect you have some things to say."

Torres sagged against a generator. "Why did you go directly to a mutiny?"

The sense of violation returned, and with it, the lump in my throat. "She threw me off the ship. In an ocean filled with monsters that eat ghosts, that's tantamount to attempted murder. She'd already murdered Wayne. I couldn't trust that going to Bickley first, or through the chain of command, was going to do anything. For all I knew, that would tip her off."

I leaned back against a generator. "I'm sorry. I know I messed up tonight. I just go so angry, I got tunnel vision about it all and made a bad decision."

"They might remove you from the ship yet," Bickley said, crossing his arms and shaking his head. There was no good humor on his face. "Your human record doesn't count, nor does Captain Hollander's guilt over killing you. You've been acting wild since getting on the ship. Running to see the dragon almost got you eaten. And then there was the whole bomb thing, which I was part of too, but it's still there on your record. People remember that you wanted to leave. You're not in the greatest standing, Rach."

"So what am I now?" I asked, no inflection in my voice. "Are you going to chastise me by calling me selfish?"

That's what they did, because it worked. It always worked. It was a swift kick in the butt for me, regardless of whether or not it was true. And now, *it was not true*. I was a lot of unsavory things, but I was not selfish.

"You *are* being selfish," Torres insisted. "You're so worked up about your own feelings that—"

"Bullshit."

Their jaws dropped. They probably didn't believe that I knew that kind of language, since sweet, religious Rachel Goldstein had never sworn in front of them before in English.

Anger flooded through me, and I pushed away from the generator. "Torres, did it ever occur to you that I'm entitled to feel strong feelings when people harm me? I was angry that Captain Hollander wasn't apologizing, but you called me selfish for actually feeling something about it. Someone just tried to kill me again, and you're shooting straight from the hip because I went and did something you wouldn't have. I protected the entire crew by throwing up the flag, knowing full well that this could be the end of my career on the ship. So maybe I screwed up by not respecting Captain Hollander enough to go to him, but what I did, I did out of concern for my shipmates, not selfishness. Back off."

Bickley slowly put his arm between us. "Okay, let's all just cool down."

Torres and I were still scowling at each other, but I broke eye contact and looked at Bickley. "It's my shift now. You can go back to berthing." Despite my suspicion that I'd be targeted in the engine room because of its solitude, I didn't want to so much as look at anyone at the moment.

I stepped onto the small dais where each nuke worked during their shift, placed my hand on the sphere in its spindly perch, and gently guided the magic into my core. My friends hadn't moved, and instead we're just watching me.

"Rachel," Torres said quietly. "Let's talk."

"Go away."

"Please, let's talk about this."

"I said leave."

"I—"

"I'm *working!*" I screamed, the connection snapping as a result. I whipped around. "Don't you *get* it? That's all I want to do! I just want to be able to do my job! But I can't, because I've got you calling me selfish over here, Commander Gagnon trying to murder me over there, people flying planes into ships, monsters killing Yeoman Hanson, I'll never see my parents grow old, I'll never turn twenty-two,

I'll never do anything except be a nuke in this engine room! So *let me work!*

I turned back to the sphere and slammed my hand down on it, tears streaming down my face.

And just to make matters worse, the sound of footsteps in the passageway was coming closer. I was about to have one more unwelcome visitor. Maybe, if I were very lucky, it was Chief Buntin with handcuffs. Isolation sounded nice.

The door opened, and in stepped Captain Hollander.

We all stared at each other. Torres and Bickley were apparently too taken aback to stand to attention, and I had a hand on the sphere, the power gently flowing from it into my body.

Captain Hollander's face was a novel all on its own, a story of regret and failure.

"What is it, sir?" I asked, turning away. "If you're coming to keelhaul me, I'll be up in a minute. I'm carrying a lot of magic right now and it shouldn't be released into the ocean like that."

"I'm not going to keelhaul you. I came to inform you..." He trailed off, and out of the corner of my eye, I saw him look down. "We lost Commander Gagnon. She stole a RHIB and escaped through the weak spot. I thought it was appropriate that you hear it from me."

And that was that. She'd tried to kill me, and she'd gotten away. She'd won.

We made eye contact, and I hoped my expression communicated just how thoroughly I'd been let down.

I turned back to the sphere. "Thank you for telling me, sir. If you relate the details to Torres and Bickley while you all leave, I'm sure they'll give me the report after my shift."

*Please leave. Please turn around and shut the door. Don't speak. Just leave.*

"I'll leave you to your work, then," he said, his voice low with emotion. "Chief, Petty Officer, let's go."

Finally, something was going my way.

They left me in the engine room, and if they gave me one last parting glance, I did not turn around to see them. Instead, I just siphoned magic, converted it, and put it into the ship's systems, again and again. Ironically, my new duties were much closer to the sarcastic "refining uranium" I'd alleged to Captain Hollander.

But as I worked, left alone in peace as I'd asked, the isolation became overpowering. I rested my head against one of the engines, power seeping into it, and closed my eyes. Perhaps we could still eat and sleep not because we needed comfort, but because we still truly needed refreshment from the drudgery naval life offered.

After a minute, I stood up straight, and began to convert energy again. I placed my hand on the sphere—and immediately saw that it was empty. I'd been so taken up with my pity party that I'd neglected to see that I'd sucked the last bit out.

Sighing, I grabbed the empty sphere and placed it in a crate set aside just for that purpose, then went over to the cage where we kept the raw magic, stored in the back of the engine room. On my way, I retrieved the hidden key from behind one of the panels in the wall.

But the cage was already open. The lock had been broken.

"No, no, no," I breathed, rushing inside. All around me, evidence of Commander Gagnon's theft laughed at me. The boxes and crates were empty, the sawdust containing just round little indentations where the spheres had been. She'd stolen an unimaginable amount of magic.

"*No!*" I threw one of the crates against the bulkhead, the sawdust flying everywhere in a dusty yellow cloud. I sank to my knees and bowed my head, crying in earnest.

There was a low boom in the distance, audible above the din of the engines.

I raised my head. What now?

Another boom, and the ship shuddered.

I held up three fingers, ticking down to what I knew was coming. Three... two... one...

"*General quarters! General quarters! All hands report to your battle stations! This is not a drill!*"

We were under attack, and this time, our enemy had our magic.

# 16

M y legs couldn't move fast enough as I sprinted down the passageway and up the stairs to the security office. Chief Buntin and his men had an entire armory filled with weapons, all of which could repel a pirate invasion. Combined with the jets and cannons, today didn't have to turn into a bloodbath—for us, anyway.

I skidded to a halt at the security door and pounded on it. "Chief Buntin! I need to talk to Chief Buntin! It's Petty Officer Goldstein! Someone's stolen all the magic!"

Nothing.

I raised my fist to bang on the door again, then paused. I put my ear to the door.

Still nothing.

"Hello?" I asked as I cracked it open. "Chief Buntin? Anyone?"

The security forces had been absent from their posts when I'd found the corpses in the brig. I hadn't given it much thought at the time, but now that they were conspicuously missing from the only other place they were usually found...

I pushed the door wide open. The large security office was deserted, each desk neatly arranged and empty. The armory, a large cage, was unlocked and stripped of the guns we so badly needed.

I hung my head. If the security forces had taken to arms because of the imminent battle, they'd still be loading up here, in the office. They'd have left at least one person behind to watch over the cage and sensitive items.

They'd probably been gone for hours.

Another explosion, louder than before, boomed in the distance. All around the ship, my shipmates were shouting to each other, calling for aid, munitions, an extra pair of hands, anything. Before long, the ship would run out of power, and then they'd start calling for me.

I closed the door of the security office and began to walk toward the flight deck. I wouldn't give in to despair until I knew what was coming. Perhaps it was a small flotilla, as before. Half a dozen decent-sized missiles had taken care of that in no time.

I pushed against the crush of sailors running here and there, moving with purpose as I made my way to the flight deck.

Another explosion. The ship shuddered.

I turned the last corner to the flight deck, then stopped dead in my tracks. Captain Hollander was standing by the door in his flight suit, an aviator's helmet in his hands. He was looking down at it. The blankness on his face was eerier than the explosions in the distance.

"Sir? Are you okay? Why aren't you on the bridge?" The last question was a bit impertinent, but fair all the same. We needed a strong captain at the helm more than ever.

He didn't answer, nor even look up at me. I came up to him and peered up at his blank face. "Sir?"

He finally looked at me, albeit with a faraway glaze. "Chief Buntin helped her. All the security forces did. My ship is full of traitors."

I swallowed a stab of self-consciousness. "Why aren't you on the bridge?"

"I need to show everyone that I can be a strong leader. I'm going to lead the mission against the ships." He pushed open the door. "I think we need every aviator available."

Eight ships were flanking us, each a rusting warship armed to the teeth. Their guns were lobbing ballistic ordnance at us, the ordnance exploded against our shields—though already I could see small cracks in the magic, the spidery fractures spreading over the ship like webbing.

On the flight deck, aviators were getting into their planes and taxiing on the runway. Captain Hollander watched them, the same faraway look in his eyes.

Regret, toxic and painful, swirled in my stomach. I'd done this to him, and still I had to add to it by bearing to him the bad news. I'd never felt such remorse for anything in my life, and I ached to travel back in time a few hours and slap some sense into myself. Why a mutiny? *Why* had that been my first choice?

But there wasn't time to mull over my mistakes. Not now.

I shut the door. "Sir, I must inform you that it appears that Commander Gagnon robbed us of our magic stores. The cage is empty. I don't even know when she did it."

Still no response from him, other than a subtle heaviness descending into his eyes. He closed them, then said, "I heard you saw your memorial service on the *Taft*."

"I, uh, yes, I did," I said, sideswiped by the sudden change of subject.

"How were you remembered?"

"Fondly, I guess. My officers and coworkers liked me."

Another explosion rocked the ship.

"Do you know how I'll be remembered, Petty Officer?"

"I'm sure the air wing misses you, sir. And of course, your parents and fr—"

"As a failure," he said, his voice hard. "I will eternally be remembered as the aviator who screwed up and killed twenty-five people. Nobody will ever care about anything else in my life. That is the story of me. And now, I'm going to be the captain whose executive officer was colluding with pirates, whose security forces robbed him blind, and whose crew mutinied because I was so crappy of a leader."

I'd pushed him into despair. This was the most human side of Arthur Hollander, what was beneath the braiding and bossy voice. A guy who'd screwed up, and his judgment was that he'd have to live with the people he'd killed. That sucked in a way I'd never experienced, nor did I want to.

But he was still the captain of the ship. We needed someone who would lead from the front, not someone who was having an emotional meltdown.

I took a breath, then planted my hands on my hips. "Sir, I'm not going to waste my time with a pep talk. The ship chose me to be its heart, and she chose *you* to be her captain. Now, get your helmet on, get in that plane, and *go defend your ship!*" I ripped the helmet out of his hands and shoved it into his chest. "And with your permission, I'd like to fight the pirates myself because otherwise there's nothing I can do!" *Why did I just yell that?*

My shout must've snapped him to his senses, because he tucked his helmet underneath his arm, gave his head a shake, and said, "Fine, yes, get out there, Petty Officer. Tell the other nukes to do whatever you need to. You have my permission."

He opened the door and ran out, and I followed.

The flight deck was alight with people running everywhere, crews carrying ordnance to planes and arming them with all speed. Jets were flying off the deck, their roars drowning out all other sound.

The eastern horizon was a dusty pink, allowing all to see the enormous force bearing down on us.

I pressed myself against the outside bulkhead and studied the ships. If all I had to work with was the raw power in my stomach, what was the best way to use it? I squinted, searching the ships for an obvious weakness. They were lined up... except for one. I knew immediately it was the ship with the captives.

The eighth ship, smaller than the others, floated well behind the others. It lobbed no bombs at us, nor did it even move. Instead, it hovered around the weak spot that was plain to see—the familiar lights of the Virginia Beach boardwalk appeared where there should've been open ocean. Standing tall above the other hotels, my family's premier oceanside resort served as a beacon. If I were a marauder seeking people, I'd automatically choose that building first.

And since they'd come *from* the weak spot, which meant they'd already been in the waters off Virginia Beach for at least a little while. What had called them back?

I stood up a little straighter. *We* had.

This was the final flotilla, and this was the final battle to protect Virginia Beach, and the entire world of the living. They'd sailed into Virginia Beach's waters hoping for booty, high in the belief that their mole had disarmed us and rendered us useless.

"Their mistake," I muttered to myself. I still had magic left in me, and as long as I did, I had a weapon. And with that weapon, a plan formed.

Better still, a plane released an enormous missile on the lead ship, finally breaking through its shield. If their shields fell as quickly, my plan was going to be easier than I had thought.

I sidled alongside the bulkhead back to the door, then sprinted down the passageway to the engine room. "Bickley! Torres! Where are you?"

Torres and Bickley poked their heads out of the engine room. "It's general quarters!" Torres said. "Where have you been? What happened to all the magic spheres?"

I pointed behind me. "Commander Gagnon," I said by way of explanation. "I spoke with the captain and told him about the magic. He said we can do whatever we have to do to fight the pirates."

"You have a plan?" Bickley said. "I know that look in your eye."

I grinned. "Can either of you drive a boat?"

---

"FAIR WARNING," Bickley said as he gripped the wheel of the RHIB. "I've only ever piloted my granddad's boat on the Hudson. Never done anything in a sea battle before."

We were bobbing up and down next to the ship in the only spare RHIB that the security forces hadn't stolen. Torres and I had clasped hands, allowing me to pour some of my unspent magic into her. When we had an even amount, I let go and tossed her an ax. "That's fine," I said, buckling down in the RHIB. "Just don't crash."

"We really have the captain's permission?" Bickley asked over his shoulder. "Nuke's honor?"

I crossed my heart and kissed my fingers. "On the grave of Admiral Rickover. Now, to be fair, he probably didn't envision something like this, but he said we could do, and I quote, whatever we need to, unquote. I have determined that we need to do this."

"Then hold on," Bickley said. The engine roared to life. "It's about to get bumpy!"

Torres and I braced ourselves as Bickley steered the speedy boat out of the shadow of the *Rickover* and into the open water. Our way was clear, lit by the orange sunrise in the clear sky. Though shaky, he maneuvered the RHIB well, and we zipped right past the first heavily damaged pirate ship.

"Machine gun!" Torres screamed. "Two o'clock, Bick!"

A pirate fired his machine gun wildly, the bullets throwing up cascades and columns of water next to us. Bickley swerved, nearly tossing me out of the boat. I raised my head to shout at him, but Torres pointed to the sky. "Bickley! Move!"

A *Rickover* jet swooped down low and took out the boat, throwing up wood and people in an enormous explosion. We wheeled around in the water, zipping past the debris and heading for the other ships, all of which were armed with machine guns and other crew-served weapons.

I gripped my ax. If the other gunners were as bad of a shot as the first guy, this was going to be easy.

A shadow moved under the water, long and feminine. I sighed. *I just had to go and jinx it, didn't I?*

"It's her!" I shouted. "It's Scylla!"

Scylla seemed to fly out of the water, rising up so fast that I barely had time to take in what was happening. She came to a stop when her torso was out of the water, her snake-hair slithering in various shapes and angles. Once again, her toothy grin was far too wide for comfort, and her eyes darted endlessly in their sockets, never focusing on any one thing. Her deep belly laugh turned my stomach.

The pirates cheered their champion, but I stared up at the thing that had killed Yeoman Hanson, hate like I'd never felt clawing at my insides.

Oh, I was going to kill her. For millennia she'd preyed on humanity, cementing her loathed visage in our myths and legends, haunting sailors as they sailed the corners of the globe. But no more. She'd killed a good man, and now she was going to die. Her time was well overdue.

"Torres, link up with me," I said, holding out my hand and focusing on my hatred. "You'll know what to do."

Bickley mounted the machine gun on the bow of the RHIB and began to fire at her stomach.

She hissed and bent down to reach us, just what I'd hoped she do.

"Now!" I screamed. Torres opened the "poltergeist" link that had caused so much trouble all those weeks ago, and into it I poured my anger, my hate, and my fear for my family—the perfect recipe for an absolutely perfect psychic storm.

Scylla was blown off balance by the wave of power that hit her, flailing and falling backward into a ship. The ship capsized immediately, bowing and snapping underneath Scylla's enormous frame. We bobbed up and down in the waves as Bickley fired some more. Scylla was floating on her back, partially impaled by bits of the ship she was on.

Pirates dove off the vessel, waving their arms helplessly as they tried to grab onto whatever piece of flotsam they could. Nearby, jets were taking out more ships, cracking their shields and blowing them to kingdom come.

"Get me next to her," I ordered, clutching my ax. "It's not over yet."

Bickley maneuvered the RHIB to where Scylla met the water, and I jumped off, right onto her flat white belly. I began to swing my ax.

She screamed, trying desperately to grab the tiny person hacking into her stomach. Whenever her enormous fingers came near, I unleashed another blast of hate. I ran up her chest, between the mounds of her breasts, and raised my ax to her throat.

*For John. For Jordan. For the ship. For me.* I infused the ax with my remaining magic and brought it down into her neck.

Her high keen morphed into a low, guttural moan that shook her entire body. I lost my purchase, falling down into the ocean water by her head. Green blood pulsed out of her throat, dripping down into the water. As it washed over me, I felt a familiar, instinctual tug.

Magic! There was magic in her blood!

I spread out my arms and welcomed the magic into my body. It wasn't as raw as the magic in the spheres, and therefore not as powerful, but it was magic all the same. Plants could survive on sunlight through a window, and I could absorb the magic in an evil beast's veins.

With a huge, pained sigh, Scylla slipped underneath the water, her white body growing dimmer and dimmer each second until, quite suddenly, she winked out of my vision.

*Huh. That actually* was *easy.*

Someone grabbed my neck.

I thrashed against my assailant, immediately trying to hit them with my ax. I caught glimpses of him; he was a pirate, all white and green and sparkly, and pissed off. My head went underwater, held down by large, masculine hands. Not dangerous, but disorienting—which *was* incredibly dangerous in battle.

His hands clamped on my throat.

Pain in every inch of my body caused me to seize and stiffen, unable to escape from the source. Something inside me began to move, inching out of my body into his, crawling in my veins like lava. It was like an obscene parody of what happened when I released the magic into the ship. This was forced, and it was horrible.

His hands went slack, and he slid underneath the water with me. There was an enormous gash in his head, billowing blood into the murky water.

I popped my head out of the water. Torres was hanging off the side of the RHIB, her ax dripping blood. "Sorry about the wait."

"Help me up!" I held up my hands, and Bickley and Torres hauled me inside the RHIB.

"Can't hang around," Bickley said, turning the wheel. "The prison ship just went through the weak spot."

I looked around at the chaos. The seven ships had been ripped apart either by bombs or giant naked women falling on them, and their crews were in the water. Some were desperately trying to stay above the surface, while others were floating face-down. Body parts drifted by in the current. The flotilla was history—but the threat still remained. We had to stop the final ship from harming anyone in the world of the living.

Behind us, the *Rickover* was suffering, large columns of smoke rising up a thousand feet in the air. The lights were flickering, puttering along on the last of the power I'd put into the ship. The shields were broken, and large dents and scorch marks in the side of the hull provided large targets to anyone who wanted to attack.

The three of us were the only ones in a position to storm the final ship.

I took a deep breath. "Bickley, get us alongside the hull. I'm going to blow it open." None of us had enough power to take on an entire crew, but a ship in distress was a ship in distress—they'd have to throw all their efforts into fixing the damage, freezing them where they were.

Bickley piloted the RHIB through the floating carnage while Torres and I hacked at the pirates trying to grab on. We passed through the weak spot with ease, the only noticeable difference in the temperatures of the two worlds. It was August in the world of the living, and therefore immediately muggy.

More bullets rang out, blowing water into the air. Bickley shot back at the small machine gun on the stern of the prison ship. Within seconds, we were immediately alongside the ship.

Torres, Bickley, and I clasped our hands together and locked onto the hull.

Pirates began shouting in alarm as a huge strip of rusting metal was pulled back from the ship as easily as a label was pulled off a soup can. Water flooded into the empty compartment. The ship began to list.

We jumped out of the RHIB and into the compartment, axes in hand. The compartment was an office, by the look of it, and I sloshed through the water to a light socket, where I placed my hand on it and tapped into the power supply. Every system on the ship died at once, plunging us into a shadowy dimness only punctured lightly by the fingers of sunlight shining through the breached hull.

Torres and Bickley came up to me, and I rationed out the power into thirds. I was trembling from the power surging through me, but I knew I couldn't let it go to my head. We were at a disadvantage, since we didn't know the layout of the ship, didn't know what was waiting for us, and—I watched water creep up my ankles—we'd soon be in a capsizing vessel.

"Spread out, keep your axes up," Bickley ordered. "Our only goal is to find the prisoners."

I shoved open the door, bracing for an onslaught of pirates... but nothing happened. The passageway was empty, devoid of any being, living or dead.

"What are they waiting for?" Torres asked, her eyes darting around. "They know there's only three of us."

A gunshot somewhere above us made us flinch. Bickley motioned for us to get behind him, and we began inching our way down the passageway. There were more gunshots, followed by shouts and thuds of furniture moving.

We all exchanged confused glances. "What do you think is going on up there?" Torres whispered.

Before I could answer, we passed a door with bars on the windows. I peered in. It was a brig, and it was filled with people.

"Guys, it's our officers," I said, eyeing their insignia. Their uniforms had changed, too, even as they'd been captive on a pirate ship. I raised my ax to break the small window, but Bickley held his out and motioned for us to move back.

"Let me. You too, find the others. Use your power to blast them to hell."

Torres and I hurried down the passageway, our steps in time with Bickley's assault on the door handle and window. There were no pirates to be found anywhere, but it was no comfort. There *were* pirates on the ship, so why were we being allowed to free the officers? And where were the enlisted captives?

"Psst," Torres hissed. "Check out this door. There's a padlock." She'd stopped at a narrow door at the end of the passageway, right at the bottom of a stairwell. "It's probably a holding cell or an armory."

"More likely a holding cell, since they knew we were coming. Stand back." I raised my ax to break the lock.

"No!" Torres screamed.

A bullet missed my head by inches, ricocheting wildly around the passageway. Commander Gagnon was at the top of the stairs, holding her service weapon and staring at me with so much hatred it was a wonder that I didn't burst into flames. Torres and I grasped hands.

Gagnon flew backward, out of sight.

"Get that door open!" I shouted, holding my ax up. "I'll take care of her!" I scrambled up the stairs, searching for the treacherous officer who'd tried to kill me twice now. "Where are you, you little..."

I trailed off, grinding my teeth. The stairs led to an intersection of three passageways, all lined with doors. She could've been in any one of them. Worse yet, because I'd leeched the power out of the ship, they were all dark.

"Come out and face me!" I shouted. "It's over, Gagnon! We've won!"

I shoved a door open and ran into the room, ax up, but was met with only an empty berthing. Meals sat half-eaten on some of the racks.

I stepped out of the berthing and opened the next door. Galley storage.

The next door. Another berthing.

The next one. A men's head, complete with unwashed urinals.

I opened the final door on the left side of the passageway. My jaw dropped.

Sacks of gold and silver coins gleamed in the low light from the passageway. Row upon row of chests were similarly filled, jewelry and other baubles spilling out of them. Stacks of American dollars lined one wall, directly opposite a wall of magic spheres tucked into sawdust boxes.

Apparently these pirates were interested in people *and* regular booty.

I walked over to the magic spheres and picked one up, the magic automatically rushing into my hand. I held it up, smiling despite myself. The white light illuminated the small compartment, as well as my pale, bloodstained face, visible in the reflection. I could clearly see a gash on my cheek I didn't know I had.

Something in the reflection moved.

I moved just in time. Gagnon's bullet tore through my right shoulder, eliciting a scream from me. I crashed to the floor, the sphere still in my hand, the magic still rushing into me.

Gagnon's finger moved, but this time her gun just clicked. Cursing, she tossed it aside and jumped on me.

"It was mine!" she screamed, swinging her fists pell-mell at my face. "It was all mine! You took this from me!"

I tried desperately to block her strikes, but my useless right arm meant that I was almost defenseless.

My leg, however, worked just fine. I landed a sharp kick in her stomach, causing her to fall to the ground. I rolled onto her and straddled her stomach, bringing down my ax onto her head.

She blocked the ax and dug her nails into my wrist. I hissed, then fisted a handful of her hair and slammed her head into the deck repeatedly. "Why?" I asked through gritted teeth. "Why turn on us?" I stopped banging her head. "What was worth betraying your countrymen and your ship?"

She gave me a look of deepest loathing. "We're *dead*, you stupid cow. I don't owe anything to anyone. Money is the only thing that matters in both worlds. All of this was mine. They wanted ghosts to suck the juice out of, and I wanted gold. Simple transaction. Until the *Rickover* came along. Even summoning Poseidon didn't work."

I faltered. "You summoned him?"

"Yes. But, oh oh, you were all cuddly with Fish Man. So I had to resort to other measures to weaken the ship. If I couldn't kill that idiot captain, I had to pick something else."

While she talked, I glimpsed the chain of the magic cradle beneath her collar. If I could just—

She kneed me in the solar plexus, making me fall to the side. My ax was suddenly in her hands, and she had the blade to my neck. "Nice try. Any final prayers from Rachel Goldstein?"

I spat on her face.

"You little—"

I clamped my hands on her face and unleashed the magic I'd absorbed from the sphere.

There was a blinding burst of light.

I laid my head down on the stacks of cash, my shoulder bleeding beneath me, and closed my eyes. The last thing I was aware of was a female voice calling my name.

## 17

R *achel.*

A thousand people were calling my name. Simultaneously near and far, their calls were all just one word: my name.

I focused on it.

*Rachel.*

Now it was Peggy's voice.

I opened my eyes. I was in a hospital bed in a small, bland room, almost certainly off the main wing of the sick bay. My bedside table was littered with mementos from visitors: origami flowers I recognized as Torres's handiwork, a challenge coin from an officer, a tasty-looking pastry on a plate, and a card bearing many signatures. Best of all, the superhero novel I'd been reading on the *Taft* sat beneath everything. The lone porthole showed the starry night sky, still and cloudless. I'd been out for at least twelve hours.

I was still deciphering the signatures when a gentle knock on the door made me look up. "Come in."

Peggy opened the door. "You're finally awake! I've had a long line of visitors for you, but you've been asleep for nearly thirty-six hours. How are you feeling?"

"Achy. Sore. Tired." My whole body felt like it had fought the flu.

"Gunshots can be like that," Peggy said. "Dot and I removed the bullet, but—"

"Dot! Dot's here? Send her in!"

And then Dot was there, standing in the doorway in her new coveralls, her mahogany hair pulled into a modern ponytail. She was bearing a lunch tray and beaming at me. "It's been too long since I heard your voice, Petty Officer. Lunch?"

She set down the tray on the sliding over-bed table, and I threw my arms wide. She returned my embrace, hugging me for a long time. Finally, I sniffed and rubbed my eyes with the heel of my hand. "I'm so happy you're safe. Commander Gagnon said the pirates were going to suck all the magic out of you all."

She sat on the edge of the bed. "Yes, that was the plan, I believe. They were aiming for a land invasion of Virginia Beach and had hoped to use our innate magic to power their weapons."

"Is everyone safe?" I asked. "Were we too late?"

"We're all fine," she assured me, patting my hand. "Don't you worry about a thing, except maybe what you're going to eat first. Petty Officer Torres told me that you eat from the kosher counter, so I got something from every tray there." She handed me a plate loaded down with noodles and sauce. "As the chief nurse, I can say that you're not allowed out of bed until you finish this entire tray. Food is for the soul as much as the body."

"It kind of makes us holy women, you know," Peggy said, leaning against the doorway. "We've been looking after people's souls for decades."

We all shared a goofy grin, and I began to dig in.

While I was eating, Peggy and Dot filled me in on what had happened after I'd fallen unconscious.

"Chief Bickley got the officers out, and they ran up to the bridge and found the entire pirate crew had been shot by Commander Gagnon," Dot said soberly. "It appears that she'd hoped to double-cross the pirates and make off with their booty."

"Sounds like desperation to me," Peggy said, still in the doorway. "She freaked out when her master plan fell apart."

"We were liberated not long after that, by Petty Officer Torres," Dot said. "And we all rushed to get the boat back into the Oceanus. The United States Coast Guard had hailed us already, and we needed to slip away through the weak spot. After all, if they'd boarded, they would've found dead pirates of another species, and all the magic spheres, not knowing that the ship was piloted by ghosts. Best not confuse or scare them."

"Who found me?" I asked through a bite of buttered bread.

"I did, actually," Dot said. "Lying there in a pool of blood, surrounded by a king's ransom, with little bits of Commander Gagnon floating around in the air. It was all rather Shakespearean, I must say."

The sound of the sick bay door opening made us all look up, and Peggy moved aside. "Sir."

Captain Gorman stood in the doorway, ever calm and stern. He was holding a stiff blue folder bearing the seal of the US Navy. "Nurses, might I have a private word with Petty Officer Goldstein?"

I swallowed a thick bite of bread. Heroics aside, I'd still started a mutiny on his ship. I wasn't out of hot water with that one, I just knew it. That envelope was probably holding my dishonorable discharge paperwork.

Dot and Peggy cleared out. Captain Gorman pulled up the lone chair and sat next to my bed. "How are you feeling, Petty Officer?"

"I've been better, sir, but I'll survive."

His eyes shone with an emotion I couldn't name. "Because of you, many people aboard this ship right now can say the same, including me."

I ducked my head. How was I supposed to answer that?

Captain Gorman opened up the folder. "Without the power of the US Congress behind me, I can't award medals, no matter how much I want to. But this letter is from myself, asserting that your actions, and that of your coworkers, were worthy of the Bronze Star." He handed it to me. "I only wish I could've seen you three in the RHIB with my own eyes. Thank you for you valor, Petty Officer."

I opened the folder and removed the handwritten letter, which was written on thick card stock with Navy letterhead. I looked up at him, my eyes wet. "The Bronze Star?"

"Nothing less."

I closed the letter and wiped at my eyes again. "Sir, I don't deserve this."

"Petty Officer Torres told me you'd say as much when I gave her letter to her. Something about a mutiny?"

I nodded.

"My, my, things did fall apart when I was gone, didn't they?"

I nodded again, too ashamed to look him in the eyes.

He sat back in his chair, his hands folded on his lap. "While I will never condone mutiny, Petty Officer, it does not mean that I will immediately condemn your actions. An officer had tried to kill you, and you knew yourself and your shipmates to be in immediate danger. I wrote your letter knowing exactly what had happened that night." He leaned toward me. "If you'll let an old man impart some wisdom?"

I nodded again, my eyes wide.

"Do not rid yourself of that fire, but learn to be judicious of when you use it. Not all battles require a gunfight. Many more are won through patience, cleverness, and diplomacy. I suspect you were mastered by your own justifiable anger and fear that night, and being David to Gagnon's Goliath was your immediate course of action."

"Yeah, that sounds like me," I whispered. "Gotta shout down whoever makes me mad."

Captain Gorman reached over and picked up the superhero novel. "A favorite of yours, I assume? I heard that the entire series materialized in the ship's library when the ship upgraded. When Nurse Majors upgraded the ship, some rather shocking romances were suddenly on the shelves." He laid the book back down and patted it. "What I'm saying, Petty Officer, is to remember that you are a sailor in the United States Navy, not a super-hero, as it were. You must fight your enemies differently. The time will come when you can fight them with an ax," he said, giving me a knowing smile, "But the rest of the time, try not to immediately jump to a mutiny."

I nodded again, then laughed and hid my face in my hands, then uncovered it. "Sir, are you the captain again?" Hashem, I hoped so.

"Actually, no. I haven't received my command voice back. Captain Hollander has dubbed me Captain Emeritus Gorman, but I'm just a crewman, now."

"What will you do?" I asked, taken aback. "There can't be two captains."

"Indeed," he said, rising slowly from his chair. "The ship knows it." He gazed out the porthole for many seconds, then looked back to me. "Petty Officer, how old do you think I am?"

"You look to be in your sixties, sir."

"Very good. I was born in 1881. I died in the Second World War." He looked back out the porthole. "I haven't seen my wife and chil-dren in a lifetime. Louise and I were childhood sweethearts. We married under a willow tree on a sunny day. That was rather fancy-free back then, you know." He walked closer to the porthole, never even blinking. "We had three children, and all of them died from Spanish flu in the same week. Theodore, Mary, and Evelyn. Such beautiful children. Louise died of a broken heart that Christmas."

*Where was this coming from?*

"Sir?" I said, pushing back the blankets. "Are you all right?"

"Can you hear them?" He didn't turn his head. "Their voices... I can hear them. They're calling me."

A shadow fell over the room as fog encased the ship, blocking out any view from the porthole. "Sir, I think you should—"

*Rachel.*

The voices that had woken me were near now. Just outside the porthole, even. A thousand voices, no, a million, called to me, singing jubilant songs in a cacophony of languages. Men, women, and children were calling to me, bidding me to come. Among their songs, the sound of my grandparents' voices were clear to hear.

I slid to my feet, and Captain Gorman and I walked out of the sick bay. Dot and Peggy were standing by their station, their eyes glazed over as they listened. They bowed their heads a fraction as we walked past.

Captain Gorman led us down the passageway to the flight deck. We didn't talk. Instead, I just listened to the singing. Such old songs— songs of praise, of happiness, of lost children now found and safe. My brain didn't know the words, but my heart did.

My people were waiting for me.

Captain Gorman opened the final door. A thick bank of fog had encased the entire ship, but instead of the murky cold I knew from life, this fog was warm. Hug-like. Welcoming. In the distance, at the barest edges of my vision, I could make out an island in the fog.

Commander Muree met us on the flight deck. "I hear my brothers," he said softly. "The Muree triplets have been apart for so long." He looked at Captain Gorman. "Ed, it's been an honor."

Captain Gorman bowed his head. "Go. Thank you everything, George."

Commander Muree walked ahead of us, disappearing into the fog. I wasn't sure, but I thought I could just make out the sound of three men shouting for joy.

Captain Gorman took off his hat. "If you excuse me, Petty Officer. I hear my wife calling, and it's rude to leave a lady waiting." Tears were streaming down his face.

"Go on," I said, tears falling down my own without ceasing. "Go."

He left me on the flight deck, disappearing into the fog immediately.

The calls of the people were all around me now. I could hear laughing children, singing women, men calling to each other. I could almost feel them touching me, jostling me in their excitement.

*Come home, Rachel. Come home. It's time. It's time!*

There were two voices I could not hear, and their lack of presence spoke the loudest of all to me.

I closed my eyes. "I want to speak to the fog, please." If the ship could appear as a person, so could the fog.

The shouts fell away. There was a whisper of sound, and then a man's voice said, "I am here."

I opened my eyes. He was hooded and cloaked, his face in shadow. Still, I sensed no danger from him. I pulled my shoulders back. "I made a deal with the ship. I stay on here until my parents pass on. *Then* you come for me."

"The ship has released you from your obligation."

"Why?"

"You did not truly want to stay."

"The terms were that I would stay until my parents died. They haven't changed. I don't want to be seen in bad faith."

He nodded. "Very well."

"One last thing, though."

"Yes?"

"Are you the Angel of Death?" The Angel appeared in many Jewish stories. If this was him, I needed to tread lightly.

I saw the slightest hint of a smile on his lips. "You may call me that, if you wish."

I let out a long breath. "If that's so, how can I be sure that you don't feel cheated or anything? In all our stories, you always end up getting what you feel you're owed." Usually via killing someone in a bloody, ironic way.

"Your contract with the ship supersedes my claim, Rachel Goldstein. There is no cheat here. But don't worry, I'll be back for you before too long." He said it in such a way that it sounded like a consolation, not a threat.

Before I could say anything further, he melted away into the fog. Immediately, the fog rolled back, pulling away from the ship and dissipating like steam. The island was gone, replaced by iron-gray water and the call of seabirds.

I was alone on the flight deck, a small person on a vast sea of tarmac. On the other side of the flight deck, a few sailors were speaking to each other, no doubt recounting whatever it was that they'd heard in the fog.

I dragged my feet all the way to the door again, the pain in my shoulder flaring anew. Peggy and Dot would fuss horribly, but as long as I had a soft bed to land in, I didn't care.

My hand was on the knob when Captain Hollander's voice made me pause. "Petty Officer."

"Captain?" I looked around.

He was lingering in the shadow of a jet, still in his flight suit. He came up to me. "I was out here overseeing repairs on the squadron when the fog rolled in. Did I hear Gorman and Muree with you?"

"They went home, sir."

"And you didn't?"

"I couldn't just go and leave my ship, could I?"

"It's my ship. I'm the captain."

"No, it's my ship. It's the *Rickover*."

He fought a smile. "Agree to disagree." He pulled out a small box from his pocket. "This is yours, by the way. It was salvaged from the room you were found in."

I raised an eyebrow and accepted the box, then opened it. My magic cradle glowed softly, its white light lighting up the area around us. "You saved it!"

"That, and all the spheres, plus enough money to buy a small country." He sighed. "Or should I say, enough money to buy new weapons from the dealers in Port des Morts. Turns out, I personally blew up the security team and all they'd taken with them."

"You don't sound very cut up about it, sir."

"I'm not."

It was my turn to quell a smile. "Thank you for retrieving it, sir." I slipped the necklace over my head and secured it under my collar. "And sir, I really am sorry about what happened. I got a good lecture from Captain Gorman about it. I'll, uh, dial it back in the future."

Captain Hollander nodded. "That's good to hear. And thank *you* for the kick in the pants when I needed it. If there's ever anything I can do, just tell me."

We shared a warm look, and I turned to go back inside. However, a thought struck me, and I turned around. "Sir, there's one thing."

"What is it?"

"I'd like to take some leave while we're near Hampton Roads. Let's stop at a port of call."

---

As BEFORE, I could see the effect of the wind, but I could not feel it. I understood this now to mean that I was not part of this world in the way I'd been before. The sounds didn't meet my ears correctly, nor did the earthy smell of parched grass, fresh dirt, and wilting bouquets of flowers tickle my nose as they would've had I been alive in this place.

I walked through the quiet graveyard, pulled by a preternatural knowledge of where my earthly remains had been interred. Even if I didn't know, it would've been easy to guess; there was a fresh grave in the northwest corner of the cemetery, the simple marker bearing more stones than any other grave around it.

I came to a halt at the foot of my grave. The small marker wasn't the permanent one—that would be installed next year. Instead, a simple plate now bore my name, birth and death dates, and rank in both English and Hebrew. My parents would've had the option to inter my remains at a national cemetery, even the one in Arlington, but they wouldn't have entertained any other choice besides the Jewish cemetery near our home. Surprisingly, they'd honored my career by placing an anchor on the marker.

I kneeled down and brushed my fingers over the stones left by my mourners, which were so many that the plot appeared to be cobble-stoned. I'd had many friends in life, people from school, my synagogue, my neighborhood, and other places. My family would've flown in from all over the country.

What had they said at my funeral? The older adults would've whispered to each other that my parents were *horim shakulim*, orphaned parents. How sad, they would've said. Perhaps death will come to them early, they would've whispered. Their only child, lost so young, so tragically.

I removed my Bronze Star letter from my pocket and laid it on my grave. There it would stay, forever, unless I or another ghost removed it. I stood and inhaled deeply, trying to lock onto a scent. Perhaps my mother had been here recently and her perfume was wafting on the breeze.

I'd prepared a message for my parents, as formal as the letter I'd just laid down. But I needed it to be formal—otherwise there was a high risk of me crying while I spoke. Formality provided distance.

"I have a message for all of you," I said. "I'm speaking to the living, and I know my words will stay here long after I've gone back. I forgive you for the words you said when I joined the Navy. You spoke in anger and fear. You called me selfish and ungrateful. Let me assure you that I have never been ungrateful for all you gave me. As for being selfish, I don't think it's wrong for an adult to follow their heart and make a way for themselves in the world. But please know that I've left this letter here as a testament to the honor I will always try to bring my family."

My family would come here again and again, and perhaps, deep down, they'd hear the sentiment echoing down through the realms, landing in their heart and entrenching themselves there. A blessing from the beyond, my soul kissing them.

The breeze picked up, and I looked up at the green leaves of the tree that stood guard over my grave. My liberty period was almost up —it was time to leave.

I closed my eyes and felt myself slide back through space, onto the gangplank of the *Rickover*. The quiet of the cemetery was replaced by the clamor of bells, whistles, sailors calling to each other, and jets taxiing on the flight deck. Nearby, in the hangar bay, sailors were forming up in their dress whites for the exit into the Oceanus again.

I walked up the gangplank and signed back onto the ship. The liberty officer snapped his logbook shut. "You're the last one. Go get into formation."

I was already in my dress whites, knowing that this moment was coming. Besides, I wouldn't have visited my grave in anything less.

One of the chiefs blew a whistle and directed us to stand along-side the edge of the ship, at the rails. "Hold out your arms and stand arm's length apart, then stand at parade rest."

I took my place at the rail, gazing out at Naval Station Norfolk. Across from us, the living dockworkers were preparing the dock for the USS *Taft*, which was scheduled to come in to dock today. I could see it out in the river, slicing through the water.

The *Rickover*'s horn blew. A dockworker piling rope at a pillar stopped and looked over his shoulder.

We began to move, silently sliding away from the dock, unencumbered by the friction from this world. I stood at parade rest, my face blank. Captain Hollander had ordered this ceremony, one last nod to the ship the four of us had called home.

We neared the *Taft*, and I almost broke into a grin. A glowing figure was sitting on the rails, waving to us. Rollins was still in his bloodstained uniform, but otherwise he looked great.

Bit by bit, the ships passed each other, so close, yet so far—separated by the sheer but ironclad veil of death. I held my head up a little higher. The *Taft* was coming home from deployment in despair, bruised and bleeding from the heavy losses she had taken. Little did they know that four of their own were still sailing, in a way more alive than we'd ever been. The fighting spirit of the Navy.

Soon the ship was behind us, and we were in the open ocean. Virginia Beach passed us, the tall hotels and attractions of the boardwalk bright and clear to all. My senior prom had been in one of those hotels. I'd been in the queen's court. That part of me was now buried in a cemetery in Norfolk. The deeper part of me, the eternal part, was what remained.

The ship picked up speed, and then I felt the pressure of the weak spot all around me. Virginia Beach grew smaller, a fractured image inside an endless sea of lost souls.

Well, not all were lost. I knew exactly where I was.

I was where I was supposed to be.

### THE END

---

THANK you for reading *Sea of Lost Souls*! If you enjoyed the journey, please consider leaving a review on Amazon. The review rating determines which books of mine receive sequels, so if you want more books in the Oceanus series, please leave a review!

Are you ready for the next chapter in Rachel's story? The next books is called *House of the Setting Sun*, and it will debut in late 2019. In the mean time, keep reading for a preview of my superhero urban fantasy series, Battlecry.

# ACKNOWLEDGMENTS

A second series isn't easier to write than the first, and I must acknowledge the people who helped me along the way.

First and foremost, all glory and thanks to our Lord Jesus Christ. Without daily prayer for inspiration and guidance, I wouldn't have gotten anywhere.

Secondly, I dedicated this book to Sarah Spivak for a reason—it's her book more than mine. Sarah, I never could've written *Sea of Lost Souls* without your incredible and never-ending support. You put up with my dumber questions, answered everything with patience and understanding, and helped form a beautiful narrator. I hope that Rachel is the kind of character you would've wanted to read growing up, and that you saw a measure of yourself in her.

Special thanks go out to Angela Sanders, my editor. Angela, you're proof that God is real. I never could've dreamed that my editor would be a retired Chief. You brought this book to the next level, and I'm terribly eager to keep working with you. Similarly, special thanks go out to my beta readers Katherine and Emily. Your comments helped mold this story into something really great.

Many, many thanks go out to my husband Alex. One half of Rachel was formed by your stories of being in the nuclear navy, and I hope that you also found someone to root for in the nukes I created for you. I love your navy stories. Being married to you is a great adventure all by itself.

Finally, endless thanks go out to my fans and readers. You're why I do this, and I adore you all.

# ABOUT THE AUTHOR

Emerald Dodge lives with her husband Alex and their two sons. Emerald and Alex enjoy playing with their children, date nights, hosting dinner parties for their friends, and watching movies. They are a Navy family and look forward to traveling around the nation and meeting new people. When she's not writing, Emerald likes to cook, bake, go to Mass, pray the rosary, and FaceTime with her relatives.

Her favorite social media platform for interacting with fans is Tumblr. Message her on her Tumblr page!

If you'd like to receive Emerald's newsletter, please sign up here. Emerald regularly sends out newsletters with updates on her books, exclusive book promotions, and book bargains.

# EMERALD DODGE

WHO SAVES
A HERO?

BATTLECRY SERIES – BOOK 1

# BATTLECRY

# ABOUT BATTLECRY

For one superhero, the good guys can be deadlier than the bad guys.

Jillian Johnson, known as the mighty Battlecry, was born into a superhero cult. She craves a life of freedom, far away from her violent and abusive team leader, Patrick. With no education, no money, and no future to speak of, she's stuck in the dangerous life... until she meets the mysterious and compelling Benjamin, a civilian with superpowers. When Patrick confronts her, she fights back--and then runs for her life. One by one, her ex-teammates join her until a new team has formed.

But Patrick will not let his upstart teammates get away so easily. Humiliated and hellbent on vengeance, he waits for his chance to strike back and kill the new team, and he is happy to murder super-heroes and civilians alike. On top of that, Benjamin has joined Jillian and her comrades, angering his own lethal family. Jillian's enemies begin to close in from all sides.

Desperate and in hiding, Jillian must shed everything she thinks she knows about what it means to lead. Can she rise up to the challenge of defeating Patrick? Can she save Benjamin from his family? Or will she die like every other superhero who's dared to challenge the cult?

*If you like the gritty, understated superheroes in Netflix's* Jessica Jones *and the raw urban fantasy of Veronica Roth, you'll get sucked into Emerald Dodge's* Battlecry!

**Pick up Battlecry, and join Jillian's team today!**

# BATTLECRY - CHAPTER ONE

The eighteenth bomb exploded.

Flattened against a wall beside a stinking dumpster, I crouched and maneuvered my finger beneath the fabric of my mask to remove a piece of shrapnel caught there. I was so grateful the media couldn't photograph superheroes.

A nineteenth bomb exploded down the street.

I straightened and peered around the corner. The bombs didn't frighten me. I'd faced worse in my six months as a superhero on my city's team. Adrenaline surged through me during battles leaving no room for fear. My teammates were out there. A volley of explosions had forced us to scatter fifteen minutes before. They now hid somewhere among the twisted wreckage, abandoned ambulances and police vehicles, smoking shells of cars, and shards of glass. Before I made any decisions, I had to know their whereabouts and condition.

I sprinted across the broken road. The blood rushed in my ears so loudly I could barely hear the maniac's yells from where he stood on top of the overturned armored car. Civilians huddled sporadically around the scene, clinging to each other. Others were pinned beneath rubble, trapped there when the man's fireballs exploded and threw out shrapnel.

My quick glances towards the armored car revealed that I stood the closest to the masked bomber, since I couldn't see anyone else. It was up to me to do something, even though I was just as vulnerable to fireballs as the rest of my teammates. I didn't mind the death-inviting responsibility. My teammates were, with one exception, far more likable than me. My death wouldn't make that much of an impact.

I'd already counted four burned bodies. If the gathering clouds overhead emptied themselves on us, we'd have storm damage to deal with on top of bombs and mangled people pinned under rock and twisted steel.

Skidding to a halt behind a cement planter in front of the ravaged bank, I crouched as low as I could and surveyed the scene. Craters and broken cars covered the wide downtown avenue. Large enough to accommodate traffic for Saint Catherine's population of a quarter million, it was now a daunting battlefield.

Skyscrapers loomed large above me, though they provided little shade against the late-morning sun that blazed down despite the increasingly ominous threat of a storm. The summer heat, Georgia's defining seasonal attribute, pressed me from all sides. Not for the first time, I wished my fighting clothes were any other color besides black. I wiped sweat off my face with a gloved hand and peered around the planter.

I'd been smart to change locations, because I could now see three of my teammates, busy climbing over wreckage. My fourth teammate, our leader Patrick, was nowhere in sight, but I knew that he'd never be far from the Destructor. At least, I thought that was the name the bomber had shouted at us over the screaming of civilians when Patrick had ordered him to identify himself.

I'd had to suppress the urge to laugh; since when did supervillains have codenames like us? And if they were going to pick codenames, why pick one so *dumb*?

The Destructor lobbed another explosive at an unseen person in the distance. Not risking a melee, I picked up a tennis ball-sized rock and waited for the right moment. A rock thrown at just the right spot would knock him down long enough for me to take him out. Between my enhanced strength, speed, and agility, I wouldn't miss my target.

He whipped around and looked directly at me. "Did you think I wouldn't notice you?" he shouted as another blazing orb appeared in his hand.

I ran, my speed allowing me to barely escape the blast. Shards of glass and stone soared past my head, and a searing burn on the back of my neck followed by a wet trickle alerted me to a fresh wound. I'd have to deal with it later.

I dove behind a car with bloody handprints on the door. I peered through the window— he was looking my way. There was no hiding now.

Beneath his red-and-black mask, his eyes gleamed with the anticipation of my death. For a fraction of a second I felt both insulted that he was trying to kill me and invigorated that something was finally happening, though both were stupid reactions at a time like this, or any other time.

"Come out and fight," he said with a snarl, another glowing ball already in his hand. "A dead little girl would brighten my day."

I pursed my lips, since I knew better than to correct him. If he thought a twenty-year-old was a "little girl," then he'd already underestimated me. I needed him just cocky enough that he'd make a fatal error.

The Destructor jumped off the armored car and sauntered towards me, bandying his fireball about as if it were a beach ball. I slowly unsheathed the knife on my belt. Just a few yards closer, and I could throw it into his shoulder with such accuracy that I could sever the nerves without damaging an artery. He'd have quite a time hurling fireballs if he couldn't move his shoulder.

He stopped and tossed a fireball from halfway across the street. Once more, I ran for cover.

I was fifteen yards from the car when it exploded.

The blast threw me into a crumbling brick wall that promptly collapsed, unable to withstand both the shockwave and my weight. I tumbled a few times and the knife sliced my leg. I lay face down on the ground for a moment. A ringing sounded in my ears. Adding insult to injury, it started to rain.

"Battlecry, you okay?"

I heard the words from somewhere but the flashing lights in my vision distracted me from figuring out who said them. Weirdly, my dislike of my codename was the first thing I thought of while my vision cleared. I much preferred to be called Jillian.

The ground trembled, followed by walls of dirt and stone springing up between the Destructor and me. Earth-moving--Reid's power. It had to have been him who'd spoken. With shaking arms, I pushed myself off the ground. A sharp pain ran through my right shoulder, and I winced. Likely it was a sprain—it wasn't the first time I'd received such an injury. Fighting would to be that much more difficult for the next few weeks.

"I'm okay." I flashed the thumbs-up to where he stood on a levitating piece of pavement. He returned the gesture and, after straightening his blue mask and cracking his knuckles, flew away in the direction of a large car pile-up.

Screams filled the air again. Around the earthen wall, the

Destructor bore down on a group of three injured businessmen huddled against the side of an overturned hot-dog cart. Cursing, I unsheathed another of my knives and prepared to charge him.

The Destructor threw his fireball. It sailed through the air in a perfect arc with a horrific hissing noise. The businessmen closed their eyes.

The fireball hit an invisible wall and disintegrated into thousands of sparks.

Patrick was here.

He emerged from behind a pile of rubble, his inhuman fury visible even from a distance. I swallowed the lump in my throat and returned behind the dirt wall, listening to Patrick and the Destructor trade curses. Every time the Destructor attacked, Patrick shot back an enraged response and I held my breath, my whole body tensed and ready to run far, far away. But I didn't run—I stood in my little enclave, clawing at my brain for a plan.

Footsteps a few feet beyond my hiding place made me look up.

Marco rushed in. "Hiding, B? I'll join you," he said, panting. "That guy nearly turned me into pudding and now Patrick is working on him."

An ugly gash marred his face, and blood dripped onto his ripped tunic. One of his sleeves had been completely torn off. He looked every inch the hardened fighter the public expected us to be, instead of what he really was: a seventeen-year-old who'd lied about his age to the police when he'd registered with the city.

"I'm not hiding," I snapped. "I'm planning. And don't call him his real name right now."

Patrick caught the Destructor's volleys and crushed them in psychic force fields—apparently the rain made the bombs more manageable. Sweat beaded on his forehead as he directed all his physical strength into his telekinesis. The only one of us who went unmasked, he looked even angrier than before. Rumbling thunder overhead completed the picture.

"Planning," I repeated, more to myself than Marco. *You're a super-hero, Jillian. Do something.*

"Plan something fast. *Atropos* is furious that this is taking so long."

I couldn't help but smile at Marco's tone when he said our leader's goddess-themed codename. "What makes you say that?"

Already Marco's presence had lifted my mood, but his words worried me.

Instead of speaking, he merely tapped his temple.

Ah, Ember. The team telepath had told him.

"Great." There was more acid in my voice than I intended. "Can you blind him?"

Marco harnessed solar power and could redirect the heat and light. One good blast of concentrated sunlight would end the fight... although he rarely unleashed his power like that in public because of the risk of blinding a civilian or one of us.

Marco shook his head. "No, too many people are around, and even if there weren't, it's too dark from the cloud cover. I've used so much of my reserves already cutting through rock and steel that I'm practically going cold."

I held the back of my hand to his forehead—he did feel cooler than usual. My heart sank. This fight was probably going to drag on for hours.

"We need to get in the air." I glanced up to see if I could spot my skinny twenty-two-year-old teammate on his flying pavement.

Marco lowered his voice. "Em told me Atropos said he needed to get people out of the rubble."

I frowned. "Where is Ember, anyway?"

*I'm helping out with the rescue effort.* Ember's mental voice filled the back of my mind in the strange whisper-echo tone of telepathy. *And now that I have your attention, Patrick's got some orders for you.*

*Of course he does.* The rain started falling harder, which didn't help my mood. *Have you been eavesdropping on me? I hate that.*

*Not now, Jill. Please. And I was in Marco's mind and heard your question.*

*Fine. What does Patrick want me to do?* I crossed my arms, hoping the attitude came across.

*He says go to the top of the Bell Building and signal when you're up there. I'll give you the rest of the orders when you're on the roof.*

*No! No more open-ended orders. Remember last time? I got shot because he didn't tell me a gang meeting would be going on.*

*Stop being an idiot! This kind of crap from you is why he's the way he is. And besides, the bullet only grazed you.*

I told her where she could put his orders.

*Jill, listen to me. I get that you don't like not knowing what you're running into, but please think of the rest of us. You're not the only one on this team.*

My resolve crumbled and was replaced by guilt. Ember didn't deserve my anger. *Okay, fine.* My shoulders sagged, causing a searing pain that took my breath away.

*Thank you.* A long pause followed—she'd slipped out of my mind for a few seconds. *The Destructor's not thinking about you at all. If you act fast, you can probably get to the entrance of the Bell Building without attracting his notice.*

I explained to Marco what I was about to do, then took a deep breath. With only a glance to double-check that my way remained clear and unseen, I started the hundred-yard dash, darting behind cars, massive upturned pieces of steaming pavement, and other large items that littered the street. The weather worked in my favor; the rain acted as a curtain of sorts and the howling wind, thunder, and cracks of lightning disguised my footfalls.

I jumped through the shattered glass doors of the Bell Building into the cool dimness of the marble lobby. Though glass and bits of marble littered the floor, it remained relatively untouched. Even the hidden speakers still worked, playing a tuneless melody that offices seem to prefer.

A snuffling noise came from behind the reception desk, and behind it was a woman curled up next to her desk chair, weeping softly.

"Where's the stairwell?" I demanded, trying to project authority with sopped clothes and hair plastered to my face.

She pointed a shaking finger to a door at the end of the foyer. I thanked her and ran to it, gearing up for a sprint up twenty-five flights of stairs.

I arrived on the roof, panting and wincing from the burning pain in my shoulder. I stumbled to the edge and located Patrick below, a dark little figure surrounded by tiny floating items. He had moved to the top of the armored car. The Destructor was desperately trying to land a hit on him, but Patrick's telekinesis wasn't allowing it. Dozens of fireballs sailed through the air and dissolved into steaming, fizzling sparks when they hit Patrick's shield.

"Hey, Atropos! *Atropos!* I'm up here!"

He didn't turn around. The storm drowned out my shouts.

I flicked open a pouch on my belt with an aggravated sigh, pulling out a small flare and igniting it. After waving it for a few seconds, Patrick noticed me. He shouted something to Reid. For a moment I couldn't tell what Reid was doing, but then—

"Oh, hell," I breathed.

The ground rumbled and shook. A small patch of earth sprang up under the Destructor, six feet wide but soaring hundreds of feet into the air—far too quickly for the Destructor to jump to the ground. My team hurried from their locations to the base of the tower to watch.

Ember's presence tickled the back of my mind once again. *I picked up from him that he's afraid of heights when he was standing on the armored car, so we're lifting him up to throw him out of his comfort zone. Patrick wants you to give him a beat down.*

The mental image of me kicking the Destructor in the stomach over and over again while he begged for mercy flitted across my mind. That wasn't my fantasy but Patrick's, relayed by Ember.

Of course. How many times had Patrick used me as the team's muscle? Sure, Reid could control lava, Marco could harness the *sun*, and Patrick himself could move things with his mind. Heck, even Ember was one of the few superhumans lucky enough to have two powers, telepathy and control over animals. Our leader had made it clear to me that I was useful for my fists and nothing more. I ignored the leaden weight in my chest and geared up for the fight, my feet automatically sliding into a defensive stance.

The earthen tower reached the roof and stopped. The Destructor huddled on it in the fetal position. Ember had downplayed his feelings about heights. He wasn't just afraid, he had a phobia. Beneath my surging adrenaline lurked something almost like pity, because a trembling, sniveling adversary just wasn't respectable.

Still, I'd rather have jumped off the Bell Building than reveal my true feelings to a supervillain. I stuffed down my pity and worked my face into a steely glare.

I jumped from the roof onto the muddy tower, my boots skidding on the wet pavement and only stopping an inch from his head. He yelped.

"Scared?" I sneered. I lifted him by his shirt with my one working arm, the blood pounding in my ears. "Good."

I threw him off the tower onto the roof and then jumped after him. He scrambled backwards and held up a hand. "Don't come any closer! I'll—I'll blow us up!"

"You'd have done it already," I said coolly. Energy manipulation like bomb-making virtually always required the Super to have working hands, so without a word I stomped on the hand clutching the ground with my steel-soled boot while simultaneously crushing the hand he was holding up with my own vise grip. Despite my pity, the crunches and his cry of anguish were highly satisfying.

I mentally reviewed the steps I was supposed to take next. Punch, kick, maim, the usual. But this pathetic man was down, and doing anything else just seemed...*mean*. I looked at him while he cradled his useless fingers and marveled at the irony of someone so powerful being so weak at the same time.

"You disgust me." I put my hands on my hips, ignoring his sobs. "I've been told to kick your head in, but I think you've learned your lesson. The police will be here in a few minutes. Have fun in prison."

I turned to go to the edge and signal the all-clear. The moment my back was to him, he swiped a leg under my own and I fell.

My injured shoulder took the brunt of the fall, and my head bounced against the ground. He awkwardly ran towards the edge. My groan turned into a growl of anger. That had been a rookie mistake.

"Get back here!" I yelled, jumping up and blinking away white spots in my vision.

He glanced back at me, eyes wide, his fear of heights battling his fear of me. I bridged the gap between us and grabbed his wrist just as he went over the side of the building.

"Let me go," he pleaded, crying again. "I can't spend the rest of my life in the Supers' prison! Have some mercy on a fellow Super." His wide eyes were slick with terror, but the shooting pain in my shoulder reduced my previous pity to dust. I just wanted this disgusting man out of my sight.

"You didn't show any mercy to the people down there," I replied with some difficulty, as he wriggled and pulled against me. Normally pulling a man up with one arm wouldn't have been a problem, but the pain in my shoulder compromised my strength. A deafening crash of thunder preceded even more sheets of rain. Rivulets of water ran down my arm onto his, making my grasp slippery. A few more minutes of this tug-of-war and the Destructor would get his wish.

*Patrick says drop him.*

"Shut up, Ember!" I yelled into the storm.

*Patrick will catch him.*

*Yeah, right.* Powerful as Patrick was, he struggled to catch falling people—as we'd witnessed during a suicide two months earlier. Gritting my teeth and cursing the Destructor's ancestors, I ignored Ember's further protests and with a burst of effort pulled the Destructor back over the edge. A quick punch to the temple knocked him out cold.

*He's down.*

Adrenaline drained out of my system and left a cold creep in my veins, the same creep I felt after every mistake and poor judgment call. Though I could feel Ember in my mind, she said nothing. When the police arrived on the roof, I didn't leave the scene until they asked me to.

Back on the street, Patrick was surrounded by soaked teenage girls holding umbrellas and a copy of a tabloid that had done a feature on "Saint Catherine's Heroic Heartthrob." After signing autographs, he fielded questions from reporters. Their ability to converge at a scene just minutes after an incident never failed to amaze me.

One particularly aggressive woman pushed her way to the front and stuck a microphone in his face. "Atropos, how did you feel when you were fighting the Destructor?"

He ducked his head, grinning sheepishly. "Well, every fight is a thrill and a challenge. I didn't have any time to be scared for myself, though. I'm always one hundred percent concerned about the safety of my team and the citizens of Saint Catherine."

Another reporter pushed his way to the front of the throng. "Atropos, our readers want to know what it's like being the leader of a superhero team."

Patrick's crooked grin made several girls giggle. "It's the best job in the world. My team loves me, I love them, and we're a well-oiled machine." His eyes flickered towards me.

Nobody else seemed to notice his momentary glare, though Ember clutched my hand. *I'm here for you no matter what happens.*

The reporter referred to her notes. "Our viewers voted on our final question: any tips for prospective superhero leaders out there?"

What a stupid question. You were born into our life or you weren't, and leadership was for men in elder families only.

He laughed. "Sure. Lead with a firm hand, and you'll have the respect of your team and your city."

The rest of us looked on in the rain while Patrick fed the crowd his smooth replies. We made sure to never stop smiling for the public in case they looked our way, just as we'd been told for years.

After all, if we didn't smile, people might guess the truth about us.

# BATTLECRY - CHAPTER TWO

"Jeez, Jill. What did you do to yourself?"

Marco examined my shoulder.

My cousin and I were in the sick bay, a cramped room with peeling white paint, lined with wooden shelves of medicines, pain relievers, bandages, and other supplies. The only furniture was a chair and an examination table made of a material that always stuck to my skin.

"I didn't do it to myself." I was unable to keep the bitterness from my voice. "A bomb knocked me into a brick wall and then that freak gave me trouble on the roof."

He prodded my shoulder and frowned deeper. "Well, you were right, it's a sprain. You're going to be in a sling for a while. I don't like the look of those cuts in your neck and leg, either." He took an arm sling off the shelf and handed it to me. We'd made Marco the team's official medic, simply because he had read more first-aid pamphlets than the rest of us. He'd even understood a few of them.

"That's just excellent," I muttered, putting the sling on and securing it. "Every team needs a useless member."

Marco casually redid my attempt to secure the sling. "Stop that. Nobody on this team will ever be useless."

I sighed, then pointed to the ugly gash that marred his light brown face. "Does that still hurt?"

He playfully smacked my hand away from his face. "Yeah, but I'm going to have a cool scar to brag about, so who cares?"

The front door slammed. We froze.

"Maybe all the swooning girls improved his mood," I whispered. Patrick's stomping footsteps through the house caused my heart to pound.

"In my office, *now!*" Patrick's harsh tones made my mouth go dry. His tone made him sound much older than twenty-five.

Marco visibly swallowed. "Maybe a missile will hit the house in the next sixty seconds," he whispered back. He helped me off the table and gave my shoulder one last worried glance. "Let's go."

We walked to Patrick's office and were joined outside the door by Ember and Reid. Ember's long red hair still smelled of smoke and death, and her skin was even paler than usual. She wouldn't meet my eyes. Reid's mouth formed a thin line, and his gray eyes contained the same hard apprehension that curdled in my stomach.

I took a deep breath and opened the door. We all filed in.

Inside, Patrick, tall and blond and terrifying, sat on the edge of his desk with his arms crossed, a look so chilling on his face that I had to fight the urge to step back. "Shut the door."

Everyone flinched, but he spoke only to me.

I closed the door as quietly as I could, trying not to seem fazed.

Patrick looked directly at me. "Jillian, we're going to talk about what happened today."

I gathered my nerve. "We fought the Destructor and won. Because we followed your orders."

Everyone nodded and murmured agreement. Patrick's eyes narrowed. I struggled to keep my breathing steady. Already my fight-or-flight instinct was screaming at me to escape.

"If you followed my orders, why didn't you drop the Destructor?"

The question cut into my core. My eyes itched with tears, but if I let them fall, he'd say I couldn't control myself.

"Because, um..." My gaze darted around the room as I tried to stifle the shame that my team had to watch what was coming. "Because..."

Patrick abruptly stood and took a step towards me. Everyone else moved back. "Because what, Jill?"

My mind was racing. I couldn't pick out a coherent answer. Patrick was my leader and I had to listen to him. As a member of a non-elder family in the camp, my position in life was to be under another person's authority at all times. No exceptions. To defy the authority of my leader was unthinkable—practically as unforgivable as defying an elder directly. The turmoil of being at a loss for words began building up inside of me.

"I was worried he wouldn't make it," I finally blurted. "A lot was going on and it was a long fall, you know."

An invisible force slammed me into the wall.

"How many times do I have to tell you that you *do not have permission to question my orders*?" He strode towards me. "You *stupid*, insignificant piece of crap! I let you stay here and this is how you repay me? This is how you treat me? Who are you to question what I'm capable of?"

"I didn't mean it like that, I swear!" The words struggled to come out through the pressure on my chest and neck. I couldn't control the tears any longer, and my fear transformed into naked humiliation that my team was watching me not just get punished, but cry about it like a child.

"Then how did you mean it? Were you questioning my authority?" His fist clenched.

Reid moved to stop him, but pulled back his hand after a second, doubt and fear warring on his face.

"I'm sorry," I managed to whisper as I hung my head, tears dripping down my nose. "I just...I didn't want him to die."

"What have I told you? Nobody cares about what you want!" The invisible hand of Patrick's telekinesis threw me into a bookshelf, where several heavy tomes of *Leadership and Wisdom* fell on top of me and made my shoulder light up with excruciating pain.

I squeezed my eyes shut, willing myself to stay still. If I kept quiet, there was no way he could think I was fighting his discipline. Marco rushed over to help me up. His hand brushed the laceration at the back of my neck and I could tell that it had opened up again.

"You're going to make her shoulder worse," Ember said, her voice shaking.

She crashed into the desk. "Now *you're* questioning me?"

My chin lifted against my will, forcing me to look into his hard blue eyes. New tears appeared. The telekinetic force grabbed my collar and hoisted me to my feet. The chalkboard we used for strategy notations floated over and landed next to me. My fingers plucked a piece of chalk from the air.

Patrick crossed his arms. "Draw the chain of command and explain it to us. I want to hear from your own mouth that you know our law."

I gulped and started sketching, struggling to control my trembling hand. "The chain of command is like an umbrella," I began, using the same words my teachers had used over the years. "Elders are at the top, followed by team leaders, then your father and mother." I drew a crude likeness of an umbrella and sectioned it horizontally, labeling the lines. The umbrella analogy was very old, created when people in the camps still had umbrellas.

"Go on." He gestured for me to continue.

"If you go out from under the umbrella, you'll be exposed to danger. If you mix up the parts of the umbrella, the umbrella won't work and you'll also be exposed to danger."

Patrick nodded. "Tell me the core character traits of a good superhero."

Those had been drilled into me since I was three. "Obedience, joy, loyalty, and silence."

"Tell us how you will model all these traits during our next mission." His voice was suddenly softer.

I breathed easier now that his ire appeared to be fading. "I'll obey you without question. I'll do so happily because you're my leader, and I'm loyal only to you. And, um, I won't talk much?" Silence had always struck me as an odd concept to call a "trait."

Patrick's face relaxed and he rolled his neck. "You guys all know I don't enjoy these types of meetings. But I carry the burden of leadership. If you don't obey, it is my responsibility to discipline you." He looked at Ember. "Em, we're going to have a discussion tomorrow about interrupting me during discipline sessions."

She gulped and nodded. Even though I could still feel the tingle in my injuries from his punishment just minutes ago, I had to quash the desire to beg him to not hurt Ember, too. Was I demented?

With that, he turned on his heel and walked out of the room. I'd survived.

We were all slow to move.

"At least he only wanted the four traits. I'd have been screwed if I had to list the principles under pressure," Marco said, erasing my drawing on the board and sliding it back to its storage place.

"I can review them with you," Reid offered, gently brushing chalk dust off my arm. "Cautiousness, deference, deci—"

Ember bent down to help me pick up the books that had fallen. "Spare us. That's the last thing we need right now. Jill, how're you doing?"

"My shoulder hurts," I mumbled, trying not to sniffle. "I'm going to go to the clinic." The free clinic downtown was our answer to injuries that basic first aid couldn't address. Most of their patients came in with gunshot wounds and knives sticking out of them, so they didn't ask questions about things like broken bones, sprains, or serious burns.

"Are you well enough to walk?" Marco started to fuss over my injuries again, but seeing the hard look I gave him, he stepped back. We finished putting away the books in silence, and I hobbled to my room.

Before I headed to the clinic, I would need to change into civilian clothes. As I undressed, I laid my uniform out on my bed: gray mask, bulletproof vest, khaki pants, utility belt, combat boots, and black gloves, undershirt, and hooded tunic. Gazing down at my battered, bloody uniform, I briefly thought about what it would be like to never put it on again. I was blessed with powers and the chance to defend innocent people with them, and here I was, disobeying my leader and daydreaming about abandoning my team. Loyalty, I reminded myself.

I pulled on a pair of worn jeans and comforted myself by putting on a pretty blouse speckled with blue flowers, the latter with some difficulty because of my sprain. After gently unwinding my regulation waist-length hair from its messy bun, I sat on the edge of my bed and brushed it.

I caught a glimpse of myself in a windowpane. Bruises and cuts crisscrossed my thin, pale face like splattered paint, though they couldn't distract from an obvious black eye, a leftover from a fight a few days prior. My thick hair was such a dark brown it was almost black, and it was matted with dirt, blood, and who knew what else. It was painfully clear that I wasn't pretty on the outside and, as Patrick was fond of reminding me, I was too obstinate and impulsive to be pretty on the inside.

After braiding my hair tightly in two sections, I scrubbed my face and put on foundation over the black eye, which didn't really conceal it. I topped off my disguise with thick-framed glasses that slightly obscured my dark brown eyes. I took a moment to gaze at my reflection, and all I could see was an unfortunate young woman, as forgettable as she was powerless.

Before I left base camp, I signed out in our log, writing my name, the date, time, location I was going to, and how long I expected to be gone. With any luck, my outing would be unremarkable.

# BATTLECRY - CHAPTER THREE

T he downpour mirrored my mood while I walked towards the clinic. I mentally dared every hypothetical mugger and rapist to try me, but I walked down the street in miserable safety. I kicked a soda can into the gutter.

I'd said I'd be gone for an hour. The clock was ticking.

When I arrived at the double doors with the large red cross on them, I only paused for a second before continuing on my way down the street. I didn't know where I was going. I passed the park where I'd once stopped a shooting, the office building where I'd chased a man who could chew metal and spit it out like bullets—three people died that day—and the road that led to the bridge where just six months ago I first met Patrick, Ember, and Reid. An ice storm had encased the city—Marco and I had been dispatched to help the other three, and our team had finally become complete.

Soaked to the skin and shivering uncontrollably, I turned down Davis Street, a fancy neighborhood filled with boutiques, specialty bookstores, and ritzy little restaurants that catered to the city's wealthiest.

As I approached a coffee shop called Café Stella, a customer opened the door with a jingle, and the swirling aromas of coffee and spices enticed me to enter. My hand met the door handle.

There was no way to justify this act of rebellion. What if a teammate saw me? But the café looked so warm and cozy, I decided to step in. Just for a minute or two. Patrick couldn't punish me too harshly for just wanting to step out of the rain.

The café was almost empty. The glass counter off to the side held rows of glistening pastries filled with chocolate and jams. Two glass jars on top of the counter were labeled "biscotti" and "amaretti." Other jars showed off types of cookies for which I had no name. Behind the counter hung a chalkboard listing the café's offerings. With a stab of embarrassment, I realized I didn't know most of the words. What the heck was a macchiato?

The digital clock on the microwave reminded me that I had forty-five minutes left.

"What would you like, sweetheart?" The middle-aged man behind the counter smiled at me. His name tag read Lee. I bit my lip.

"I've never had fancy coffee before," I admitted. "What's your most popular?"

Actually, I'd never had coffee, period. It wasn't available in the camp where I'd grown up, and if it had been, we probably wouldn't have been allowed to drink it. Elder St. James often lectured to children that anything that alters the mind, besides medication, was dangerous, though he never explained why. The coffee smelled so good, and the old lady in the corner who sipped on a large mug seemed to enjoy it.

He thought for a moment. "If you've never had a specialty drink,

I'll start you off with a latte. It's just coffee and milk, so if you want something more, I can give you some syrup or chocolate."

He poured my coffee and gave it to me with a wink. I handed him my money, donated by a thankful almost-victim of an armed robbery, and sat in the corner on a squishy loveseat, grateful for Patrick's generosity. He allowed us to keep three percent of any money donated to team members. Because I didn't spend often, I'd accrued about twenty dollars in six months.

Before I indulged in the coffee, I took one last glimpse around me to make sure nobody was watching.

A fashion and entertainment magazine rested on the table next to the loveseat. I turned it over so as to not be tempted to look at it, because looking at media not sanctioned by the camp elders was a very serious infraction, far more serious than sipping coffee. Coffee just temporarily intoxicated the mind. Most, if not all, movies, television, books, music, and magazines could pollute it forever. If I thought hard enough, I could probably trace my character flaws to some rock song I'd overheard while grocery shopping with Ember.

I settled back into the loveseat and started flipping through memories, looking for a song or image that had left a bruise in my psyche. I took a sip from my latte. It was bitter, but I decided I liked it.

The door of the café opened again with its friendly jingle.

"Hey, Lee!"

I looked over to see a handsome young man about my age walk in with a thick book in his hand.

Lee looked up from cleaning a coffee pot and grinned. "Benjamin! How are you?"

Lee and Benjamin shook hands and chattered for a few minutes. I didn't normally listen in on civilian conversation, but Benjamin's deep voice and bracing northern accent were pleasant to listen to.

Lee pointed to the menu. "So what'll it be? I've got all the usual stuff and the new seasonal menu. Three new pastries, too."

Benjamin waved his hand. "Just my usual order, thanks. I'll take a chocolate croissant, though."

"You got it." Lee got to work, and I couldn't help but notice that Benjamin's "usual" involved a lot of chocolate syrup.

After Benjamin paid for his order and took it from Lee, he looked around for a place to sit. I returned to mentally reviewing all the civilian songs I'd ever heard—it wasn't a long list.

Far in the distance, many blocks over, wailing sirens made me pause in my thoughts and turn my ear towards the door. No explosions or gunshots...probably just an accident. Civilian authorities preferred that we wait until called in for those.

"Do you mind if I join you?"

I startled and looked up.

Benjamin stood next to me, smiling pleasantly. He gestured to the empty spot on the loveseat. "Not to be weird or anything, but the loveseat is the best spot in the place."

I doubted that. An identical couch sat in another corner near a pretty girl with spectacular hoop earrings. She'd been shooting glances at Benjamin since he'd come in.

I scooted closer to the arm of the loveseat, my own automatic smile stretching my face as I made room. "Er, no, that's fine. Make yourself comfortable." I certainly wasn't comfortable. Speaking with normal people outside of strict superhero business was so forbidden I half expected to spontaneously combust.

He sat. "Thanks." He stuck out his hand. "I'm Benjamin."

I awkwardly shook his hand with my left, a thrill shooting up my arm when he touched me. "I'm Jillian. Sorry about the sling."

He did a double take. "No apologies necessary. If you don't mind my asking, what happened? You look like you went through a harvester. Er, I mean, you look fine," he said sheepishly.

His embarrassment was touching. "Don't worry, I know I look bad. I got hurt at work today."

Benjamin's face hardened for a moment but then smoothed over. "I'm sorry to hear that."

I lifted my left shoulder in a shrug. "It happens."

We sat in silence for a few seconds. I tried to rework my face into something other than a grin. He seemed to search for a topic of conversation.

I glanced at the microwave. Thirty-three minutes.

Finally, he said, "So, first day of hurricane season. Scientists are saying we're overdue for a big one. Do you think it could happen this year?"

"Don't they say that every year?" I murmured into my latte.

He nodded. "Yeah, I guess they do. So, are you a student down at the university? I'm thinking about going there myself, and I wouldn't mind an insider's perspective."

"Sorry to disappoint you, but I'm an assistant gym teacher at one of the city schools." My usual lie came out easily. The job was ordinary and explained bruises.

He nodded and sipped his chocolatey drink. "You're braver than I am. I'm not sure I could work at a job that beat me up like that. What did you do, fall down some bleachers?" His words were polite and friendly, but I thought there was a tiny speck of sarcasm in there, too. He reminded me of Marco.

"That's exactly what happened." I was purposely neither enthusiastic nor dismissive. It was best to let civilians think what they wanted to think. The conversation was focusing on me far too much for comfort, so I pointed to his book. "What are you reading?"

A woman outside the window answered a phone call. After a few seconds, she gasped and took off running in the direction I'd heard the sirens.

Now I was intrigued, but I had to wait for the call to report to the scene—I was technically supposed to be at the clinic, much too far from the sirens to hear them.

He held it his book. "A nursing textbook. I'm thinking about quitting my job and applying to the nursing school down at UGSC."

"Nursing. Wow." I was impressed—The University of Georgia at Saint Catherine was the largest university in the region. "I don't know much about it, but I've heard that it's hard. Lots of long hours and cranky civilians. I mean, patients." *Whoops.*

"It can't be harder than my current job." There was an edge to his words. He hadn't appeared to pick up on my mistake.

"What do you do?"

"I'm an errand boy for my parents' human resources consulting firm. And before you ask, no, the work isn't hard. Being with my family all day is hard." He sank back into the couch. "I'm actually supposed to be on a job right now, but I decided to ditch." He looked sidelong at me. "I'm glad I did, though. Normally the company here isn't so nice to talk to. Pardon me for being so bold, but I love your Georgia accent. It's thicker than others I've heard."

Heat crept into my face. How should I even respond to that? "I— I'm also ditching. My boss would freak if he knew I was here. But I'm glad I came, too."

I'd never had a real conversation with a young civilian man before, and Benjamin *was* incredibly nice to look at. Every once in a while he'd turn his head and his mop of light hair would bounce slightly, shifting into his eyes. He'd shake his head a little to clear it away, and I'd see his crinkly hazel eyes once more.

Benjamin grinned. "So how about we waste more time? Tell me about your bad boss and I'll tell you about mine."

His wide smile warmed my stomach. Against my better judgement, and the microwave's half-hour warning, I started talking.

"My boss isn't really bad, just difficult to work with. He...Patrick is kind of controlling. He yells a lot and gets really angry when I make a mistake. He's just really hard to please. But it's usually my fault," I added quickly. "I mess up, a lot and there's so much on the line when I do. I deserve what he does." I picked at a spot on the couch. "You wouldn't believe how much I mess up at work."

Benjamin raised an eyebrow. "I can't believe that. And your boss shouldn't yell at you. Although...I'm being hypocritical, because my dad yells at me a lot and I never tell him to stop. But Patrick's not your family."

Patrick actually was a distant cousin of mine. "Sometimes I think about quitting but then I feel terrible. Besides, Patrick would be so angry; he hired me and I owe him everything."

Benjamin set down his cup. "Jillian, I don't know what this Patrick guy has been telling you, but you can quit your job. And you know, if he's such an ogre that you're afraid to give two weeks' notice, you may want to report him to the school board. That sounds like a really bad place to work."

This was the downside to my cover story; it only worked at the surface level. "It's not that easy," I said softly. I looked up at him. "Tell me about your boss."

The lights flickered. Lee stopped cleaning and frowned at them.

Twenty-nine minutes...but I didn't want to go.

Benjamin exhaled in a long breath. "I should start off by saying that my mom and dad are under a lot of pressure all the time. When things get bad, they lose control and start screaming their heads off.

Dad'll get gruff, mom will say something nasty to my brother, he'll reply with an attitude..." He trailed off and sighed heavily. "And then everyone jumps on the crazy train." He stared off into the distance for several long seconds, lost in thought. After an awkward second, he turned beet red and ran a hand through his hair. "I—I'm sorry, that was a lot to unload on you. Um, let me go get you another latte." He jumped up and headed towards Lee, still red as tomato sauce.

Smiling into the latte I was still drinking, I worked through his words, looking for the part that was supposed to be "bad." Authority figures had a right to rein in their inferiors through any means necessary, and sometimes that included yelling, even hitting. It was just an unpleasant part of life, like hail or sickness.

Still, I sensed that Benjamin thought this was unusual behavior in some way, so I sipped my coffee and decided not to comment on his family drama when he returned.

When he sat down again with a new latte in hand, a few awkward seconds passed before Benjamin spoke. "So if you quit your job, where would you work? Could you teach something else?"

I shook my head. "I don't know what I'd do. This is all I'm good for." The pain in my shoulder flared and I winced. I'd have to go soon, whether I wanted to or not.

He reached out to touch my shoulder, then drew his hand back. "I don't believe that. Give yourself a chance."

I was tired of this part of the conversation, but I didn't want to stop talking to him altogether. His black t-shirt said the word Nirvana on it and had a bizarre yellow smiley face below. "What does your shirt mean?"

Two shrieking ambulances raced down Davis Street, followed by a firetruck and police cars.

He pulled the bottom of his shirt to straighten out the front. "Nirvana? They were a nineties grunge band. You've never heard of them?" He was surprised, but I didn't hear any suspicion in his tone.

"No. Are they your favorite band?"

I could hardly judge him for enjoying a band, since he was a civilian and had no limitations on what media he could consume. I wondered what Nirvana's songs sounded like. They couldn't have been too bad, if Benjamin liked them—he was just so polite. Nearly all civilian music could corrupt, but I'd always gotten the impression from our lessons that some music could corrupt faster and more completely than others. Nursery rhymes and traditional ballads were alright—I even knew a few. Nirvana, whoever they were, were probably on the safe end of the scale.

"Eh, not really. They're okay. The shirt was last year's birthday gift from my sister. She's visiting right now, and I wanted her to see me wearing it."

I sipped my coffee to hide my smile. I didn't know what I'd expected from talking to this young civilian man, but such thoughtfulness about his sister's feelings wasn't it. I was moved.

"What bands do you like?"

*Dang it.* "Um, there aren't any specific bands, but I've always liked singing with my family. We used to sing around campfires when I was young." Those days seemed very far away. "Singing while we played in the meadow...while we worked...while we ran through the trees. I love to sing." I hadn't sung in six months.

Benjamin's eyes shone. "Were you in musicals when you were in high school? I wasn't good enough to be on stage. I ended up doing debate and forensics, plus some other stuff. What did you do?"

I knew what "debate" was, but not the other activity.

However, before I could bluff my way through an answer, my phone rang. A quick peek at the screen showed that it was Marco. I mouthed to Benjamin to hold on a minute while I took the call over by the bathrooms.

"Hello?"

"Jill, come home. There was a break-in at a bank and Patrick is freaking out 'cause you're not back. Tell me you're close."

So there it was: a robbery. Didn't criminals in this city ever sleep?

"Of course I'm on my way home. I just left. Give me fifteen minutes." I hung up and returned to the couch. "That was a coworker." I hoped my anxiety wasn't written all over my face. "I need to go."

Benjamin jumped up, and I saw for the first time that he stood at roughly six feet, just like me. "I had a great time talking to you," he said, taking my trash. "I'll just come out and say it: would you like to meet me here again?" He looked hopeful and shy at the same time.

His words hung in the air between us.

Nobody had ever asked to see me socially before. Back home, my only friends had been other children in the camp. Here in Saint Catherine, I had to be careful. Everything about the situation felt wrong. Forbidden. I could think of a dozen reasons to say no, the first one being the risk of Patrick pounding my face in for breaking a cardinal rule.

"Yes, I'd love to," I blurted. "How about next week, same day and time? In fact, let me get your phone number." I dug around in my pocket for my phone.

He told me his contact information and I saved it, making sure to label his contact file "Snitch #5" in case Patrick felt like randomly searching through it as he'd done in the past.

When I was done, I stuck out my left hand. "It was great to meet you."

He shook my hand and a spark of electricity traveled up my arm into the back of my neck and down to my thigh. "And you, Jillian. I really hope you'll consider what I said about your boss."

I nodded and we parted without another word.

I was walking out the door of the café when I realized that my shoulder didn't hurt anymore.

---

To read on, check out *Battlecry*, available now!